WHAT DEVILRY IS THIS?

SAM CHEEVER

ELECTRIC PROSE PUBLICATIONS

ABOUT ROME

Crafting worlds is crazy good fun. Authors love to make stuff up. Sometimes locations that are created for books seem like real places, even though they're not. That's actually good, because it means the author has done her job well. My fictional town of Rome, Indiana is not based on a real place. I've created a location that lives in my mind—one that fits the stories I wanted to tell. Hopefully you have enjoyed the picturesque town of Rome with all its paranormal challenges. I'm thankful for the opportunity to share this fictional town and its inhabitants with you.

xo

Sam Cheever

PRAISE FOR SAM CHEEVER

"You have that essential Je ne sais quoi that it takes to tell a story so mesmerizing you cannot stop reading once started. You are not telling stories to your readers...you are taking them with you on your adventures so that the experience can be shared by all as it happens and not simply replayed like a memory on the page of a diary! You are indeed gifted and it is my pleasure to read your books!"

Valerie Irwin

Psst! Can I tell you a secret? Midlife is a c-r-a-z-y ride. Not what I expected at all. But, I'm having a ton of fun in between the...you know...near death experiences and bladder-testing moments of complete terror.

Curse, curse, swear! How did midlife get so out of control? All I wanted was to make my own mark on the world. Start my own business and celebrate the end of an uninspiring marriage. Instead, I have a bat in my belfry. Not a metaphor...a REAL bat. The woods in my back yard is full of something dark from my nightmares. I've got a mysterious and sexy neighbor who seems to appear out of nowhere and knows more about my life than he should. And my best friends? Yeah, they're witches.

What the..?

My life has become a carnival and I'm sitting at the OhMyGoddessNo! spot on the most heart-stopping roller coaster.

Things are getting hairier than my chin. And midlife is definitely not shaping up to be the calm and graceful phase I'd been expecting.

But, I've got a good grip on my granny panties and I'm taking the ride. What could possibly go wrong?

STAY IN TOUCH

Sam doesn't give away a lot of books. But she values her readers and, to show it, she's gifting you a copy of a fun book just for signing up for her newsletter!

SIGN UP FOR SAM'S NEWSLETTER!
https://samcheever.com/newsletter/

A GUARDIAN FOR THEE

With the kindest heart and purest soul, though Fates
above will take their toll, the Lares' guard will
oversee, a kindly protectorate for thee.

A guardian does her petitioners cherish,
For all that evil would not perish,
And with a hand made sure with magic,
Stays the destructive winds and tragic,
Keeps them safe from wicked forces,
Allowing for the natural courses,
And if she fails, her plans amiss,
Her actions drawn by Faustian wish,
If every soul within her purpose,
Embraces right o'er evil service,
The Lares' magic makes them whole,
Although the fates will take their toll,
An understanding forged with love,

Shall know her bounty from above,
A devil's bargain met and dashed,
A terrible cost, a danger vast,
When all seems lost and death is nigh,
And in the end, a child's faint cry,
A faithful guardian's touch will quiet,
A terrible foe, emotions riot,
Extend her hand to sever vice,
And ease a soul not once but twice,
One by one and two by two,
The Lares' resolve will see it through,
And when at last death's courses run,
The Lares' tears will see it done.

A GUARDIAN DOES HER PETITIONERS CHERISH...

The taillights grew smaller as distance swallowed them a fraction at a time. The gravel country roads stretched away from where I stood, one intersecting the other, like an enormous cross that lay upon the ground.

At least, that was the way my fanciful imagination pictured the country roads, topped with stark white gravel. As I stared at it, the stone seemed to glow with a pale light.

I smiled.

Since I was standing in the front yard of a beautiful white country church, which as of two o'clock that afternoon had become my new home slash candle shop, the glowing cross felt like a good omen.

When I blinked, the cross image disappeared, leaving behind only a crossroads that the little church on the hill seemed to watch over with a benevolent eye.

Turning around, I rubbed my arms as the cooler evening air slipped along the ground, bringing a pale fog up from the sun-warmed ground.

I sighed. I'd left the lights on inside the church. They shone out through enormous arched windows like a warm, golden beacon to anyone who needed the icon's comforting embrace.

At the moment, that was me. Aggy Lenore. A forty-five-year-old divorcee who'd never really had her very own place. At five feet six inches tall with hazel eyes, I'd been just an average middle-aged woman whose greatest indulgence over the last few months was to get the tips of my long, straight black hair tipped in silver highlights. But that was changing. I'd not only gotten my own living space, I was also going to be a businesswoman, turning a beloved hobby into a livelihood.

I was terrified, excited, horror-stricken, stoked, and petrified all at once.

Shivering, I rubbed my arms more briskly. Where had the cool air come from? It had been a hot mid-summer day, and the weather hadn't even hinted at the drop in temps I was feeling.

The fog rose around me, swirling and agitated. It spurred an answering nervousness in me, and I felt a sudden urge to get inside.

Rome, Indiana was known for its strange fogs.

Nobody understood why. But they always seemed to start at the Rome Lutheran Church, which was no longer a church. It was my new home and would eventually be the *When in Rome* candle shop.

Mist licked at my elbows, and I started walking.

Thank goodness the lights inside the church were so bright. By the time I got to the front door, that golden glow was about all I could see.

A deep-throated barking greeted my entrance into my new home. Nails clicked over the well-worn wooden floors, punctuated by the determined woofs of my distrustful roommate. "It's just me, Monty," I said as the fluffy form of my black and tan standard-sized long-haired dachshund bounced into view. His shaggy tail wagged happily at the sound of my voice, his soft brown eyes sparkling with excitement. I bent down and scratched his ears. "Have you been terrorizing the resident bugs and boogies?"

Monty barked again and spun around, running back the way he'd come. He probably had the crickets I could still hear inside the building on the run. As long as there weren't any rodents, I was okay with his hunting ways.

I was less excited about tripping over a headless mouse corpse in my passage through the mess of the big room.

I stopped in the extra-wide door that led to what had been the sanctuary of the church and stared at the mountains of boxes.

Sighing, I realized I was hungry and tired. The idea of unpacking anything else was unpalatable. No matter how excited I was about being there.

"Come on, Mont," I called toward the sounds of snorfling and sniffing across the room. A shaggy tail rose from behind a box in the corner, wagging enthusiastically.

"I'm going to find your food and bowls," I informed him.

Yes, I was one of those people who talks to her pet. I'd always done it. Since I was an introvert of the highest order, there were many days when Monty was the only one I talked to. My private circle of friends and loved ones was small, consisting mostly of my mom and my best friend Bev, who also happened to be kind of my sister. Long story.

I had a wide group of casual and work acquaintances from living in a small town all my life, but I rarely interacted with most of them. Especially since I'd been let go from my job as receptionist at the Senior Living home on the edge of town in a cost-cutting measure. I didn't really mind. I'd worked there for almost ten years, and I was ready to do something for myself. Though I did miss some of the residents and staff there. I made a mental note to go for another visit soon and that thought lightened my step.

I followed a trail of boxes, tape balls, and packing paper to the kitchen at the back of the church. It didn't take me long to find the box marked "Monty." It took me a bit longer to find the box cutter to open it up. But as soon as Monty heard his kibble hit the bowl, he abandoned his buggy prey and flew toward the kitchen. I smiled at the sound of his nails tapping out a path through the house.

Filling his water dish, I placed both bowls on the special feeding mat on the floor that read, "Set the food down and back away, and nobody will get hurt."

True to his dachshund nature, Monty wasted no time diving into his bowl. He made short work of it.

I opened the retro refrigerator, whose curved lines matched the rounded tops of the windows throughout the picturesque old church, and pulled out the salad I'd had the foresight to put in there when I'd arrived. I didn't have the energy to cook, and there was no way I was getting into my car to drive back to town. Even though it was only a couple of miles. Since I'd turned forty-five, my eyes didn't much like driving at night. And the fog only made that situation worse.

Monty and I ate in companionable silence. He ate a few bites of my chicken, as well as most of my carrots and cucumbers, and I ate the rest. Yes, I was also one of those people who fed her dog human food when she ate. It was only one of many things that had annoyed my ex-husband about me. Fortunately, the thought no longer had the power to worry me. Quite the opposite, actually. I'd been about half relieved when Troy had gone off on a golf outing with a couple of his college buddies two years earlier and had never come back.

If my talking to and feeding my dog had run the man off, I had no regrets. After all, Monty was a much better companion. He was more loyal. And he didn't judge me at every turn.

All in all, I'd gotten the better end of that deal.

Monty licked my toes, and I smiled down at him, giving him my last bite of chicken. "That's all now, Mr. Chubby," I told him. "We've worked too hard to get that extra pudge off your waistline. I don't want you to get fat again."

Goddess knew I understood how hard it was to lose the weight once it had found its way onto my thighs, hips, and belly. I'd actually managed to lose mine lots of times.

Unfortunately, it always found me again.

After cleaning up the dinner mess, I forced myself to unpack the boxes in the kitchen. I'd spent the hours between closing on the house and arrival of the moving truck washing out all the kitchen cabinets and lining them with pretty shelf liner.

Even as exhausted as I was, seeing my beloved antique dishes arranged carefully behind the glass doors in the maple cabinets made me smile. I'd found the set at my favorite antiques store outside of Rome and had fallen in love with them immediately.

They seemed the perfect thing for my brand new, old kitchen.

Unlike the rest of the church, the kitchen had been updated to private rather than religious use before I'd purchased it. The seller had clearly intended to do what I planned and turn the quaint building into a private home. Yet, they'd done a good job of making the additions fit the age of the church, giving the renovated space a grace and dignity a haphazard updating might not have accomplished.

Unfortunately, the rehabilitation of the space hadn't gone much beyond the kitchen. Which was probably okay since I needed to create a unique, business slash private space out of it. And I had my own ideas about how I wanted to do it.

After breaking down the boxes and throwing them into the small breezeway that led to the back door, I turned off the overhead light, leaving only the pale glow of nightlights to guide my way. "Come on, little man. We need to find the bedding and make up the bed. After that, I'm done for tonight."

Monty bounced alongside me down the hall, tail happily wagging. I couldn't help smiling at the little dog. He approached even the most mundane event like it was an adventure.

While I looked for sheets, Monty snuffled happily around the room, shoving his long nose into dusty corners and sticking it under furniture in search of fresh victims and deadly intruders. I found my sheets, enjoying the freshly-laundered scent as I shook them out over my naked mattress. I had all four corners of the bottom sheet in place before I remembered I needed to put the mattress pad on first.

Sighing, I yanked the sheet off again and went in search of the mattress pad box. Fifteen minutes later, my bed was finally made. I yawned widely as Monty and I took an adventure down the Nile river...a.k.a. the hallway leading to the front door...to lock up for the night.

I stopped in the wide archway leading to the sanctuary and reached for the light switch. My fingers halted as I looked into the room that had sold me on the place the minute I stepped into it.

A smile spread on my face at its beauty.

Wide golden oak planking covered the floor. The walls and thirty-foot-high arched ceiling were painted a fresh, stark white. The wall facing the crossroads was dominated by a tall, arched window set into a pentagon-shaped alcove that had smaller, matching windows on either side. When I'd looked at the building, I'd decided the alcove would be a perfect spot for my sales counter.

The window itself was bisected by wide, golden framing in the shape of a Y that transformed it into two vertical windows, with a small, diamond-shaped window at the top. Slender Y-framing carried the same architectural device into the two vertical windows. The gorgeous focal point was set at the oak floor level and rose twenty feet high inside its alcove.

The previous owner had hung delicate, pipe and amber-globed lights along the length of the long ceiling. Two ceiling fans dropped from the same slender piping down the center line.

The four original oak church pews arrayed along the walls had been refurbished. I planned to use them in the shop as both seating and creative display pieces.

Pleasure bloomed in the center of my chest at the beauty of the room. Even filled with furniture that had been dropped without consideration for location and boxes stacked three high over much of the space, it was still a beautiful space.

I flipped the light switch, sending the room into darkness, except for a wide ribbon of silver moonlight painting the center of the cluttered floor. Back in my room, I discovered that Monty had already climbed his doggy steps and had burrowed into his favorite spot in the center. I stood next to the bed and stared at him a moment, grinning.

The covers rose and fell with his wagging tail, and his bright brown eyes found mine. As usual, he was completely under the covers except for his sleek head, which was resting on a pillow like a little human's.

In his customary response to my chuckle, he

rolled over onto his back, his tail still creating havoc under the covers. "You're a goof, Mr. Monty," I told him, earning myself a kiss on the nose as I settled beneath the covers.

I tried to read for a while before going to sleep, thinking my excitement would keep me awake. But I soon found my eyes drooping closed and gave up.

Snuggling with my adorable companion, I fell asleep almost immediately.

A deep, booming gong brought me upright with a pounding heart. "Cuss!" I yelled. "What in the cuss, swear, cuss is that?"

Unfortunately, I'd had a lifelong habit of swearing too much. Saying the words cuss and swear instead of actually indulging in the practice of cussing and swearing was my admittedly weird attempt to change that. It mostly worked like a charm.

Monty jumped up too, tail wagging manically as he barked with alarm.

My eyes skimmed to the cell phone on the bedside table and I reached out, tapping the screen.

Midnight.

I dropped my head into my hands as another gong sounded. The bell. I'd forgotten about the bell.

Jeezopete! What was the bell doing going off at midnight?

Gong!

I considered just waiting it out. By my calculations, I only needed to survive ten more gongs, assuming it was chiming out the hour like a giant grandfather clock.

I rubbed my face, exhausted. But as the bell gonged again, I knew I wouldn't be able to sleep until I'd seen what I could do to stop it. With my luck, the thing would keep chiming every hour until I found the *Off* switch.

With a long-suffering sigh, I shoved back the covers and climbed out, feeling every minute of my forty-five years, three months, ten days, eight hours, and some number of minutes which I refused to consider.

I mean, that would just be psychotic.

Gong!

Monty bounced happily across the bed and bounded down his dog steps, his bright gaze fixed excitedly on me.

What I wouldn't give to have a tenth of his energy.

Le sigh.

"Come on, handsome. We're going on a middle of the night adventure."

I slid my feet into my favorite pair of fuzzy slippers with the hard soles. I'd only ascended the bell tower stairs once, and I remembered the wood had been a little rough.

No splinter souvenirs for me, thank you very much.

Gong!

Remembering the cool mist from earlier, I grabbed a robe I'd thrown over a chair earlier and tugged it on over my nightgown.

Monty bounded ahead of me, his long ears bouncing and his entire back-end wagging with excitement.

I opened the narrow wooden door off the kitchen and realized there was no light on the steps. Fortunately, I'd brought my cell. I tapped the flashlight icon, and light flared into the narrow stairwell.

Monty was already at the top of the steps, his nails clacking over the rough wooden floor above.

Gong!

The sound of the bell was much louder inside the stairwell. I wondered if it would strike me deaf by the time I got to the top.

Static electricity bit at my skin as I started up. Sparks flared where my fingers tugged my gown up to keep from tripping over it. The stairwell smelled of ozone, as if there was a storm coming. The hairs on my arms lifted from some unseen energy.

I hesitated. If there was lightning in the atmosphere, was it smart to climb to the highest point in the building, like some kind of living lightning rod?

Gong!

"Cuss, swear, cuss!" I muttered under my breath. I needed to woman up and just get 'er done.

Monty started to bark. Was the little idiot barking at the bell?

"Hush, little boy," I called out.

Gong!

He whimpered, and panic flared. "Monty?"

I started to run. The staircase stretched out ahead of me like a nightmare. The rising steps seemed endless as I heard my dog running around the belfry, whining and whimpering.

"Monty, come!"

Gong!

My heart slammed against my ribs. My thighs burned. Still, the belfry seemed a hundred miles away. What in the goddess's good name was happening?

Gong!

Light flared from the belfry, a silvery light that burned my eyes like the sun and gave off physical heat.

Monty yelped.

I dug in and tried to run faster.

"Monty?!"

Gong!

The light eased slowly away, the heat going with

it, and the sound of Monty's barking dulled, seeming far away. My ears were plugged. Panting and feeling as if my legs were going to buckle out from under me at any moment, I ran on, not knowing what else to do.

Gong!

Suddenly, my ears popped, and I blinked. I was standing at the top of the stairs. The big brass bell was pocked and corroded with the years. The metal clapper in the center trembled as if some unseen force was jiggling it.

Gong!

By my count, that had been twelve gongs. I should be able to find the brakes for the thing in peace.

"Monty?" Nails danced toward me from the other side of the belfry. I breathed a sigh of relief when the little dog trotted out of the shadows, tail wagging.

"Are you okay?" I asked him, crouching down to run my hands over his soft fur. He seemed perfectly fine...although he was vibrating like the clapper on the bell.

"What in the world happened?" I asked, wishing he could actually answer.

Gong!

I went very still. Thirteen gongs? No. That wasn't right.

Monty suddenly whipped around and ran back into the shadows. "Monty, come back here." I hurried after him. The belfry was giving me the creeps, and I decided I'd wait until morning to fix the bell. If I had to, I'd put earplugs in my ears to get through the rest of the night.

My little dog watched me approach with my light. He stood on his back legs, his front paws resting on the short belfry wall. Whining, he danced excitedly as I reached him, begging to be lifted.

"You can't go up there," I told him, eyeing the narrow ledge around the top of the short wall. Rising from the wall on all four sides were open archways that would allow the bell's music to travel across the countryside.

I looked out on the graveyard in the back, shivering at the sight of the fog roiling over the ground. It looked like a scene from a Halloween horror flick. I pulled my robe closer as I stared out over the fog-shrouded tombstones.

The graveyard was old. Really old. With tombstones that were broken and falling over. The grass and weeds had grown up all around the stones, in some cases obscuring them entirely.

Maintenance on the little plot had been neglected for years. I was going to change that. The ground below me was sacred. The lives within it were important. Giving them back the resting spot they deserved was at the top of the list of things I planned to take care of as soon as I got settled.

Distant lightning spiked from the sky in a jagged

spear of light and energy. A moment later, a soft boom told me thunder was hot on its heels. A cool breeze washed over me as Monty started to bark.

Lightning stabbed downward again, significantly closer to my little piece of paradise. We needed to get out of there. "Come on, Monty. We'll come back in the morning." With relief, I watched him bolt across the belfry and bound eagerly down the steps.

I started to follow him. But something caught my eye in the graveyard. I turned to look and felt a jolt of fear. Someone was standing out there among the broken stones. I went very still, my eyes locked on the tall form. He...and I was pretty sure it was a man...stared back at me. Though I couldn't make out any features, just the gentle tilt of his head, I could feel his gaze like a brand against my skin. With a sudden, inexplicable certainty, I knew he was looking directly at me.

We stared at each other for a beat as the fog swirled around his long legs, and then he slowly lifted a hand as if in a wave.

All the hair rose on my arms again.

The belfry exploded into light–detonated in a cacophonous boom.

And the world turned charcoal gray beneath it.

2
_____

FOR ALL THAT EVIL WOULD NOT PERISH...

"Dingdingdingding...Your mother is calling, answer the phone."

I jerked awake on an unladylike snort and tried to open my eyes.

"Dingdingdingding ...Your mother is calling, answer the phone, right now."

"Jeezopete," I complained, scrubbing at my face.

"Dingdingdingding...Your mother is calling, answer the phone, or I'm telling your father."

I reached blindly for my cell phone, my eyes not quite wanting to open to the bright sunlight streaming into my room. "Why did I leave her in a room alone with my phone?" I muttered to myself.

"Dingdingdingding ...Your mother..." I grabbed my phone off the nightstand and stabbed my finger on the screen, halting the torture. "Could you have picked a more obnoxious ringtone?" I growled into the phone.

Mavis giggled happily. "I thought the dinging at the beginning was a nice touch. It has that startle factor that I knew would really bunch your boxers."

"Har," I said grumpily. I shoved upright on the bed and pushed my shoulder-length black hair out of my face. Next to me, Monty stretched and yawned, making a little sound as he rolled to give me his belly. As usual, I couldn't resist. I started scratching even as I succumbed to my own yawn.

"...needed help today."

I forced my mind back to Mavis's end of the conversation. "Hmm? Oh. I'm not sure. I'm at that stage where I don't know where to start or where to go."

She gave me her trademark husky laugh. "How about if I bring lunch by later? You should know by then if there's anything I can do, right?"

"Perfect," I told her. "Thanks."

"It's my pleasure, honey." There was a pulse of silence. If my mind hadn't been mushy, I might have been able to gird my loins before she said those six dreaded words. "I spoke to Troy last night."

My fingers must have dug a bit too hard into Monty's soft underbelly because he started licking them with too much enthusiasm. I pulled my hand away, sliding it over his sleek head. "Oh?" I didn't know what else to say. I really didn't want to encourage her to start talking about her son. He'd gone his way, and I'd gone mine. Despite the fact that she'd taken my side in the split, she was his mother, and I didn't think she could keep herself from thinking we might someday work things out.

I heard a sigh. "Don't worry, honey. I'm not going to beg you to get back together with him. I know you've moved on with your life. I'm really excited about what you're trying to do. It's just..."

The pregnant pause made me soften. Mavis had been my mother in every way that counted since I'd lost my birth mom to cancer when I was fifteen. Troy's family had lived right next door to us then, and he and I had started circling around each other when I turned sixteen. Mavis had opened her heart and home to me from the day my mother died and had never wavered in her support or love.

I couldn't love her more if she were my birth mother. "I am moving on," I told her. "But Troy and I are still friends. That's the best of both worlds."

"It is," she responded, her tone full of forced cheerfulness. "Anyway, I just wanted to check in with you. Make sure everything was okay. I'll be there at noon. You'll call me if you need anything before then?"

"Absolutely." I disconnected, feeling just the tiniest bit guilty. I mentally flogged myself for the emotion. I hadn't done anything wrong. Following my own dreams wasn't bad. It was a positive step for my future.

But even though I knew Mavis, and even Troy didn't begrudge me my new life. Somewhere deep down inside Mavis, I knew she'd always hoped her son and I could pick up the pieces of our broken marriage and get on with our lives.

That wasn't going to happen. Mostly because I didn't want it to.

I pushed the covers back and plodded into the tiny bathroom attached to my small bedroom. I had plans to turn a large room across the foyer from the sanctuary into my master bedroom suite with a walk-in closet. The space had been added to the old structure a dozen years earlier and it had been used as a meeting hall. It was perfect for what I had in mind.

Overall, the church was desperately short on closets. But I'd make do for a while. I figured I could stack a lot of the boxes that were filled with stuff I wouldn't use right away in the meeting hall space until I got around to the upgrades. Fortunately, I had the money for the renovations tucked away in the bank, the result of selling a house Troy and I had shared for ten years and splitting the money between the two of us.

I just needed to get my bearings and get organized before I started thinking about that project.

As I washed my hands at the pedestal sink, a

sharp pain sliced through my head. Sucking in a gasp, I closed my eyes and willed it to pass. A moment later, I reached for the towel to dry off and stilled when I caught sight of my arms. A thin network of pink lines covered the skin of my hands, running all the way up to my shoulders, and disappeared beneath my gown. In a panic, I tugged the gown off over my head and saw that the lines covered my entire body.

I stumbled back a couple of steps, running into the wall before I was forced to stop. "What?"

I blinked, looking down at myself again, and saw only my sun-deprived pale skin. Sans lines.

"What just happened?" I asked Monty because he was the only one in the room with me.

He wagged his tail and gave me his "I'm starving, feed me" bark.

Being a dachshund and therefore fully focused on eating twenty-four hours a day, Monty emitted that particular bark a lot.

"It must have just been the lighting," I told him. He happily agreed via another wag of his tail and a few enthusiastic bounces.

I decided to get dressed since I'd already basically stripped, and then headed wearily toward the kitchen. All of my muscles ached. Every single one. Getting old sucked. Apparently, just the effort of carrying boxes and moving a few pieces of furniture was enough to turn me into a walking zombie.

Sighing, I fed Monty before making coffee because, if I didn't, he'd pester me relentlessly. It was just more peaceful that way. I quickly found the coffee pods and offered one to the coffee goddess in the form of the single-serve machine I'd had the foresight to set up the day before. When it was done, I grabbed a bagel and headed into the sanctuary with my breakfast. Monty bounded along ahead of me, no doubt hoping to score a piece or five of my bagel.

There was probably a solid chance that would happen.

The sun was exceptionally bright in the sanctuary. Balancing the bagel on top of my coffee mug, I settled it on top of a box and grabbed the purse I'd thrown on the couch, digging my sunglasses out of its messy depths. As I reached for my coffee, an image flashed through my mind and I staggered, nearly falling.

The picture I flashed on was of dark brown eyes, silky mahogany-brown hair falling attractively over an unlined forehead, and a wide, sensual mouth. I squeezed my eyes shut and opened them again. What had I just seen? I didn't know anybody who looked like that.

I dropped to the couch and dug around in my purse until I found some pain pills. I swallowed three of the little red pills. The way I felt, I needed them. Especially since my headache seemed to be making me see things.

I'd been planning to pull a chair into the alcove to enjoy my breakfast. I wanted to enjoy the beauty of the front yard, with its dense, green grass and variety of mature trees dotting the wide, flat hill where the church sat. But I decided that was too ambitious a project for the moment and, instead, just stayed on the couch.

Monty jumped up and snuggled next to me, resting his head on my thigh.

I bit into my bagel, grinning as I chewed. His bright brown eyes followed the bagel's every movement, up to my mouth and then down again. Up to my mouth and then down. Over my head and then whirling in a circle above it.

I laughed. "You are a goofy boy."

A door closed at the back of the church. I jolted upright in pure shock. "What?"

Monty took off running.

"No, wait, Mont!"

His nails clicked energetically down the hall.

I hurried after him, my sore muscles forgotten in a rush of adrenaline. "Monty, come!" That curse, swear, swear dog never listened to me.

A gruff voice, like gravel over concrete, brought me up short, my heart pounding.

"Well, hello, my man. It's nice to see you again."

I felt my eyes go wide. *Again?*

The good news was that whoever it was didn't seem to be hostile. The bad news was that he'd just walked into my home without knocking.

Shoving fear aside, I forced my feet to move and stepped through the kitchen door.

Then jolted to a stop again. "Erp!"

The man across the room lifted a gnarly hand from where he'd been smoothing Monty's fur and looked at me, smiling. "Hello, Madam Lares."

"Uh..."

He blinked at me, frowning. "Is something wrong, Madam Lares?"

"Er..."

He straightened to his full height.

"Oh, curse swear! No, don't do that!" I shrieked.

The frown on his thick features deepened. "Do what, Madam L...?"

I flung up a hand to block my view. "I'm not Madam Lares. I think you've wandered into the wrong..." I swallowed hard, sneaking another peek just to make sure I hadn't lost my mind. "...the wrong kitchen." I flapped a hand toward the door. "Go. Out!"

A look of pain crossed his homely face. It made me feel a little bad. But not bad enough to let him stay.

"Have I displeased you, Madam...?"

"Please stop calling me that. My name is Lenore. Aggy Lenore. You're in the wrong house." I determinedly kept my gaze locked somewhere above his thick, hairy chest. "And you're naked."

He lowered his head, skimming a beady black gaze down his dense form and then resettling it on me. He looked perplexed. "Yes, Madam Lares. I am gardening," he said as if that explained everything.

Still holding my hand up to block the pertinent areas, I responded in the obvious way. "What does that have to do with you being naked in my kitchen?"

He held blocky, work-roughened hands out, palms up. "Well, the kitchen doesn't really have anything to do with it."

I bit back a frustrated growl. It was like talking to a politician. No matter what I said, I got only gibberish back from him.

I scanned a glare down at my erstwhile canine protector. He happily wagged his tail. *Traitor*. "Look, whoever you are..."

"Niele Waxman at your service, Madam Lares." He gave me a little bow. "Today is pruning day."

He said that as if it explained everything. I determinedly kept myself from observing Mr. Waxman's own "prunes," but it was a close one. The thought made me giggle a bit hysterically.

Niele Waxman smiled widely. "There ya go, Madam. I like to see you smile."

It was my turn to frown. "Have we met before, Mr. Waxman?"

"Niele, if you please, Madam." He gave me another one of those bows, which were elegant enough for an English drawing-room.

Not easy to pull off when your stick and pebbles are exposed to the world.

"We've not met formally, Madam," he responded with some perplexity. "But I'm here to remedy that." He gave me another bow. "I'm the greenskeeper."

I thought about that. "Greenskeeper?" Was there a golf course back behind the graveyard?

"I believe you call them gardeners in this part of the world, Madam."

What other part of the world would he be from? He did have a slight accent. Not British, really. Maybe Irish?

Then I had a thought. "Do you tend the graveyard?"

He frowned, his thick brows lowering over small eyes. "Ah, no, Madam." He vigorously shook his head, shaking the stick and pebbles in a very disconcerting way. I blinked, internally flogging myself for allowing my gaze to be drawn downward again. "I wasn't sure if I'd be welcome there," he said in a sad voice.

Dragging my attention back to the conversation, I finally registered what he'd said. My eyes widened. "Why wouldn't you be welcome?"

He shrugged. "The spirits haven't requested my presence there, Madam."

I threw up a hand. "Please stop calling me that. You make me feel a hundred years old."

He grinned, showing large blocky teeth. "No, Madam. Yer much older than that."

Umph! That one hit me right in the solar plexus. I glared at him. "Well, that was unkind."

He simply looked confused.

I moved on because I didn't want to risk taking any more emotional body blows. "So, you're telling me you work here? At the church?"

"Yes, Mad..."

I held up a hand and his mouth contorted, his eyes going kind of crossed. I figured he was trying to figure out what to call me. "My name's Aggy."

Relief swept over his blunt features. "Madam Aggy." He grinned. "A lovely name, for sure. Like lilacs in the summer sun."

I sighed. "Okay, Niele. Here's the thing. We'll address your employment after I've had a chance to settle in a bit. In the meantime, you need to wear pants when you work. That's not negotiable."

He took on a crestfallen expression but didn't argue. "Yes, Madam Aggy."

Inspiration struck. I'd wanted to tackle the graveyard anyway. I might as well make use of the resource who was already on site. Making a sudden decision, I said, "I'd like you to start grooming the graveyard. It's a mess, and that's disrespectful to the people whose eternal rest is under our care. Don't you agree?"

He squinted, his lips moving without managing to eject any words, but then he nodded. "As you say, Lares. It will be done."

Electricity zinged through the air with a snap, and I blinked in surprise. "Uh..."

He turned toward the door. "I'll get right on that, Madam."

I barely managed to avert my gaze as a pair of hairy buns swung into view. "Don't forget the pants," I called out as he headed outside.

Monty looked at me with a doggy grin, tail flailing the air.

"Yeah, you think it's funny," I told him. "Dogs are fine with nakedness."

He barked and hurried over to the cabinet where I stored his dog cookies, scratching at the door.

Naked greenskeepers, electrified air, unfriendly spirits in the graveyard...nothing gets in the way of a dachshund's appetite.

3

AND WITH A HAND MADE SURE
WITH MAGIC…

I was staring at the narrow wooden door in the back corner of the kitchen, sipping coffee, when the front door opened. "Hello?"

I blinked out of my reverie and responded. "In the kitchen."

My best friend Beverly, who was also my sister in every way that matters, tromped down the hallway in her flip-flops. She didn't bother to restrain the flapping sound from her shoes, making more noise than a slender woman of forty-six should.

Bev jolted to a stop in the doorway, her gray eyes wide with surprise.

Monty bounced around her feet, wagging his back end in an enthusiastic greeting. She barely noticed him.

Alarm filled me at her expression. "What?" I rubbed a hand over my face and smoothed my hair.

"Is there a bat in the cave or something?" I covered my nose.

"What happened to you?" she asked, blinking.

I narrowed my gaze. "I...moved. I know I'm probably a mess, but you try lugging boxes around and crawling over the floor putting stuff away."

She shook her head. "No. You look fine. I'm talking about..." She waved her hands around in an indecipherable message that did nothing to clear up my confusion. "What?"

"You're glowing."

I snorted. "Now I know you're messing with me."

Bev came over and all but fell into the chair next to mine. She reached out and ran a hand over my arm, her expression filled with awe.

I jerked my arm away. "What is wrong with you?"

"You have Lichtenberg lines." Her gaze shot up to mine. "Did you get struck by lightning?"

I stared at my arm, a feeling of dread making it hard to breathe. There were no lines. I didn't see anything. The memory of a fleeting glimpse of faint pink lines that morning flared to life in my mind. "I..."

"Aggy, talk to me." Her pretty face was so earnest I felt like I should reassure her. Even though I had no idea what to say.

"I'm fine," I said, laughing. "Stop looking at me as though I have two heads."

Impatient with being ignored, Monty jumped up and put his paws on her knee.

Bev finally looked at him. "Hello, handsome. I'm sorry I didn't give you a proper hello" She scratched his floppy ears, and he kissed her chin.

"Do you want coffee?" I asked. "Mavis is bringing lunch at noon."

"Oh good. I was hoping she'd bring food. I'm starving."

I looked her over, seeing the messy blonde pony-tail and the damp ringlets around her face. Her cheeks were flushed and it only made her look more attractive. She had Mavis's fine bone structure and peaches and cream coloring. I suspected the deep-set eyes came from her father, though I'd never met him. Like mine, he hadn't been around when we were growing up. Unlike my dad, he'd *never* been around. At least Andrew Lenore had come home in between work trips. "Did you just come from the gym?"

She nodded, tearing a chunk off of my second bagel and stuffing it into her mouth. It wasn't as bad as it sounded. I hadn't finished either of them. By the time I got back to the couch after the naked greenskeeper fiasco, Monty had already liberated the rest of my first bagel and tucked it securely inside his chubby tummy. I'd been too busy unpacking to finish the second one. "Coffee?" I asked again.

"Sure, thanks."

I felt Bev's gaze on me as I went about the task of making her coffee. It made me self-conscious. Then I realized Niele Waxman hadn't said anything about any lines on my skin. I tried to shove my fear away on the subject. But Bev wasn't going to let that happen.

"Tell me about the lightning," she said when I set the mug down in front of her.

"There wasn't any lightning," I insisted. Even to my own ears, I sounded a little defensive.

She tilted her head, giving me an admonishing look.

"I had a dream about being up in the bell tower, and there was a storm," I told her. Then I blinked in surprise. Until the words had come out of my mouth, I hadn't remembered the dream. I looked down at my arm and ran a hand over it. The skin was pale and smooth, with no visible lines. "This morning, for just a beat, I thought I saw markings. Then they were gone."

Bev sipped, looking thoughtful. She glanced toward the small door I'd been staring at all morning. Something about it had me intrigued. I had no idea what it was. "Is that the door to the tower?" she asked.

I looked at it and frowned. I really didn't want to go up there. And I had no idea why. "That's it."

She pushed to her feet, heading for the door.

I stood too. "Where are you going?"

Bev didn't react to the nearly hysterical tone of my voice. She just reached out and opened the door. It opened smoothly. I would have expected it to stick like most of the other doors in the building. Age and settling had taken everything in the place just a bit off square.

Sort of like turning forty-five had done to me.

Bev jogged up the stairs, Monty bounding up ahead of her.

Everyone but me seemed happy to explore the tower. I stood at the bottom for a minute, my pulse pounding. Vertigo swamped me as I took the first step. I paused, my hand finding the wall of the narrow staircase to keep me from falling on my butt.

The world swam behind my lids. A striking face loomed over me. Fog swirled around broken and crooked grave markers. And jagged black wings fluttered on the air above me.

Wings?

"Are you coming?"

Bev's voice jerked me out of...whatever that had been. Taking a deep breath, I opened my eyes to find the world stationary again. With a resigned sigh, I started up.

There was no sign of Bev when I reached the top. I looked around, my gaze going to the open arches on all sides. Panic flared again. "Bev?" I clutched the railing, locked into place by visions of her broken body sprawled on the ground far below us.

Her head popped up from behind the bell. "Over here. I found something."

I hurried around and found her on her knees, her hands skimming along the floor. Monty stood nearby, nose down and tail whipping. "What is it?"

She pointed to a large, muddy footprint. "These just appear here and trail toward the stairs." She frowned. "Then they just stop." She pushed to her feet. "And then there's this." Near the railing, on the floor, was a small spot of blackened, charred wood. "I'll bet lightning struck while you were up here." She looked at me, her eyes narrowing. "You're lucky to be alive."

I shook my head. "That's impossible. How did I get down to my room then? Why don't I remember?"

She snorted. "The not remembering part is easy. You were shot with millions if not billions of volts of electricity. Does the term 'fried my brain' do anything for you?"

I glared at her. "My brain is not fried."

"No," she said in a thoughtful tone. "It isn't." She reached out and touched my arm. "And the lines aren't visible either."

"Why do you look about half disappointed by that?" I asked, frowning. "And you said you saw them."

She flapped a hand dismissively. "I didn't *see.* see them."

My frown deepened. "What does that mean, exactly?"

She gave a little shrug. "People inexplicably survive these things all the time. What else do you remember?"

My initial reaction was to refuse to go into it with her. But it was really starting to bother me, and it would be good to talk to Bev about it. "A loud noise, a face..."

"What? Tell me about the face."

"I don't know. As I said, I can't remember."

"Was it a man's face?"

"I think so..."

She waggled her brows. "Was he good-looking?"

Gorgeous, my traitorous brain said before I could stop it. But at least I hadn't said it out loud. Bev would be all over me like ants on melted ice cream if I had.

"Gorgeous, huh?"

I winced. *Oops.* My traitorous face had given me away.

She nudged my shoulder with hers. "You dog you."

Monty barked gleefully. Sometimes I wondered if the dog had special powers. He sure acted like he understood human speech.

"Ha!" I replied. "I told you it was just a dream." I

recognized my mistake immediately...as soon as I saw the look of delight crossing her face. "You're dreaming about hot men. You double-dog you."

Monty barked again.

To avoid responding to Bev, I turned to my dog. "What is your deal?"

He was turned away from us, his nose pointed toward a high corner of the belfry. Something small and black clung to the wood up there.

"Is that a...?"

Bev glanced up and went rigid for a beat. Then she shuddered, gave a terrified yelp, and barreled back down the steps.

I could have kissed my dog. "Nice damage control, buddy," I told Monty.

His only response was to bark again.

"Okay," I told him. "You can stop now. She's gone."

But he didn't stop. He continued to bark, the sound growing more insistent by the moment. "It's just a bat, Mont," I told him, feeling only a little silly for talking to my dog like he was a person.

"Bark, bark, bark, bark..." His furry little body pinged off the floorboards with every bark, his agitation continuing to increase.

I reached for him, "Stop that. Come on, let's go downstairs. The bat is sleeping. It's not bothering us." I glanced up as Monty evaded my clutches and gasped.

Did the bat look bigger?

No. That wasn't possible. "Come on, Monty. We're going back down."

The little dog leaped into the air, growls mixing with his barks as he worked himself into a lather.

Unable to stop myself, I glanced up at the bat again, twitching in alarm. Okay, that was just weird. The thing looked several inches larger than the last time I'd looked. I started to back toward the steps. If I headed back down, Monty would follow.

The bat slowly opened its wings and I gave a little scream, diving on my dog. I managed to grab him before he could dodge away again and turned toward the stairs. I really tried not to look up at the bat as I started down, but I couldn't seem to stop myself.

I immediately wished I hadn't.

The creature was definitely bigger. Its wings spread a good twelve or fourteen inches, fluttering against the wood behind it. To make things even weirder, it had been hanging upside down before. But it was upright, still somehow clinging to the wall. And its eyes were open.

Midnight black orbs in a terrifying face. Staring directly at me.

4

STAYS THE DESTRUCTIVE WINDS
AND TRAGIC...

Bev was still in the kitchen shuddering when Monty and I came inside. I tried to shove my own agitation aside, certain I was losing my mind, and gave her a smile. "You don't care for bats?"

She shuddered so hard I was pretty sure she levitated off the floor. "Flying rats. Disgusting. You need to get an exterminator."

I was beginning to think that what I needed to get was an exorcist.

"Helloooo!" said a chirpy voice from the front of the church...house. I needed to stop thinking of it as a church. It was my home. And I'd soon have it feeling like one. The thought allowed me to greet Mavis with a wide smile as she came down the hallway.

"Hey, mom," I said, hugging her around the assortment of bags she was carrying. As usual, me calling her mom made her eyes shiny with ready tears. Mavis was one of those people who teared up a lot. She was a very emotional person. A very loving person.

It was that very characteristic that had made her embrace a sad, lost fifteen-year-old and give me a second home where I could enjoy a woman's touch and understanding.

My dad had tried, but he'd always been kind of a remote father who traveled a lot for business and was rarely around for the important stuff. He'd seemed to believe that if he paid for my mom and me to live comfortably, he'd done his part. The one exception had been Christmas. Dad had always made it a point to be around for three days every Christmas. He'd gone with us to pick out a tree, helped us decorate the house, and enjoyed our squeals of delight on Christmas morning.

Mom and I had learned to lay the joy on a bit thick just for his benefit.

Thoughts of him made me a little homesick. I wondered what country he was currently visiting and hoped he'd find time to check in. I wanted to tell him about the ch...house.

I grabbed the bags from Mavis, rolling my eyes and moaning at the delicious smell. "What did you bring? It smells wonderful."

Mavis tucked her short, blonde bob behind one

ear and winked. "Your favorite. A meatball sub from Capricios."

"There's more than a couple of subs in all these bags," I said. "Not that I'm complaining. I really need to get to the grocery."

She laughed gaily.

"Hey, mom." Bev pulled her mom into a tight hug. "Aggy has bats."

Mavis's gray eyes went wide. "Bats!" she screeched.

I laughed. Apparently, the bat phobia was genetic. "One bat. In the belfry." I laughed at my own little joke. "I have a bat in the belfry."

Bev rolled her eyes. "I've been telling you that for years."

Mavis started emptying bags onto the counter. "If you need an exterminator, I have a really good one."

"Who?" asked Bev, snagging a bag of chips.

Mavis slapped her hand. "Let Aggy choose first. This lunch was for her."

Bev danced away so her mom couldn't retake the bag. "You always did like her better," she fake-pouted.

I laughed. "That's only because I listened to her. You were always the bad one."

Rather than being offended by my comment, Bev waggled her brows at me. "Which is why I had more fun than you."

I looked at all the goodies on the counter. "You

went to the grocery for me." I gave Mavis another hug. "Thank you."

My surrogate mom chuckled. "It's the least I could do after the new ringtone."

"When you put it that way," I said. "You have a point." I snagged my phone off the counter and shoved it into the pocket of my jeans. "I'm keeping this close until you leave."

Mavis laughed with delight.

I pulled three subs from the pile on the counter and two bags of chips. Bev was well on the way to finishing the third. Mavis had gotten me cottage cheese, potatoes, half 'n' half for my coffee, a box of dark roast coffee pods, cinnamon bagels, whole grain bread, butter, grape jelly, and natural peanut butter at the grocery. "You're my hero," I told her, tucking the groceries away like a squirrel storing nuts.

Mavis grabbed a bottle of iced tea and poured three glasses. Then we sat down to eat. My eyes rolled back in my head with the first bite of my meatball sub. "Goddess, this is good."

Mavis and Bev exchanged a look.

"What?" I asked.

"Goddess?"

I blinked. *Where had that come from?* "Heh. I guess I've been reading too many paranormal romance novels."

To my surprise, they shared another look.

We chatted about the move and my challenges for the house. Mavis had a few great suggestions for how to overcome the closet issue, and Bev offered her design advice. Beverly had always been good at decorating. I was terrible. She and I could start with the same three items to decorate a room. My choices would do nothing to enhance the space. But she could place the three things into a room in such a way as to transform and tie it all together. I'd always envied her that ability.

"Maybe you could help me arrange the sanctuary after lunch?" I asked.

She nodded enthusiastically, swallowing a bite of sub. "Sure. It'll be a joy to decorate that room. It's so gorgeous."

"It is!" Mavis agreed. She looked around the sunny, updated kitchen. "I'll admit when you told me you were buying this old church, I thought you'd lost your mind. But I can see why you did it now. It feels..."

"Like a refuge?" I offered.

She sighed. "Yes. That's it."

I thought of Niele, and a grin formed on my face before I could stop it.

"What?" Bev asked, grinning with me.

"You won't believe who wandered into my kitchen this morning."

Both women leaned close, eyes wide with interest. "Who?"

When I told them, Bev squealed, clapping her hands together. "Seriously!"

"I wouldn't lie to you about a naked man in my kitchen."

She and Mavis squealed again, beyond delighted. Mavis jumped up and ran to the window, stretching her five feet seven inches to look out over the empty backyard. "Is he still here?"

I shrugged. "No idea. I've been busy all morning in here. But if you're hoping to get a gander of the stick and berries, you're out of luck. I told him to put some pants on."

Mavis giggled like a schoolgirl. "Stick and berries. Hilarious. Aggy honey, only you could move into a house with a naked gardener," she told me, her eyes alight with pleasure.

I did a mock curtsey. "Thank you very much." Gathering up the refuse from our lunch, I dropped it into the trashcan. "Would you like a tour?" I asked them.

"Absolutely!" they said in unison.

Monty chased a ball of packing tape across a sunbeam, sporting moves that even a cat would be jealous of. We laughed at his antics, sipping bottles of water as we contemplated the canvas laid out before us.

Mavis was content to sit on the couch and watch us work.

Bev had donned her decorating savant demeanor and had whipped my new living room into shape. There was just one last sticking point upon which she and I were at an impasse. "I don't know, Ags," she said, frowning. "That alcove is the focal point of this whole enormous space. It seems a sacrilege to stick a sales counter into it."

"Then where do you suggest I put it?" I'd asked the same question several times, in a variety of forms since we'd begun the discussion, but she still hadn't given me a satisfactory answer.

She gnawed on a knuckle and stared at the glory that was the alcove at the front of the big room. She was right. It was the focal point. It was one of the major reasons the former sanctuary was so stunning. But I'd purchased the structure with a plan to turn it into a candle shop. Having a place to actually display and sell the candles was a key aspect of that.

"How about the meeting hall?" Mavis offered.

I turned to her, confused. "What?"

"The meeting hall is nearly as big as this room. It's located at the front of the building, so it's just as easy to get to. Why don't you put the shop in there? That way, you can keep people out of your private living space and have a dedicated shop."

My initial reaction was to reject the idea. I'd had my heart set on putting the shop in the sanctuary. I figured the "wow" factor of the space would do as much to bring in customers as the merchandise would.

"I don't know," I said. "I was planning to make that into a master suite."

Bev stared at the door across the hallway from the sanctuary. "That's actually not a bad idea. Come on." She headed toward the door, a gleam in her eye.

I almost dug my heels in, not wanting to be talked into giving up my dream bedroom suite. But, in the end, I decided it wouldn't hurt to listen to her ideas. I didn't have to agree with them.

Bev threw open the heavy oak door, and we walked into a large room. She was right. It was almost exactly the same size as the sanctuary. It had been finished much as the sanctuary had too, with polished golden oak planking on the floors, a high, peaked ceiling, and a large arched window at the front. In addition, two smaller, matching windows adorned the long outside wall that overlooked the grounds, including one end of the small graveyard.

"It's perfect!" Bev announced. She hurried toward the back wall, painting the vision in her mind with the swing of one arm across the space. "Sales counter here." She indicated the sidewalls near the counter. "Shelves for stock on either wall and on self-standing shelves there and there." She pointed to the open floor in front of and to either side of the counter. "That way, your displays won't block the counter, which can be built of oak and steel to match the light fixtures, with stained glass inserts in keeping with the church theme you've got going."

I frowned up at the ugly chandeliers blaspheming the peaked ceiling. "But there are no cool steel and amber glass fixtures in this room."

"You can add those. It wouldn't be a big deal. You could build a wall across the back if you wanted, shorten the room by about ten feet, and that could be a storage and work area. That would still leave you with a store that was plenty big enough."

I was starting to picture the shop the way she was seeing it, and it wasn't a bad picture at all. But... "I really wanted to turn this into a master suite," I repeated, sounding disappointed.

She frowned. "I know..." Her pretty face lit with inspiration. "Okay, how about this idea. That dark little room next to your bedroom..."

"The pastor's office." I clarified, nodding.

"That's the one." She pointed to the back wall. "It's behind this room, right?"

I nodded.

"What if you shaved another six feet from this room, tore out the wall between the pastor's office and your existing bedroom, and created your dream bedroom suite from that? It might not be quite as huge as what you'd had in mind, but it would still be roomy. And, to be honest, an enormous suite wouldn't really match the feel of this place anyway. Also, if you added a couple of smaller windows to match these arched ones on the side, it would be bright and beautiful."

I thought about her suggestions. The picture she'd painted was slowly forming in my brain and I really liked it. "That would be..."

"Perfect!" said Mavis.

I looked up to find her leaning against the doorframe.

She was right. "It would be perfect," I told Bev, giving her an excited hug. "And probably wouldn't cost any more than what I'd been planning." I could admit to myself that I was happier with the idea of not having strangers going in and out of my living space all day. "I love it!"

Bev's expression lit with purpose and planning. "Can I help? I have lots of ideas to run past you. It would be fun."

It would be more than fun. It would be wonderful. "I'd love for you to help. I have no vision when it comes to this kind of stuff. In fact," I glanced at Mavis. "I was wondering if you two would like to help me in the store? As many or as few hours as you'd like to give me. That would leave me more time to make candles in my new workroom." I grinned at Bev. "I can't pay you a lot at first..."

"I'm in!" Mavis said, clapping her hands together

in front of her face. Her eyes shone with unshed tears. "I'd love it."

I looked at Bev.

"Maybe weekends?" she offered apologetically.

She had a job as a pharmaceutical representative. I knew that. I'd just gotten caught up in the moment. Suddenly, I felt terrible for putting her on the spot. "Oh, I forgot about your job. I'm sorry. Don't worry about it. If mom helps..."

Bev shook her head. "No, I want to help. I just can't during the week. But if you plan to be open on the weekends..."

"I do now," I told her. I hadn't been sure I wanted to commit to seven days a week working the shop all by myself. But with help... "Let's start with just Saturdays for now. I can adopt the 'day of rest' concept for Sundays in keeping with the church theme. What do you think?"

"I think that should work." Bev dropped an arm around my shoulders. "This is going to be fun."

5

KEEPS THEM SAFE FROM WICKED FORCES…

T ired of being inside all day, I headed out to the patio with my glass of wine after a late dinner. It was a beautiful night, the full moon tipping the leaves of the trees in silver. The night was still warm, but a gentle breeze made the overarching branches of a nearby tree dance over the small patio. The iron table and four chairs were covered in acorns and leaf debris. I brushed off a chair and lowered my weary body into it, sighing with pleasure.

After a solid day of unpacking and moving furniture, it felt good to sit down. A sense of contentment filled me. The house had come a long way in two days. I planned to make some calls to contractors in the morning. I'd get a few bids on the cost of the changes I wanted to make, starting with the shop, and then hopefully get started on the work within the month.

It was an aggressive plan. But I'd been conceiving of it for a long time, and with the footprint of my new shop clear in my mind after Bev's help, I was antsy to get started.

Something caught my eye in the graveyard. Turning to look, I saw a black cat with bright yellow eyes staring at me from atop one of the tilted stones. I glanced down at Monty. He was under the table, totally oblivious to the usurper in his kingdom.

He'd be really mad if he saw the cat. I willed the creature to stay away so the two wouldn't be tempted to try to maim each other. Right at that moment, I wasn't interested in chasing them around the yard. All I wanted to do was sip wine and enjoy the serenity of a perfect evening.

A soft chirping sound pulled my gaze upward. A bat fluttered by overhead, ducking and diving for bugs I couldn't see in the velvety dark. I wondered if it was the bat we'd seen in the belfry and smiled, thinking about how Bev had scurried out of there like a frightened deer. Her rep as a tough guy had been squelched forever in the wink of an eye.

The bat was soon swallowed up by darkness. I sat in a gentle pool of light from the kitchen window. Monty stirred, yawned, and rolled belly up. Unable to resist, I shed my flip-flop and rubbed my toes over his soft belly. He gave a little sigh.

"Beautiful night, isn't it?"

I jumped, slamming my knee on the underside of the metal table and yelping unattractively. Surging to my feet, I toppled my glass of red wine. Monty jumped up too and started barking, tail aggressively high and whipping the air.

I reached down and picked him up before he could run over to the intruder.

The tall stranger who strode out of the darkness gave me an apologetic smile. "So sorry. I thought you'd seen me."

I backed away from the arresting figure and he noticed, a frown finding his perfect face. He held up two hands and stopped moving. "I didn't mean to scare you. I was just out for a walk, and..."

I glowered at him. "On my property?"

He opened his mouth and then snapped it closed, inclining his head. "You're right. I apologize. I'm not used to this place being occupied." He looked around, the gentle expression on his face calming me a bit.

He seemed sincere.

"It *is* occupied. And you're trespassing."

Something about the man's face struck a chord in my memory. But I was sure I'd never met him before. I'd surely have remembered him.

He looked to be over six feet tall, with broad shoulders and long legs. His dark hair fell in silky ribbons across a smooth forehead, and his eyes were dark too, impossible to tell the color in the dark. But the hoary light couldn't mask the beauty of his sharp cheekbones and perfect lips. Or the way his nostrils flared as though scenting me.

"Welcome, Lares. It is a joy to finally meet you." He swung an arm. "This place..." He shook his head, an action that sent a dark strand of shiny hair into his smoldering gaze. "It has needed you for a long time. Especially lately."

I frowned. "You're the second person who's called me that."

Dark brows lifted in apparent surprise. "What? Lares?"

I nodded. "What does it mean?"

There was a stark moment of silence between us. His expression seemed to flow from surprise to concern and then to amusement. Finally, something shrewd filled his gaze. "A Lares is a guardian. You are guardian to this beautiful place."

Technically, that was sort of true. But it was an odd thing to call me. "That sounds like a title from a long time ago."

He nodded. "Yes. From very long ago."

"Did you call the previous owner that?"

His dark head tilted slightly, and the sense that we'd met before strengthened. "Previous owner? Not at all. There has been no guardian here before you."

I just stared at him. I knew that wasn't true. The realtor I'd worked with to buy the place had assured me the building had been on the market for less than a year. But I pushed it aside. Clearly, the man was looking at the whole "ownership" thing differently than I did.

"Do you live around here?"

He inclined his head, then gave a jolt. "Goddess, my manners," he took a step forward and held out a hand. "I'm Lungren Maker. You may call me Gren."

I glanced at Monty, unwilling to put him down to shake the man's hand. I didn't trust the intruder and had no idea if he'd harm my dog.

Lungren caught my glance and retracted his hand. "I'd be pleased to know your name?"

He had an odd way of speaking that reminded me of historical novels I'd read. Maybe he was from another country.

"Aggy Lenore."

He bowed. "Honored." His gaze slid over me, narrowing slightly. I tensed in response to his focused stare.

"You should go," I told him.

He inclined his head. "Yes. I'm happy that you've arrived, Lares. Until we meet again."

I watched him walk through the arc of illumination sifting through my kitchen window and melt into the darkness. Once he stepped beyond the arc of light, his large form simply disappeared into the night.

Just like the bat had done.

---

*G*ong!

I bolted upright, my heart pounding. It only took me a sleep-blurred second to understand it was happening again. "Curse! Swear!" I exclaimed. I needed to find the setting on the bell that told it to wake me the heck up in the middle of every dang night and change it.

Gong!

I sagged wearily. Did I dare go up there again? My brain was still vague on what exactly had happened the night before, but I had a general feeling of danger when I thought about climbing those steps.

Gong!

I covered my head with the pillow, determined to just wait it out.

Gong!

Monty whined, clawing at the pillow with an insistent paw.

I sighed, flinging my fluffy muffle aside. "Jeezopete!"

Shoving the covers back, I slid my slippers on and yanked my robe off the chair where I'd thrown it earlier. "Stupid bell," I complained. "I'm going to stuff it with a dang sock."

Gong!

Hurrying into the kitchen, I threw open the door

to the belfry. But Monty ran to the back door, scratching wildly at the bottom and whining as if his world was in danger of ending.

I stopped with a foot on the steps to the belfry. "Monty. Come on, boy."

He whined frantically, his digging growing more insistent.

Gong!

"Stop that! You're going to scratch the door."

He ignored me. I walked over and looked out the door, seeing the same fog from the night before swirling around the grave markers in the graveyard. I frowned. The fog seemed concentrated only in that one area.

Gong!

Monty started to bark, the sound akin to running a vegetable peeler over an exposed nerve.

Curse, curse, swear, swear! I was going to lose my mind from that bell.

In pure desperation, I grabbed the door handle and turned. A sharp wind smacked into us, sending me stumbling back as the door slammed inward.

With a single, sharp woof, Monty was out the door and tearing across the grass.

Gong!

"Monty!" I flew out after him, calling his name with growing concern as I heard his bark sharpen, becoming shrill with fear.

One of my fuzzy slippers caught on a clump of

grass, and I stepped right out of it. Without slowing, I kicked off the other one and dug in, running faster than I would have thought possible given that I was sleep-dazed in the middle of the night.

The fog reached out for me with curved fingers, caressing my legs and arms and seeming to tug me into the tiny graveyard.

Gong!

I stopped with a jolt when I realized I couldn't see anything. The mist had risen above my head, covering everything and giving me a dizzying sense of movement all around.

"Monty!" I yelled again. The sound got caught in the haze and was smothered.

My heart pounding with fear, I stretched my arms in front of me and felt my way along. I fully expected to crack my shins on a grave marker with every step.

Gong!

I couldn't see anything. The fog was overwhelming. It muted every sense I had, like a sensory deprivation chamber, until all I could hear was my own heartbeat.

Babump...babump...babump...

The mist suddenly fragmented directly in front of me. I gave a little yelp as a tall figure stepped out of it.

Babumpbabumpbabumpbabumpbabump!

"Gren?" I asked, surprised.

Gong!

He held a finger in front of his lips and reached for me. Before I had time to react, he'd grabbed my hand in his big, warm one and tugged me off the ground.

A sizzling jolt of light speared the fog behind me. I slammed up against a broad, warm chest and gasped as Gren wrapped a hard arm around my waist and held me tight. He leaned close, whispering in my ear. "You need to send them away."

Gong!

I frowned. "Send who away?"

Light speared past overhead and Gren moved, swinging me away from the spot and out of the haze. Without warning, Gren's arm tightened around me and he leaped into the air, yanking me off the ground with him.

I nearly swallowed my tongue.

We flew nearly twenty feet and landed behind a large tree.

Gong!

In a panic, I shoved free of his grip. Another bolt of lightning seared the ground an inch from my feet. With a yelp, I leaped back into Gren's arms. "What is going on?" I yelled, beyond terrified and starting to get really miffed.

"It's the devils. You need to send them away, Lares."

I threw up my hands. "What does that even mean?"

"You're the guardian of this place. It's your job..."

"What place? The church? The graveyard?"

"Yes," he said, nodding. "And the town of Rome."

I stared into his delicious face and fought the urge to punch his perfect nose.

The man was totally insane.

"I have no idea what you're talking about. I'm no Lauris...or whatever you called me." I brutally shoved the memory of Niele calling me the same thing out of my mind. I didn't need the distraction at that moment. "I'm just me. A normal person who's trying to pick up the twisted strands of her life and create a new future."

Melodramatic much? I chastised myself silently.

"You are Lares. It is preordained. And you must send the devils away."

"What devils!?" I yelled.

Fire sizzled into the tree we were hiding behind. The thing had to be hundreds of years old and bigger around than my arms could reach, but it went up like a Q-tip in a flash fire. Fire flared toward us, deadly and ravenous, the sound of its encroaching feelers like a nest of hissing snakes.

The heat was impossible. Within seconds, my exposed skin turned red. The hairs on my arms curled up as if singed. When I tried to pull air into my overheated lungs, the very air burned my insides like fire.

Gren pounded against nothing, as if there were some kind of invisible barrier there. He threw back his head and roared, his hands flying up and mini-volts of lightning flashing from them.

The invisible wall shimmered for a beat, becoming visible, but held.

Smoke billowed around us, choking and scorching my lungs.

I fell to my knees, lost to the violent coughing. I was going to die from smoke inhalation. And I was standing in the open air of the yard.

Gren dropped to his knees beside me, his lips close to my ear. For one incredible moment, I thought he was going to kiss me.

Then he yelled something above the roar of the fire. "Protector...you *must* protect."

The words reverberated through my mind, clear and strong. And, as if they were saturated with magic, they wove their way into my brain, taking hold.

It still might not have been enough. I had forty-five years of resistance to unconventional ideas working against me. But then I heard Monty yelp in pain. And it was like a door had been thrown open in my brain. I shoved to my feet on a growl that exploded into the night, flinging up my hands. An amber glow danced on the darkness around me, hitting the fog and burning it away in a single wash.

Three words scorched a path into my brain, pulsing with so much power they were impossible to retain. I had to let them loose or risk being burned alive from the inside.

Opening my mouth, I screamed them into the Universe. "Leave! This! Place!"

The amber glow flared away from me, painting the air between the church and me and extinguishing the last of the lingering fog.

Like a giant pair of scissors had cut sound from the night, everything fell silent, becoming still as a grave.

No more fire projectiles blasted toward us. Whatever had been living in the fog was gone.

I sagged downward, spent and dizzy from whatever I'd just done. Gren caught me, lifting me off my feet. He beamed down at me. "Well done, Guardian."

I shook my head. "I didn't..."

A long, pitiful whine sliced through the darkness.

I jolted. "Monty!" I shoved at Gren. "Put me down!"

He complied. As soon as my bare feet hit the cool grass, I started running. As I neared the graveyard, something moved near the ground. Gren was suddenly there, that weird energy I'd seen before pulsing from his palms.

I slapped his hands away and fell to my knees as Monty limped out from behind a gravestone. He hobbled over and slathered my face with his tongue, snuggling close. "Buddy. You're okay." I buried my face in his sweet-smelling fur. "I was so worried."

"Madam Lares, we must talk," Gren said. "They are gone. But they will be back."

6

ALLOWING FOR THE NATURAL COURSES...

I rose to my feet and looked him in the eye, anger swirling through me in hot waves. I was afraid. Really afraid of what had just happened. And it was either be mad or start crying.

I'd rather be mad.

"What is going on? What's with the thirteen gongs of the bell every night? What's with this infernal fog? What just attacked us? And why do I have a bat in my belfry that grows faster than a Chia plant?"

Gren blinked at that last one but reached out to touch my arm. "Come, let's get you and your intrepid warrior sidekick inside."

I shook off his grip and stalked toward the welcoming glow of the church lights. Monty rested his head on my shoulder and gave a heartfelt sigh.

Poor baby.

I kissed his nose.

At the church...house...I turned to Gren. "I think you should go."

His sexy eyes darkened with emotion. Anger? Frustration? I didn't know. I only knew that I'd had enough for one night.

"Madam Lares..."

I held up a hand. "Stop calling me that. I told you my name. Please use it."

He inclined his head. "As you wish. But, if I may?" He nodded toward Monty, and I frowned.

Gren touched Monty's little leg, and warm light engulfed it. I watched in fascination as the cut he'd sustained during the kerfuffle knitted and healed before my eyes.

Gren bowed and turned away. "If you need me, just call. I'll always come."

I watched him head back into the darkness, his tall form elegant and proud. Remorse replaced the anger and even a little of the fear. I should have heard him out. He seemed to know what was going on around me. At the very least, I should have let him tell me about the bell.

I sighed and pulled the door open, stepping inside and closing it again before settling Monty on his feet. No way was I going to risk him running off again. One adventure of that kind was plenty, thank you very much.

I looked at the clock and was shocked to see that

it was three in the morning already. Had I been out there in the fog for three hours? My legs suddenly felt rubbery. Something was going on that was beyond strange. But my brain couldn't wrap itself around what it was.

I stood in front of the kitchen door, uncertain what to do next. I knew I should go back to bed, but I was certain I wouldn't be able to sleep. My mind was racing, filled with questions. I deeply regretted urging Gren to walk away without answering any of them. Sometimes I was too stubborn for my own good. And it seemed I was getting worse with every passing decade.

I sighed again and locked up, turning the kitchen light off as I headed to the former pastor's office. If I couldn't sleep, there was one thing I could do. By the time the sun peeked over the trees, I was going to know what I was dealing with. And what the swear this Lares thing was that everyone seemed to believe was my proper title.

Lares: Guardian deities from the ancient Roman religion. Although they are sometimes characterized as household gods, many have much broader domains that include roadways, towns, and cities. Housed in crossroad shrines, Lares are believed to observe, protect, and influence everything that occurs within the boundaries of their chosen domains. Their calling has long been understood to be passed down through family lines, originating from either the father or the mother, but never both. These deities are allegedly strengthened by the emotions and compassion of their human sides, which is why one parent must always be human.

I stared at the words on the computer screen, feeling as if I'd fallen down the rabbit hole, and the Queen of Hearts was slapping me about the ears with a long, wet noodle.

Was everyone around me totally crazy? There was no way I was some kind of deity. I was a forty-five-year-old woman with witch-colored hair and creaky knees. I didn't have magic. If the night's events had proven anything, it was that I wasn't even capable of guarding my dog, let alone an entire "domain."

I pointedly ignored the uncomfortable realization that I'd moved into a church and lived in a town called Rome. The crossroads at the bottom of the hill didn't mean a thing either.

All coincidences.

Move along. There's nothing to see here. These are not the drones you're looking for.

Unfortunately, my denials weren't sitting well. In fact, they were giving me a serious headache. I sat back and rubbed my eyes, thinking through all the strange experiences I'd had since moving into my little church.

Gren, Niele, the strange bat, and that fog. I really was in Wonderland.

My gaze slid toward the ceiling. High above my head and out of sight, was a bell that rang thirteen times every night at Midnight. Why thirteen? There had to be some significance. Even if the significance was just that somebody had set the auto-ringing-thingy wrong.

That would be the simplest answer.

Nobody had warned me about a rogue bell when I bought the building. If the thing was defective, shouldn't that have been disclosed? I wasn't sure if it would have kept me from buying the place, but I might have demanded it be fixed before I moved in.

Whatever the cause, that bell seemed to represent the beginning of all my nocturnal challenges. It had to mean something. And I needed to find out what.

I climbed to my feet and headed into the kitchen. Glancing at the clock, I saw that it was five-thirty in the morning. A respectable time to start my day.

Sort of.

Watching the coffee stream into my favorite mug, I started a mental list for the day. I'd already had some things planned, but I added another item to the list. I was going to find Niele and Gren and pick their brains about the Lares thing.

There had to be a reason they believed I was one of those mystical deities. As soon as I knew what the reason was, I'd disabuse them of the notion.

Explaining the events of the night before was a harder problem to solve, so I shoved that aside to be dealt with later.

Feeling better about things in general, I took my coffee into my room. I'd shower and get dressed for the day. Then, when the sun came up, I'd go looking for my hopefully not-naked gardener.

He had some 'splainin' to do.

Niele was nowhere to be found. So I headed into Rome instead, intending to pick up a few things I needed for the house. I parked and entered the local discount store with a very long list of items. Even as I stepped through the doors, I thought of two more things I should get.

Happy to be out of the house for a couple of hours, I settled contentedly into my shopping.

Two bathroom rugs, a new shower curtain, five new bath towels, and a cute set of shower hooks in the shape of blown-glass crosses later, I headed for the kitchen section to see about getting new glasses and mugs. My cherished stemless wine glasses were dangerously depleted, to the point where, if I had more than two people over for drinks, I was going to have to serve somebody in a pink sippy cup.

Don't ask me why I have a sippy cup in my cabinet. I can't remember. I have a distant recollection of somebody's grandkid visiting once and forgetting the cup when she left. The bigger question was why I'd never gotten rid of it. Maybe I thought that when I got to be ninety-mpf years old, with knobby, arthritic hands and several unplanned naps in my day, I'd find it useful.

Practical. That's me.

I was reaching for an adult-sized insulated sippy cup equivalent, thinking it might come in handy when I started my planned daily walk regimen (snort), when a shrill scream brought my head snapping up.

Something about the scream scraped sharp fingernails across my nerves, urging me to act. The insulated bottle fell from my suddenly nerveless fingers.

Gong! An internal bell rang inside my head and I grabbed my cart and started running down the aisle toward the shrieks, shoving it recklessly ahead of me.

As I ran the screaming amplified into a relentless ululation of terror.

My nostrils twitched as I rounded the endcap.

Smoke rose above the product shelves from two aisles over. I abandoned the cart and took off running, starkly aware that somebody was in terrible danger.

I skidded ungracefully around the end of the aisle and spotted a small group of people, all looking horrified and helpless.

Flames licked up from a spot several feet away, and the young woman who'd been shrieking stopped just long enough to scream for someone to call the fire department.

I pushed my way through the crowd and felt my lungs clench at the sight ahead of me.

A small child, probably no more than two years old, with curly blonde hair and an adorable button nose, stood in the very center of a ring of fire that rose three feet above the floor.

Amazingly, the fire didn't seem to be burning the tiles beneath it, and it didn't seem to be spreading. It kept a perfect circle around the little girl, whose wide blue eyes were shiny with tears. She stood with her chubby little arms in the air, begging her mother to pick her up.

But the mother couldn't get to her. The child held a small pink blanket in one chubby fist. To my horror, I saw that one corner of the blanket was inches from the fire. If the child moved toward her mother, even two inches, the blanket would catch on fire and the situation would get much worse than it already was.

Gong!

I watched in horror as the mother dodged toward the wall of flames and jumped back with a squeal, holding one burned arm close. It was only a matter of time before she did something drastic that might be the end of both of them.

I couldn't let her do that. I had to stop her.

Gong!

"Coming through," called a male voice as a dark-haired man, holding a canister in one hand, pushed through the crowd. "I have a fire extinguisher. Stand back."

Relief loosened my chest, and I took a deep breath. Crisis averted.

He sprayed white foam over the fire.

Nothing happened.

Gong!

Frowning, the man sprayed more foam and kept spraying until the shelves and floor around the fire were covered in the stuff.

But the fire, the baby, and the blanket were untouched.

The gongs came fast and furious inside my brain.

My lungs seized up, and I saw stars. That was no ordinary fire.

The baby took a step, sobbing for her mommy, and the fire grabbed greedily at the pink blanket, flaring up with an unnatural appetite. The little girl shrieked as the flames shot quickly up the blanket toward her little hand.

Her mother was screaming for her to drop it, but she was too scared and didn't seem to hear.

Unable to breathe or think, I shoved the mother back and held my hands toward the flame, palms out. I didn't consider what I was about to do. Something rolled through me that I couldn't identify. I only knew that I'd felt it before…in my yard when the fog had hidden unseen enemies.

Gong!

A single word flared in my mind, throbbing with specific intent. I grabbed the word and let the energy behind it flow toward my outstretched hands. It pulsed there, gaining power as I tried to find the conduit to let it go. Suddenly, it came to me. Like the guiding illumination of cat-eyes along a pitch-black road, I saw what I needed to do.

Taking a deep breath, I let all my muscles relax and closed my eyes. The command slid easily from my mind to my lips. Though the expulsion was gentle, the power of the command was anything but. It burst from my tongue with the power of a lightning bolt. "Douse!"

A gust of air shot down the aisle, blowing my hair around my face. I stood firm against it, my palms still out and the word still anchored to my intent.

The gust of wind grabbed the blaze and ripped it away, flinging it toward the thirty-foot-high ceiling and then yanking it down the aisle, away from the child.

The flames disappeared with a soft pop of displaced air.

The little girl was free. Her mother dove in and snatched her up, sobbing with relief.

I sagged to the floor, exhausted. My bones felt like someone had sucked all the marrow out of them.

The pealing of the bell inside my head had gone quiet. My raging heartbeat slowed.

The soft murmur of conversation drifted away. In the distance, a child laughed. And my eyes shot open.

I was alone in the aisle. Everyone else had just moved on as if nothing had happened.

I stared around with shock. How was that possible?

No scorching marked the floor in front of me. I sniffed the air. There was a slight tang of ozone, like the harbinger of a coming storm, but not the smallest tinge of smoke.

"Are you all right?" A deep voice asked from behind me. "Did you fall?"

I turned to find the man who had only seconds earlier wielded the fire extinguisher. The extinguisher was gone, and he was looking down at me with a worried expression on his face.

I realized I was still sprawled across the floor. "Oh. Yeah. I'm fine."

He offered me a hand and I took it, allowing him to pull me to my feet.

"I just tripped over something."

His concern for me turned to something that looked like worry. Probably about a potential lawsuit. That was the moment I realized he was likely the store manager.

I smiled, offering him my hand. "I'm just clumsy. My name is Aggy."

Some of the worry leached from his face. He shook my hand. "I'm Paul. It's nice to meet you. Are you sure you're okay?"

"I am. But thank you for your concern. I'll just go get my cart..."

I was nearly to the end of the aisle before he called out. "Aggy?"

Turning, I gave him another smile. "Yes?"

"I'm new in Rome." He threaded his fingers together, looking uncomfortable. "I couldn't help but notice you're not wearing a ring..."

Alarm flared in my middle. "Oh!" I said, feeling instantly stupid. He was trying to ask me out. "Welcome to Rome!" I said, sounding like an idiot. "It's really nice here." *Smooth Aggy. Jeezopete!*

"Yes. Well, I was wondering if you'd like to have dinner with me sometime?"

"Um. I might. Sometime." Realizing how strange that response sounded, I winced. "What I mean is. I'm recently divorced. I don't think I'm ready to date yet. Maybe another time?"

A smile turned his pleasant face into a handsome one. "I'd like that. No pressure. Later is good. I'll probably see you around?"

I nodded. "Absolutely. Have a great day, Paul."

I left him staring after me, his gaze speculative, and hurried to my cart. It took another couple of minutes for the reality to sink in that I'd just been hit on by a nice man. A good-looking, nice man.

That hadn't happened to me in years.

I grinned. The grin stayed with me through three aisles. It clung to my face through a new set of wine glasses, new kitchen towels, two potted plants, and a partridge in a pear tree.

Okay, that last thing wasn't actually a partridge. Nor was it sitting in a pear tree. It was really more like an oversized bat with scary eyes. And it was hanging from the frozen pizza case on aisle fifty-one.

Staring right at me.

7

AND IF SHE FAILS, HER PLANS AMISS…

The bat disappeared. Just like that. In the blink of an eye. One second it was there, and the next, it was gone, leaving me to consider the strong possibility that I was losing my mind. I rubbed my eyes with the heels of my hands. The bat had just been a figment of my exhausted mind.

I glanced back up at the empty corner, high above me, and it was still empty. Good.

Shaking my head, I turned toward the checkout area. I'd had quite enough fun shopping for the day.

My phone rang as I was loading all my purchases into the back of my elderly Range Rover. I hit the Answer button without thinking. "Hello?"

Shoving the last bag inside the car, I closed the door.

"Hey!" Bev said, sounding excited. "I have a

contractor coming over tomorrow night. I hope that's okay?"

"You found somebody? I have calls in to several people, but nobody's calling me back."

"I did. We'll be there at six o'clock tomorrow night. If that's okay with you?"

I shoved the cart into the cart caddy. "Absolutely! I can't wait."

"Great! How's it going with the unpacking?"

Slipping behind the wheel, I locked the doors and started the engine. I chewed my bottom lip, wanting badly to tell Bev all about my adventures. But she'd think I was losing my mind. Just like I did. "Good. The kitchen and the bathroom are all done. In fact, I just got some new rugs and stuff to pretty them up."

"I can't wait to see them. I saw a rug that would be perfect in front of your couch. I'll send you the picture in a few."

I grinned. The house was really starting to come together. "Great. I'll see you tomorrow night."

The trip home took exactly five minutes. That was one of the things I loved most about the location of my new place. It had a definite country feel, but I was mere minutes from just about anything I needed in Rome.

It was my perfect spot.

Then I remembered the bat. Okay, that was less than perfect. Grimacing inwardly, I decided that it was time for me to make another visit to the belfry. If there was something wonky about that bat, I needed to know what it was. Because, with my recent move, my life had gone from boring and unsatisfactory to...

To what, exactly?

Exciting and unpredictable? Despite everything, I hadn't suffered even one second of regret for the move. In fact, I suddenly realized I was brimming with anticipation from the moment I jumped out of bed...or crawled painfully, shoving at the bees' nest on my head.

Potato, Potahto.

I might be living an adventure, but I was still a middle-aged woman. And dang proud of it! I'd packed a lot of experience and smarts into those forty-five years. I wouldn't go back to being twenty-nine again for anything in the world.

Well, except maybe for the ability to eat whatever I wanted and not get fat. That would be nice.

Despite my intention to revisit the bat in my belfry...I chuckled to myself every time I thought those words...I took my time installing my purchases in the bathroom and kitchen. They made the place feel like home, yet brand new at the same time.

When I was done, I felt good about the result.

With no more decorating to delay me, I decided I needed another cup of coffee before I climbed the stairs. As I stood at the coffee maker, I stared out the window and caught movement among the tombstones.

Niele!

Making a quick decision, I grabbed a to-go cup for my coffee and headed out to the graveyard to chat with him.

Monty bounded out of the house and ran ahead, chasing a random grasshopper and then getting distracted by a low-flying bird.

The greenskeeper stood behind one of the larger markers in the graveyard, his bare shoulders gleaming in the sun.

Irritation flared, and I quickly forgot my purpose for approaching him. "I asked you to wear pants," I said to the naked greenskeeper.

He turned in surprise, a ready smile finding his homely face. "Madam Lares! What a nice surprise. Did you come to view my progress?"

I took a moment to look around, discovering that he had, in fact, made good progress. Most of the stones stood straight and gleamed in the sunlight from a recent scrubbing. The grass was short, not a weed in sight, and fresh flowers bloomed in small, tidy clumps before each stone.

I blinked. "How'd you make the flowers grow so quickly?"

His grin widened. "Now, madam. A gnome doesn't give away his gardening secrets."

A gnome? I blinked in surprise. "Erm..." Yikes!

The man believed he was a fantasy creature. That was alarming. I'd have to ask Gren if Niele was safe to have around.

"I'm pleased you like my work. I have to admit it's been satisfactory returning these resting places to their former glory."

I nodded, eying his naked chest. "Niele, did you forget that I asked you to put on some clothes?"

He shook his head. "No, madam. You did not. You asked me to wear pants."

"Okay," I raised my brows. "So?"

Before I realized his intent, he stepped out from behind the marker.

I gave a violent twitch. "Oh!" And tried to cover my eyes.

"I hope you don't find this attire too presumptuous of me. I thought, given my place as the greenskeeper, that it was appropriate."

I stared at his "pants," my mouth dropping unattractively open. He waited for my approval, his smile slowly draining away when I was too stunned to give it.

"You don't approve?" he finally asked.

"I..." Forcing my lips to close, I cleared my throat. "You're wearing vines."

He nodded. "Flowering vines. In the gnomenclature, it is formal attire, not to be worn except for the King's balls. But I hoped you wouldn't mind."

I didn't mind. But the king's balls probably did.

I cleared my throat again to buy myself some time. Narrowing my gaze, I opened my lips. "Um, are those rose vines?"

He winced, one blocky hand moving toward the living loincloth as if he wanted to shift something. I felt my eyes go wide, and he stopped. "Yes, madam."

"Did you remove the, um, thorns?"

His grimace was all the answer I needed. "That wouldn't be proper, madam. We celebrate all living things. To strip the vines of their natural protection would be sacrilege."

"I see." I cleared my throat again. "But what about *your* natural protection? Those thorns must be painful."

His shoulders moved slightly in a shrug. He didn't deny it.

"Maybe if you just wore some regular pants?"

He straightened to his full height. "That would be unseemly, madam. It would go against the gnomenclature. I couldn't do that, Madam Lares."

"What exactly is the gnomenclature?" I asked. I was becoming more and more convinced that the man was a thorn short of a complete vine.

"It is our code. It governs all gnomish things."

I tried to remember if the little gnome statues at the garden center had been naked. I drew a blank on that, recalling pointy hats and bulbous noses but nothing else. Niele did have a bulbous nose. I eyed his head. The frizzy silver hair was sans a pointy hat.

Deciding not to get waylaid, I sighed. "Okay, we'll discuss this later. I wanted to ask you about last night."

His brows lifted. "Last night?"

"Yes. The fog. The attack."

It was his turn to widen his eyes. "Madam?"

"You don't know about it?"

He scrubbed a hand over his chin, looking non-plussed. "I wasn't aware my services were needed last evening, so I left the grounds."

He and I really needed to sit down and hammer out work hours and dress code. And salary. We hadn't talked about how he got paid. "No problem," I said. "It was irrational of me to assume you hang out here all the time. My bad."

"Your bad what, madam?"

I barked out a laugh at the question. "Sorry. I meant it was my mistake."

He inclined his head. "If you don't mind my asking, what happened?"

"The fog was really bad, and Monty got lost in it. I was trying to find him when someone shot some kind of fire at us."

Niele tilted his head in a familiar way. "Us?"

"Me and Gren."

Niele's face suddenly flushed a dark red. "That scoundrel Lungren attacked you?"

Scoundrel? "No." I frowned. "Gren was trying to help me."

"Help?" His voice rose nearly to a shout.

It shocked me. The man had always spoken to me with quiet deference. I took a step back.

He noticed and held up his hands. "I do apologize, madam..."

"Stop right there," I said, frowning. "I have to insist you call me Aggy."

Niele gave me a shallow bow. "Madam Aggy Lares." He looked thoughtful. "It will require more time to recite all your names. I'll have to plan for that in future conversations."

I closed my eyes, striving for patience. "Just Aggy will do fine."

"Madam Just Aggy Lares?" He counted the names off on his thick fingers. "I'll need to time it out. Brief conversations will be out of the question, I'm afraid. But no worries. We'll muddle through."

He had to be putting me on. Shaking my head, I tried again. "Gren said something about devils? Do you know what he meant?"

"Devils?" Niele glanced around the graveyard as if afraid there were devils hiding behind the tombstones. "It can't be." He wrung his big hands. "Has it been a hundred years already?" He began to pace, mumbling to himself.

"Niele?"

The gardener shook his head. "The prophecy. But, of course, that's why you're here. The last Lares..." His eyes darkened. "Well, it's best not to dwell." He stopped in front of me, his expression earnest. "I'll do some investigating, madam."

I arched a brow.

"I apologize." He gave me a little bow. "Madam Just Aggy Lares."

"Only Aggy," I tried again.

"Madam, really, we'll be out here all night if I add another name to the mix. Are you sure you need them all?"

I stared at him, trying to figure out if he was pulling my leg. I thought his lips might have twitched. Was that a sparkle in his dark eyes?

Finally, I shook my head and turned back toward the house. "Let me know if you find out anything," I told him.

"Yes, Madam Only Just Aggy Lares."

I shook my head. "You're a scoundrel, you know that, Niele Greenskeeper Gnome?"

I thought I heard a soft chuckle. "So I've been told."

I had a hand on the doorknob before I realized I'd never asked him about the bat.

Turning around, I looked toward the graveyard and saw that he was gone. "Well, that was fast."

Apparently, I was on my own.

Monty came running from around the front of the house.

He had a grasshopper in his mouth, one long, green leg sticking out the side. "Drop it!" I told him.

He did, spitting the soggy bug onto the patio. After a beat, the thing shook spit from its legs and limped away. "Come on, buddy. You and I have a date with a bat."

Even as I said the words, I couldn't believe I was actually going up those stairs again.

8

HER ACTIONS DRAWN BY FAUSTIAN WISH...

I stood next to the bell, my eyes trained on the corner where the bat had been perched the last time I'd been there.

It was gone.

Monty sniffed happily along the short walls, stopping to stand on his back legs and peer out into the yard.

I stood behind him, looking out at the empty graveyard and the yard. Staring down on it for the first time in daylight, I realized how much the yard had changed since I'd moved in. Niele had been busy. The thick grass was cut short and vibrant green. The bushes had been shaped, their leaves glossy with health. Even the edge of the patio had been trimmed, a perfect ribbon of rich black dirt giving it a definition it hadn't had before.

My gaze caught on the tall hedge-like bush at

the corner of the patio. It had been unkempt and wild when I'd moved in. I'd planned to cut it down at the earliest opportunity. After Niele's handiwork, it was shaped like a dancing woman holding some kind of bowl and horn. The detail on it was incredible.

My gaze slid to the graveyard again. Niele was indeed a talented greenskeeper. I felt a small smile tug on my lips. The place was really starting to come together.

Monty woofed. My gaze shot to the corner where the bat had been. It was still empty.

"What is it, little man? What do you see?" The words died on my lips. Something moved among the tombstones below. Something shimmery and...

I blinked. A single *gong!* sounded inside my mind. A warning? Or just a heads up that something was there?

A man knelt before a gravestone, his hand smoothing over the freshly polished surface with a sort of reverence. Was he a relative of the deceased? Without giving it any more thought, I turned and trotted down the steps. Monty's nails clacked along behind me and, by the time I reached the breezeway, he was bouncing excitedly, ready for another adventure.

He shot out the door ahead of me and ran toward the still-kneeling figure. The man straightened as Monty shot past the first marker, and he clasped his hands in front of him while favoring my dog with a welcoming smile.

"Monty!" I yelled, afraid he'd make a pest of himself. But I needn't have worried. He stopped in front of the man and dropped to his butt, his fringe of a tail dusting the grass with joyful exuberance.

The man bent to pat him on the head. "Hello, young man. It's nice to see you. What's your name?"

"Monty," I told the man as I slowed to a panting walk. I smiled. "Hello. I'm Aggy. I just moved in."

The man favored me with a pleasant smile. "Aggy." He took my hand between both of his. I noticed a couple of things at once. First, his hands were cold and his skin soft. And second, he wore a collar. "I'm Reverend Dodson. It's a pleasure."

I looked into his kind brown eyes and felt as if I'd found a friend. He was very thin, just under six feet tall, I'd guess, though his slightly stooped posture made it hard to judge. His lean face was heavily creased, his skin was an unhealthy shade of gray. But the eyes were sharp, sparking with intelligence and interest.

"You're a pastor? Did you serve here?"

He nodded, favoring my new home with a wistful glance. "For twenty years. I loved this church."

"Would you like to join me for some tea? Or I have coffee."

He didn't respond, his gaze still fixed on the

elegant old structure. "I've been hearing the bells the last two nights."

My eyes went wide. "You have? Do you live nearby?"

"I do," he said, not clarifying. "It's unusual for the bell to toll thirteen times." He frowned. "It's a concern."

His words sucked some of the warmth from the afternoon sun. "Oh? I wasn't sure if it was normal. Is there a way to turn it off?"

He gave me a patient smile. "Turn it off?" He chuckled. "No, child. The bell rings as needed. It's self-motivated."

What a strange way to put it, I thought. As if the bell were sentient. "Really?" I narrowed my eyes. "It can't ring itself. Something must be managing it."

His smile didn't waver. His expression gave me the impression he was merely trying to keep the crazy lady from losing her mind. Though, I wasn't the one who was claiming the bell rang itself when it felt like it. I decided to play along for the moment. "Why would it suddenly start ringing?"

He pondered that for a moment, his lips pursed in thought. "The bell has several purposes. It's a call to worship, of course. It also signals a celebration or, in some cases, a crisis. But in this case, I believe we're experiencing a warning."

A little more of the warmth leached from the day. "A warning? About what?"

He rested a gray hand on the rounded top of the tombstone. Rather than answer my question, he told me a story. "Mary Martin was a simple woman." He ran his fingers over the name carved in three-inch-high letters on the surface of the stone. "She loved her husband, cherished her children, and was active in Rome charity circles," he said, frowning. He moved to a marker two down from the unfortunate Mary. "Dix Walters trusted no one. He was a particularly unlikeable man whose temper ranged from ugly to downright despicable on any given day. Nobody mourned the man's death. I'll admit even I had trouble praying for his soul." Reverend Dodson hung his head, looking as if he were still filled with shame by the admission. Then he glanced at me. "Each of these stones marks a life lived. Each one records a range of years, an array of experiences. Decisions celebrated or regretted." His gaze sharpened, and I got the impression he was desperate for me to understand something. "Human beings are fallible, Aggy. We're flawed. But our true spirits are hidden throughout our lives. Our physical presence serves as a mask rather than a window into our souls. Do you understand?"

He looked at me so earnestly, I wanted to say I did understand. But I didn't. Not at all.

I shook my head. "I'm sorry."

He sighed, reaching out to squeeze my hand. "Mary Martin killed her entire family and buried them in her back yard. Believing that she'd lost her loved ones to the cruel hand of a passing stranger, Rome grieved with her, favored her with kindness. In the end, their kindness was her undoing. True evil cannot survive in a place where love thrives. She grew more unhinged by the day and eventually drove her car into a tree here in the churchyard." He pointed toward the largest tree near the road.

I'd noticed the deep, horizontal scar on the trunk of that tree. "That's horrible," I said.

He nodded.

"And Dix?" I asked, expecting him to say the man secretly loved kittens.

"Terrible man. A horror until his death. Died of liver disease. He was a mean and incorrigible drunk."

I blinked. "Oh. I thought..."

He looked sheepish. "That I was contrasting them. Maybe. But I dropped the thread. I've always been a terrible storyteller. You have my apologies."

I fought a grin. "Hey, do you know anything about the bat in the belfry?"

The reverend's lips twitched. "Bats in the belfry, huh? My story wasn't *that* bad."

I let the grin escape. "I wasn't referring to you. There really is a bat up there, sometimes. And it's been..." I hesitated because I knew he'd think I was crazy.

"It's been what?"

"I...saw it at the discount store in Rome."

His eyes widened. "You did? How do you know it's the same one?"

I winced internally. Did I really want to tell him I saw the thing change size? "Sometimes it has yellow eyes. They're alarming."

"I can imagine." He shook his head. "I've never heard of a bat with yellow eyes. Perhaps it has a condition."

"A condition," I said, trying it on for size. "Maybe."

"Well, I'm off," the good reverend told me. "It was really nice to meet you, Aggy. I'll see you around."

"Come any time. I've enjoyed chatting with you. And I might have more questions about the church. If you don't mind."

"I don't mind at all. I'll answer anything I can." He started to turn and stopped, lifting an intense gaze to mine. "Beware the thirteenth peal, Madam Lares. It portends great danger."

Then he smiled and waved, walking toward the trees at the edge of the graveyard as if he'd never given me such a dire warning.

I considered chasing after him to ask what he'd meant. But something told me he wouldn't elaborate. In fact, from the way it was delivered, almost like a prophecy or something, I wasn't sure he'd even know what it meant.

When I looked for him again, he was just...gone.

"*Heads up! It's your mother calling!*" a familiar voice shouted into the quiet. I jumped and yelped in surprise, glancing around with my pulse pounding in my ears.

"*Heads up! It's your mother calling! Get off your duff and answer the phone.*"

I closed my eyes, taking a deep breath. Mavis had done it again. Sliding my phone out of my pocket, I stabbed the Answer button before Mavis' new ring tone could renew its assault. "Where do you get these things?" I asked in a half-amused tone.

Mavis's response was an unrepentant chuckle. "I'm not telling you that. It's a trade secret."

"Oh? And just what trade would that be?"

Mavis snorted. "I just wanted to check in and see how it was going. Are you getting settled in?"

With a final glance toward the spot where the Reverend had disappeared, I headed back toward the house. Maybe the bat was back in my belfry. *Heh.* That never got old.

"Actually, I feel like I turned a corner today." I told her about my shopping expedition, sans endangered toddler and disturbing bat events, and finished with a quick sketch of my conversation with the store manager. "I think he was actually hitting on me," I told her, a smile in my voice.

"Well, of course he was, honey. Have you looked in the mirror lately? You're a beautiful woman."

I glanced at the kitchen door and then discarded

the idea of going back inside. I sat at the table on the patio instead. It was a beautiful evening, with the coming sunset painting the bottom edge of the horizon. The breezes were soft and warm, carrying the sweet scent of freshly cut grass and flowers across the yard to tantalize my senses.

Mavis's words had me fighting an automatic eye-roll in dismissal of her compliment. I'd always been bad at accepting accolades. I didn't trust them, no matter who they came from. Something inside my brain automatically translated bits of flattery into small lies that were only meant to make me feel better. "Yeah, yeah."

"You are so stubborn," Mavis said, real frustration in her voice. "One of these days, I'm going to make you see yourself as you really are."

I bit my lip, wondering if I would ever really know myself. After all the weird stuff that had recently happened and my apparent connection to all of it, I was starting to doubt my own sanity.

"So, are you going out with him?"

I blinked as her words burrowed their way past my internal dialogue. "Huh?"

"The store manager. Are you going to let him take you out?"

I shuddered at the thought. "Not now. I'm not ready to date yet." I couldn't tell from Mavis's silence if she was happy about my statement or not. I suspected that her feelings were mixed.

She sighed. "Well, don't wait too long, honey. You deserve happiness. Lots of it."

Tears burned my eyes. "Thanks, mom."

I imagined her smile at my calling her mom. She was always touched by it. At that moment, I realized I should always call her mom. She deserved it. "Hey, Bev's bringing a contractor over tomorrow to talk about the renovation. You should come too."

"I'd love that!"

We chatted for a half-hour about nothing special, but when I hung up, I felt energized and happy. Mavis always had that effect on me. She'd been a balm for my worries and sadness for years. I was beyond ecstatic that she and Bev were going to work with me on the shop. Asking them had been a stroke of genius on my part.

Monty came running up to the house, barking. I had a momentary flash of alarm as I realized he'd been somewhere at the back of the property, and I hadn't even noticed he was gone.

I frowned. I'd never explored the wooded acreage at the back of my property. I suddenly needed to know what was back there. If there was a busy highway or a railroad, I'd need to make sure to keep my dog closer to home.

Pushing to my feet, I set off in that direction, with Monty jumping excitedly around my feet. As we neared the woods, he tore off ahead of me, pretty much ignoring my screams to stay close.

Monty disappeared into a dense line of trees and was swallowed up by the glooms. It suddenly occurred to me that visiting the woods might not be the smartest thing to do so close to dusk. It would probably be easier to see and harder to get lost in the bright sun of mid-morning.

I fought an urge to call my dog back and go home.

But something drove me forward.

My need to explore the woods had moved beyond simple curiosity to almost a compulsion. An immutable feeling that something was wrong inside that wood.

And with the thought, a resounding *Gong!* sounded inside my head.

My heart pounding loudly in the dense quiet permeating the space, I stepped between two enormous trees and found myself standing in the middle of a fairytale.

9

IF EVERY SOUL WITHIN HER
PURPOSE...

The air seemed to sparkle with motes of unnatural, multi-colored light. The illumination bathed the area under the trees, its spectrum of colors giving the space a magical feel. The soft whir of tiny wings spun past me at every turn, and bursts of sparkling light briefly illuminated the dozens of fairies fluttering around beneath the enormous, slightly intimidating army of old trees.

Despite the late hour, a butterfly drifted past, its wings a pale yellow with vibrant purple and blue patterning. The stunning creature was the size of my hand. It trembled in front of me, its antennae twitching with curiosity as two dark eyes seemed to take my measure.

I lifted an arm and the butterfly drifted into my hand, light as air, its proboscis tapping along my skin.

It was a magical moment, and I was completely charmed.

A loud snap startled the butterfly into the air, where it quickly fluttered away. I watched it for a moment and then turned toward the sound I'd heard.

Monty ran from the underbrush, tail tucked and eyes wide. He slammed into my legs and huddled there, looking terrified. His muscular little body trembled against my leg. "What's wrong, buddy?"

The little dog's obvious fear brought back my own trepidation as I'd approached the wood. Something cold slipped down my spine and I shivered, rubbing my arms against a growing cold.

A cool breeze carried the putrid scent of death with it. Another loud snap had me reaching for Monty.

Large, gray shapes moved among the trees, silent and inhumanly fast.

Gong!

My heart beat a staccato rhythm against my ribs, the sound speeding as the light disappeared from the once magical spot. "Who's there?" I asked, proud of the strength of my voice, especially with my teeth clacking together like skeleton bones in a stiff wind.

Gong!

The answer to my question came in the form of another loud crack. I started to turn, Monty squiggling in my arms, and the shadows exploded toward me, a charcoal blur that smelled like a mix of rotten eggs and putrid meat. Something slammed into me, sending me skidding across the leafy dirt. Monty flew out of my arms and I screamed his name. I struggled to see him as fear for both him and me made it hard to breathe.

Gong!

I shoved at the shadowy form, my hands encountering flesh that felt like burnt wood after it had cooled. Enhancing that image, soft, gray ash fluttered to the ground from the spot where I shoved. Enormous, clawed hands held me on the ground. "Get off me!" I screamed, the words shrill with panic. My breath wheezed in and out of my lungs as I struggled, the weight of my assailant compressing my chest.

Foul air bathed my face from the creature's breath, and a deep rumble of laughter made me want to scream in rage and fear.

The warning gongs reverberating inside my brain became white noise as I fought for my life. The moon rose above the trees, finally casting a warm silvered light onto the spot where I struggled for my life. The light would have been comforting except for the fact that it better illuminated the thing above me. My gaze locked onto the wide head, which was made even wider by two curved horns on the sides. A fiery gaze...not metaphorically fiery, but actually fire-filled, with yellow and red flames snapping in their depths...stared down at me. The nose was broad and flat, with large, moist slashes for nostrils.

The monster's mouth opened, a wide slash of leathery lips containing a set of teeth that I knew would invade my dreams for the rest of my life. The thing's fangs were deadly sharp and as long as my pinky fingers. But it was the voice—too deep to be real, graveled, and dripping with ugly menace—that nearly had me peeing my pants. "Give us the key."

Beside me, Monty whined. I reached out blindly with one hand, my gaze never leaving the nightmare that held me in place. My fingers touched fur, and I felt his side rise and fall under too-rapid breaths. I kept my hand on him, but I wasn't sure if I was trying to reassure myself or Monty. "What key?" I choked out, swallowing hard.

"The key!!" he bellowed, spittle spraying the air around the nasty mouth.

I mentally chastised myself for thinking that what I was seeing was real. I was having a nightmare. Or, maybe I'd hit my head when I fell.

I squeezed my eyes closed and willed myself to wake. "This isn't real. This isn't real. This isn't..."

"Give us the KEY!" the thing screamed.

"I don't have a key!" I screamed back. "Get off me!"

A small black form flew out of the gathering dark, teeth flashing as Monty landed on the back of the nightmare monster.

"No!" I had to un-dream my dog. I couldn't let him get hurt, even if it was only a nightmare. "Monty, stop! Go home."

But, it was no good. Even in my nightmares, Monty was a dachshund. Dachshunds didn't give up on an idea once they'd gotten it firmly into their cute little heads. Especially if there was food involved.

Did the monster pinning me to the ground taste like chicken?

I was snapped out of my musings as the thing's horrible head started to turn. He'd apparently just noticed Monty chomping away on his back.

"Oh, no you don't," I yelled, and slammed my bony knee upward. I gained deep satisfaction from both the squishiness of my target and the long, pain-filled wail that followed my assault.

The thing reared up, and Monty slid off. The little dog danced away as the creature reached for him and then danced back in a determined attack, his snarls so impressive that, had I not known he only weighed twenty-one pounds, I'd have been afraid of him myself.

The weight on my chest suddenly lifted away. I shoved off the ground and scurried to Monty, tugging him close. "Buddy..." It was all I could say as tears flowed down my face.

Monty's little chest rose and fell in rapid breaths. His fur was grimy with dirt and tangled with sticks. He licked my face and whined.

My mind gradually encompassed the sounds of battle nearby, and I looked up. The shadowy monster was battling with another shadow, a large form on four legs, with a wide muzzle and eyes that glowed silver like the moon.

I climbed to my feet, snatching Monty off the ground. It was time to skedaddle.

A long, mournful howl filled the night. I shivered as the sound scraped along my nerves, clutching Monty tighter against me. "Let's get out of here," I said.

He whined in agreement.

I turned and backtracked to the yard, the feeling of being watched like fingernails clawing along my spine. Even when we were away from the woods and hurrying toward the house, I couldn't shake the feeling that we were being watched.

At the patio, I finally turned. And saw that I hadn't imagined that feeling.

The woods stretched black as pitch along the back of my property.

Except for at least a dozen fiery gazes, cutting through the darkness toward us.

I was too stirred up to eat. I fed Monty and then glanced at the door to the belfry. Stiffening my spine, I wrenched open the door and started to

climb. As soon as my foot hit the bottom stair, the
bell chimed in a single, melodic peal, and I jolted to
a stop. A beat later, I started up again, my steps
hurried.

Before I got halfway, Monty caught up with me,
still licking his lips from his hastily-eaten meal. He
started barking before he reached the top. My early
warning system.

I jolted to a stop on the top step, my eyes going
wide.

The bat wasn't stuck to the high corner of the
belfry. But there was a man standing at one of the
arched openings. He stood with his back to me, his
gaze locked on the distant tree line.

Monty, the little traitor, ran right up to the tall,
dark-haired man with the smoldering gaze. He
jumped up and put his little paws on my intruder's
leg, waiting for the scratch on his silky head he
considered his due.

"What are you doing up here?" I asked Gren.
"Did you go through my house?"

He turned an unreadable look my way. "I'm sorry
I didn't get there in time."

I blinked. Of all the things I'd expected he might
say, that hadn't even been on my radar. "Huh?"

Good one, Aggy. I scolded myself. *Sparkling
Conversational Ripostes R You.*

Lungren Maker slid his dark gaze over me...a

long, languid perusal of my form from head to toe. "You are unharmed?"

"I am. Unharmed," I finished awkwardly. I winced internally. I needed to stop hanging around all these renaissance era wannabes. I was starting to talk funny. "Why?"

He turned completely around, fixing me with an incredulous stare. "You went into the wood. Don't you think it's a little soon? You haven't even embraced your magic yet."

Magic? Nope, not going there. "I don't believe in magic." Except that I was starting to think, deep down inside, that I might possibly believe in it. And that I'd somehow fallen into an enormous vat of the stuff with my new life.

One dark eyebrow arched in disbelief. He gave me a wry look. "Oh? Then how do you explain what just happened out there?"

I couldn't hold his gaze. "Um. Monty and I went for a little walk." I punctuated my impossibly stupid statement with a little shoulder shrug.

"Ah. In the dark?"

I nodded, running a finger along the edge of the brass bell rather than look at him. "Technically, it was only dusky when I left. I was trying to see what was at the back of my property. Monty keeps disappearing into the woods, and I was worried about him." Even as I spoke the words, irritation stiffened my spine for explaining myself to him. A virtual stranger.

He stared at me for another minute and then nodded. "You are right to be concerned. That wood is a dangerous place. Neither you nor your stalwart little protector should be going into it."

I frowned. His words so closely mirrored my own thoughts about Monty that I had to wonder... "What did you see?"

Not bothering to answer my question, he stared out into the night. "They won't stop until they get what they want," he told me.

"The key?"

A smile curved across his handsome face, and I wanted to kick myself. He's tricked me into giving him information. "What *was* that thing?" I finally asked. Curiosity won out over my resistance, even at the expense of my pretending magic didn't exist.

His smile widened as he closed the distance between us. "They were magic."

If I'd have been a dog at that moment, I would surely have growled. "Funny."

He leaned against the wall and sighed, crossing his arms over his chest. I couldn't help noticing the way his shirt sleeves tightened over his muscular limbs. Whoever...whatever Lungren Maker was, he was a delicious creature.

"They are the lost ones," he finally told me. His

gaze sharpened, and he watched me carefully. "Your human mythology calls them devils."

I didn't realize my head was shaking in mute denial until he nodded. "Yes, Aggy. They are mythological creatures. Magic...creatures."

My knees threatened to give out as the reality I didn't want to face crashed into me. Even as I tried to deny it, I knew it to be true. I'd known it since thirteen peals from a bell that had no power source had enticed a magic fog into the yard and sent bolts of deadly fire in my direction.

I'd known it when a simple bat had changed size in front of me.

When I'd saved a toddler from burning to death with the use of a single word.

When something that looked like my nightmares slammed me to the ground and demanded that I give it some random key.

I slid to the floor and leaned against the wall, stars bursting before my eyes. "Magic is real."

Gren lowered himself gracefully down next to me. "It is. And you have magic in your lineage, Aggy. That is the only way you could have been called to serve as Lares."

I thought about my parents. My real parents. And realized my mother couldn't have been magical. If she had been, would she have still succumbed to cancer?

I glanced into his sexy dark eyes. "Who?"

Somehow, he understood my cryptic question. "That you will have to discover, Beautiful Aggy."

I shook my head, knowing it couldn't possibly be true. There'd been no indication at all that my father had magic. None. And my mother had been weak in both body and mind for most of her short life. Even as a self-involved teenager, I'd recognized that. Maybe I'd been adopted.

"It can't be."

"But it can, Madam Lares. And it is."

I forced myself to stop shaking my head. Denial was no longer an option. "So," I said, pulling air into my tight chest. "Magic, huh?"

His smile made my stomach do a happy rhumba. "Magic. It is everywhere if you have the sight to see it."

"Sight to see it? What does that mean, exactly? I know for a fact that I've never seen it before."

"Have you not? Have you never lived a moment you are certain you've lived before? Have you never seen a thing in your mind mere seconds before it played out exactly as you envisioned it?"

I had. Many times throughout my life. I'd always brushed it off as a coincidence or a figment of my imagination.

"Have you never seen something out of the corner of your eye that you brushed off without observing too closely? Something that seemed to strain the bounds of reality?"

I nodded. "Yeah." I slammed a fist into my thigh. "Cuss, cuss, swear!"

His midnight brows arced. "What is this language? I do not recognize it."

My lips twisted to hide a grin. "It's nothing."

He stood as gracefully as he'd lowered himself to the ground, offering me his hand.

After the briefest hesitation, I took it and let him pull me to my feet. I fell against him for the briefest moment when I found my feet and couldn't help noticing how heated his skin was and how delicious he smelled. He looked down at me with a warm gaze and then lifted one of my hands, pressing a lingering kiss to the back. "It will be an honor to serve you, Madam Lares."

Face heating with embarrassment, I turned away. "Is it really necessary to call me that?"

"Not always. In private I can call you Aggy if you'd prefer."

"I do prefer." I headed toward the stairs.

"And you may call me a deity among men."

I barked out a laugh.

His eyes sparkled with mirth when I looked back at him. "Gren, deity among men, would you like to stay for dinner?"

He followed me down the stairs. "That depends. What would you offer a deity among men? Not just any repast will do."

Feeling my entire body lighten with the banter, I

pretended to consider his question. "I have the perfect food for you. A feast christened by the goddess."

"Yes?"

I grasped the door handle and turned back. "Peanut butter and potato chip sandwiches."

His eyes lit as if I'd promised to crown him king of all men. "Milk?"

"Of course," I blew a disbelieving raspberry that he'd even asked.

He grew serious. "Only if you put it on some of that squishy white bread."

I laughed, shoved the door open, and stopped dead in my tracks, staring at the back of a skinny creature dressed in skinny black jeans and a black tunic. A straight bob of midnight hair brushed the creature's narrow shoulders, and a large nose ring pierced its small nose. The unknown entity was standing in front of my refrigerator. As we stood gaping, it turned and favored me with an incensed frown. "Dude! You don't have grape jelly? What the actual fudge is that all about?"

10

EMBRACES RIGHT O'ER EVIL SERVICE...

W hen we just stood there staring at her, the creature frowned. "What's wrong with you two? Do you have dementia or something?" She reached into the fridge and pulled out the bread. I noticed the jar of natural creamy peanut butter was already on the counter. She indicated it with a grimace. "What kind of peanut butter is this? It doesn't look very good."

Gren and I shared a look. He shrugged.

I finally shook off my shock and moved over to the counter, grabbing the jar of sweet, creamy goodness before the hostile young woman could. "This is *my* favorite peanut butter," I told her in my best "mom" voice. Okay, that might have been a stretch since I'd never been a mom, but I'd babysat a bunch of kids in my teens. "Which makes total sense since this is *my* house. Who are you, and why are you in my kitchen?" I seemed to be asking that a lot lately.

The kid glowered like a champ, her kohl-lined eyes narrowing. "I was here first."

My brows lifted. "Pardon me?"

She snorted. "Why? Did you do something you need to be pardoned for?"

I closed my eyes for a beat, then took a deep breath and tried again. "Let's start over." I offered her my hand. "I'm Aggy. I just moved into this place." I pointed to Gren. "That's Gren. He's my friend."

Gren lifted a hand and wiggled his fingers at my young intruder.

The girl eyed him appreciatively. Then she waggled her brows suggestively. "Friend, huh?"

My face heated.

Gren stepped forward and carefully took the loaf of bread from the girl's hand. "We were just about to have dinner. Would you care to join us?"

She tucked her chin like a turtle and waggled her head. "Duh."

I retrieved a knife from the silverware drawer and nodded at the girl. "Grape jelly's in the pantry. Grab that bag of chips while you're in there, please."

The girl shrugged and retrieved the items. "I guess you're not completely stupid."

I raised my brows.

"You have jelly."

"What a relief. You had me worried there for a minute. I thought I was beyond saving."

Despite her best efforts, her lips curved upward. "The place looks kind of cool."

Slathering peanut butter thickly onto a slice of bread, I glanced her way, checking for sarcasm. She appeared sincere. "Thanks. You never told me your name."

She grimaced. "Wanda." She eyed me as if daring me to make fun of the moniker. It was unusual, but not in a horrible way.

"It's nice to meet you, Wanda."

She didn't comment. The teen wandered around my kitchen, opening cabinets and checking out their contents. Her gaze fell on the door to the belfry. "You still got the bat?"

I nodded, cutting the first sandwich in half and then starting on the second one. "I haven't seen it for the last day or so, though. It might be gone."

"It isn't," the girl said. "It never leaves."

Gren cleared his throat. "Shall I pour the milk?"

"Please," I told him. "Glasses are..."

"Here," the girl finished for me. She opened the cabinet closest to the sink and pulled down three glasses, handing them to Gren.

"You said you were here first," I nudged, starting on sandwich number three. "Did you live here before?"

Her response was another shrug.

Gren set the glasses on the kitchen table. "Get the napkins, will you?" he asked the girl.

She went right to the spot where I kept them. I frowned. How many times had she been in my kitchen without my knowing?

I settled a plate which was laden with two PB&J sandwiches and a pile of chips in front of Wanda. I handed Gren a plate with two PB&C sandwiches and carried my own single sandwich to the table.

We ate in silence for a couple of minutes...if you didn't count the delighted moaning from Gren. Personally, I counted it as fodder for my dreams later.

"You were correct, Mad...er...Aggy," he told me as he swallowed his last bite. "That was indeed fit for a king."

I inclined my head. "Thank you. I've been told I make a mean PB&C. The secret is in the thicker peanut butter layer."

"And the squishy bread," Gren added helpfully.

I smiled. "And that."

"I come here every day," Wanda said quietly. "Always around the same time."

I sent Gren a startled look. "You do? I haven't seen you before."

She shrugged. "I'm good at laying low."

"Do you sleep here?" I asked, feeling silly. Surely if the child slept in my house, I'd know it. But I hadn't known she was stopping by, so maybe not.

She shook her head. "Not usually. Sometimes."

Wiping my fingers on a napkin, I took a sip of milk. I had the oddest feeling that I needed to tread carefully with the girl, or I'd alienate her. Strangely, that thought bothered me. Something wasn't right in her life. I had a feeling she didn't reach out very often. "Is there somewhere else you like to stay when you're not here?"

"No." She shoved her chair back, and I panicked. "Don't leave. Can't you stay and chat?"

She scowled at me. "You don't get it," she said angrily. "I *can't* leave. Not until..."

"Not until what?" Gren asked softly. Wanda put her plate and glass in the sink and threw her napkin away. She leaned against the counter, her hands gripping the granite behind her. "I just can't, okay?"

"Okay," I said. "We won't press for now. But I hope you'll tell me what's wrong when you can."

She pressed her lips together and thought about that for a beat. Then she gave me a tight nod.

"Good. Now, Wanda, what else do you need?"

"I'm going up to the belfry for a while."

"Okay," I said. I watched in frustration as she did exactly that. When she was gone, I looked at Gren. "Anything?"

He shook his head. "I have no idea what's going on. But I'll make some inquiries."

I nodded. "Me too. I'll ask Niele if he knows what the deal is with the girl." I frowned.

"What is it, Aggy? You look worried."

"I am. I can't help feeling like she might be a runaway. Usually, those kids are products of abusive home situations. I just wish she'd open up to us about it so we could help."

I realized after I'd spoken that I'd said *us* and *we*. It occurred to me that he might not want to be involved. "I'd like to help her if I can."

"I would as well," he assured me.

I sighed. "It's been a long day, and I'm beat. I haven't been getting much sleep lately."

He stood up. "I'll leave after I wash these dishes."

"That's not necessary. I have a dishwasher."

His eyes went wide. He glanced around the room.

"What?" I asked.

"Where is this dishwashing person? I haven't seen anyone."

I chuckled. "*This* is the dishwasher." I opened the door of the appliance, showing him its interior. He peered carefully inside, pulling the top and bottom racks out to examine them. "Astounding. And this scours the dishes for you?"

Gren was either totally clueless, or he truly was the renaissance man he seemed. "It does." I quickly rinsed the dishes and loaded the dishwasher. Then, though it wasn't quite full, I loaded a soap pod and started the washer so he could hear it working.

He shook his head, looking amazed. Then he

took my hands and kissed the back of each one before releasing them. "Take care, Aggy. Do not answer the bell's call tonight. There is danger in the fog."

I was afraid that was easier said than done. But I nodded. "I'm just going to go up and tell Wanda to lock the doors when she leaves. Goodnight, Gren."

"Goodnight, Beautiful Aggy."

Warmth and pleasure blossomed in my middle at his words. I watched him leave and then headed upstairs.

But when I reached the top, I discovered that Wanda wasn't there.

The belfry was empty.

I heard the bell in my dreams. It had already pealed several times before I managed to drag myself from sleep. Apparently, I'd been more exhausted than I'd thought. I'd taken a sleep aid, hoping to sleep right through the bell, and I'd nearly made it. But something deep inside me wouldn't allow that to happen. Something was nudging me... spiking my pulse with an urgent need to respond.

Monty trotted happily down his doggy stairs and bounced around on the floor while I slid my feet into slippers and tugged on my silky robe.

I yawned as I shuffled down the hall in my best

impression of a little old woman. Shoving at the rat's nest of my hair, I looked longingly at the coffee machine as I entered the kitchen. With Gren's words still on my mind, I didn't go outside. Instead, I climbed the steps to the belfry so I could observe the goings-on without being right in the middle of it.

The last gong lingered on the air as I opened the belfry door and started up the steps.

The bat was in its corner, yellow eyes watching as I shuffled over to the nearest window. "Hey, bat. How's things?"

It gave me a little chirp.

"That's good. What's going on out here?"

I shoved more hair out of my face and looked down at the silvery trails of fog winding around the tombstones far below.

The night sky was cloudy, heavy with unspent rain, and the moon skittered in and out of the clouds to shine intermittently over the ground below. I realized I could see pretty well even without the moon. Maybe that had something to do with the lightning strike?

I shook off my thoughts and blinked, realizing what I was looking at wasn't fog.

They were ghosts! Dozens of silvery forms inhabited the small, consecrated plot of land. They represented a variety of shapes and sizes and were dressed in human clothing that appeared to be from all eras. With a start, I realized they were *my* ghosts. They were the people who were buried on my land.

"Well, I'll be..."

It was kind of cool, really. In an extremely creepy and horrifying way.

I watched them drift in seemingly random paths, winding between the stones and occasionally stopping to perform some kind of face-to-face interaction.

Did they speak to one another? And, if they did, was it verbal or non-verbal?

Standing way up in the belfry, out of the fray, I found it all really fascinating. I was an observer. Safe and undetected in my little tower.

Another figure emerged from the fog. The new ghost was more corporeal. Unlike the others, he and his clothing weren't indistinct. The pants and shirt he wore were dark. Black, I thought, though it was impossible to tell for sure in the dark.

I shook off the snag in my thoughts and watched the figure move through the other ghosts. He was thin and slightly stooped, but he moved swiftly to the center of the graveyard and stopped, hands folded in front of him.

Like bees drawn to their queen, all the ghosts moved in his direction, appearing to wait for him to speak.

I blinked as they all gained color and detail they hadn't had before he arrived.

As he lifted his hands and greeted the assembled ghosts, I finally recognized him.

Reverend Dodson's gaze lifted to mine and he spoke clearly and distinctly, sounding as if he were standing right next to me. "Good evening, Madam Lares. How are you tonight?"

Every ghostly face turned up to me, a variety of expressions from peaceful to enraged, fixed on my cringing form.

Okay, scratch undetected. Safe? That remained to be seen. I lifted a hand. "Reverend. What are you up to down there?"

"The bells called, and we came," he told me with a wide smile. "Much to discuss."

He didn't explain any further than that, seeming to think that explained everything.

I crossed my arms over my chest as a cool breeze slid over me, carrying with it the rich and slightly sour scent of black dirt.

What did Reverend Dodson have to do with my ghosts? How did he have so much influence on them? I had no time to consider the answer to my questions. Without warning, the night boiled and shifted. The edges of the graveyard were suddenly lined with shadowy creatures whose oversized heads and curved horns were only too familiar.

The lost ones!

The horrifying creatures' blazing eyes were focused on the little group of ghosts with malevolent intent. They weren't there to discuss the rising price of a gallon of gas. They intended to cause harm.

An instinct rose up inside me and overwhelmed my good intention to stay out of the fray. The impulse felt as old as time and left me no option except to act. My mind played the scene below out to its logical conclusion. As I hit the top step, I threw a glance toward the bat. "If there's anything you can do to help, I suggest you get moving."

I didn't wait to see if the bat responded. I was already hitting the bottom step and wrenching open the back door.

Even as I ran toward the building crisis across a seemingly endless plot of grass, I had no idea what I was going to do.

Only that I needed to do something.

It was probably not the smartest decision I'd ever made.

11

THE LARES' MAGIC MAKES THEM WHOLE...

The devils raised their thick, gray arms to the sky and started chanting. The sound was a bass rumble on the night air, a strangely melodic thrum that grabbed hold of something in my center and tugged me across the yard.

As their intonations grew in strength, the trees began to sway in a violent wave high above our heads. Fog swirled up from the ground, its touch icy and hot all at once. Panic rose to choke off my breath, turning every inhalation into a struggle and every step toward the waiting danger a practice in sheer willpower.

Dodson's words played like a strident poem through my mind. *Beware the thirteenth peal, Madam Lares. It portends great danger.*

If he believed that, then why was he preparing to

face off with something that literally came straight from Hell?

At some point, I realized my footsteps had slowed to a mere shuffle. My legs felt heavy, and my skin was like ice. The fog had reached my thighs. Its touch was pain, infused with sharp motes of abject terror.

My heart pounded in my chest. My eyes bulged under emotions that felt like they belonged to someone else. My intentions, which had been thin and undefined to start with, were swamped beneath the raging need to survive.

The horned creatures' chanting collapsed into silence, the final growling notes fading slowly into the fog. A high-pitched shriek...what could only be described as a battle cry...undulated on the night air, and both factions charged.

I watched in horrified fascination as claw to mist combat erupted on my lawn.

The devils were ferocious, their claws and teeth relentless weapons against an army of foes that slipped from corporeal to spectral in the blink of an eye. I quickly understood in watching them that the ghosts couldn't do any damage without assuming a physical state. But they could also be harmed in that state. So theirs was a dance of changes, snapping into a solid form, striking, and then popping back to mist before the devils could retaliate.

Silvery figures drifted across the yard. Spectral

faces with dead black eyes fixed on me, and several of the ghosts surrounded me, their appraisals cold and hostile.

Where had they all come from? There had to be a hundred of them. The little graveyard held twenty-five souls. Something was happening that was bigger than my little burial ground.

A low, throbbing growl sent gooseflesh along my arms and lifted the hairs at my nape.

The specters around me scattered, and my feet wouldn't move. I was locked into place, like a woman-shaped popsicle whose stick had been jammed deep into the soil.

Hot breath bathed my nape. Teeth scraped over my skin, and a thick, curved horn entered my peripheral vision. I thought my eyes were going to bulge out of my face.

"Time to die, guardian," the familiar voice said. "Your little puppy isn't here to protect you this time." The creature's laughter sounded like bones grinding together.

I had to do something. I couldn't just stand there and let the thing eat me.

My gaze slid to the graveyard again. Some of the devils were crumpled in the grass, unmoving. I had no idea if they were alive and didn't much care. The ghosts were back in the graveyard, watching and waiting. The remaining lost ones stayed just beyond the boundary of the consecrated ground.

Wings fluttered overhead, followed by a chirping sound. Yellow eyes peered past me from where the bat, much larger than before, hovered on the air. Its mouth opened and it hissed, sounding more like an angry rat than a bat.

The creature at my back slammed a clawed hand onto my shoulder. Bones shifted painfully under my skin and I gasped. Then the claws dug in, and the creature gave me a violent shake that wrenched my head and sent new jolts of pain along my spine.

The bat shot forward, wings flapping wildly. I saw jagged-edged black wings and small, deadly claws slashing the air but couldn't turn to look at what was happening.

The fog surrounding me eased away under the bat's beating wings. Reverend Dodson appeared in front of me. He gave me a reassuring smile as several more ghosts popped in around him. As one, they all opened their mouths and the fog flowed toward them. My legs started to warm as the ghosts drew the mist away. I tested the new warmth and found I could move one leg. A moment later, I could move the other one. Pinpricks of pain stabbed along my calves and shins. I took a step forward and tried to shake it off. Turning toward the battle just a few feet away, I was just in time to see the devil slash a meaty hand at the bat and send it flying on a chirp of pain.

Without thinking, I threw out a hand. "Suspend!" Energy left my open palm in a gilded wash and enveloped the bat, wrapping it in a protective web.

I turned back to the lost one just as a massive tree branch flew toward its head. The branch slammed into the creature's left horn and it gave a heavy grunt before crumpling to the ground, unconscious.

Niele joined me with a worried look on his homely face. "I'm so sorry, Madam. If I'd known, I'd have come sooner."

I fluttered my fingers to release the bat from its protective bubble, and the little creature beat its wings, flying away toward the trees.

"Thank you!" I called out to the flying rodent. Its response drifted back to me on a chirp.

"And thank you, Niele." I jerked my head toward the nasty thing on the ground. The rest of the lost ones seemed to have disappeared. Apparently, loyalty wasn't a thing in their world. "What's their deal, anyway? Why do they keep attacking me?"

"It's not you, Madam Lares. The lost ones have long sought the key to return home." He stared toward a steel-gray sky, his thick body naked as the day he was born.

I forced my gaze higher and bit back a plea for him to put something on. The last time I'd done that, he'd woven himself into a torture device. I'd have to find another option. "So this is a regular thing?" I asked incredulously.

But Niele shook his head. "No, Madam. It happens every hundred years. And only during the thirteenth month, in the thirteen days of the thirteen peals."

"Thirteenth month? How often does that happen?" I asked, even as my mind produced the answer.

"Once every..."

"Thirteen years," I finished for him, shaking my head.

"Yes."

I stared at him for a long moment. "Are you telling me that I just happened to move into the church during this perfect alignment of a hundred years and the thirteens?" Could my luck really be that bad?

"No, Madam. I'm telling you that you were placed here during the Time of the thirteens to stop the lost ones from getting the key. It was pre-ordained."

Pre-ordained? My head ached at the thought. Of course it was.

The next evening, Bev and Mavis blew into the house on a chorus of laughter and a rhythmic click of heels.

The sound of their carefree happiness made me

smile, despite a great weariness leftover from the night before. "I'm in the kitchen!" I called out. Glancing at the clock, I saw that it was five PM. I knew I should get up and pour wine for them, but I somehow couldn't make myself rise from the kitchen chair.

Monty ran to greet them, followed by the usual cooing and smooching noises as they admired him appropriately.

Mavis swept into the room, her expression filled with pleasure. "Honey, the house looks amazing. You've been busy." Delicious aromas wafted toward me from the foil-covered pan in her hands.

I shoved to my feet, some of the weariness fleeing under the force of her sunny mood. "Thanks, mom." I gave her a hug, taking care to avoid the warm pan she was holding. My hug went on longer than normal just because I needed it.

She patted my back. "What is it, honey?"

I hadn't realized until she'd asked that I was crying. I quickly stepped away, scrubbing at my face with the heels of my hands. "Nothing. I'm just tired."

Bev floated in on a wave of shopping bags. She had a huge bottle of wine clutched in one perfectly manicured hand.

Monty bounced in behind her.

Her smiled died when she spotted me. "Good heavens, Aggy. What's wrong? You look all wrung out."

I grimaced, shoving at my messy hair. "I've been working all day. Sorry. I thought you were coming at six."

She shook her head, dropped the wine and the bags on the table and wrapped me in a hug, squeezing tight.

Like magic, the hug brought forth more tears.

"I'll pour," Mavis said, heading toward the counter to put her delicious-smelling bounty down. She retrieved the bottle of red wine and opened it with the special, mechanized bottle opener she'd given me the previous Christmas.

A minute later, a glass appeared in front of my face. I took it gratefully. "Thanks."

"Sit," Bev ordered. She took a glass from Mavis and sat down with me. "Thanks, mom." As Mavis filled plates with whatever she'd brought, Bev removed the shopping bags from the table and we sipped our wine.

Soon, we all had plates of homemade lasagna in front of us, and I was shoveling it up with near frantic enthusiasm. I didn't stop until my plate was empty. "I was hungry," I said, feeling better.

"You always were emotional when you needed to eat," Mavis said, reaching out to tuck a strand of my black hair behind an ear. I sighed, knowing she was right.

"Tell us," Bev said, pushing her half-eaten plate away and picking up her wine. "What's wrong?"

I stared at my chipped and broken nails, wishing I could. "Nothing. I really am just tired. I haven't been sleeping well."

Mavis's eyes went wide. "Do you have ghosts? I always wondered if these old churches had ghosts. It seems inevitable if you think about it."

Thinking of the scene in the graveyard the night before, I barked out a laugh. "You have no idea."

Bev and Mavis shared a look. Then Bev reached across the table and patted my hand. "I know somebody who can help with that. Let me make a call."

Her offer brought my head up in surprise. "No. I…" I frowned at her. "You believe in ghosts?"

"Of course," she responded, sipping her wine. "Don't you?"

I shrugged, not knowing how to answer without putting a hole in the emotional dam that was holding everything back.

"Demi Petrus had ghosts once," Mavis offered. "She claimed it was the ghost of a pool boy who'd drowned in her pool."

Despite myself, I had to ask. "Mrs. Petrus' pool boy drowned in her pool? Why didn't I know about that?"

Mavis shook her head. "Not while she was living in the house. It happened to the previous owner, apparently. They didn't disclose it. She wasn't even mad. You know Demi…" Mavis rolled her eyes.

Bev and I nodded.

"She called a priest and he came to the house. But she was more concerned with finding out exactly what types of things a ghost could do...if you know what I mean. Apparently, her pool boy ghost was really cute."

Mavis sipped her wine as Bev and I burst into laughter.

"Leave it to that woman to try to figure out how to seduce a ghost," Bev said.

I looked at Mavis. "Do you believe in ghosts too?" I asked softly.

"Oh yes, honey. They exist, you know. Lots of stuff exists..."

Bev made a sound, and Mavis's gaze shot to her daughter. Mavis paled and jumped up from her chair. "More wine, ladies?"

I held up my glass. Bev shook her head. "I'd better keep my mind clear for the contractor. We can't all be ossified during the consultation."

I barked out a laugh at the term. We sipped in companionable silence for a minute. Then my slightly muddled brain finally settled on what Mavis had said. "Mavis?"

"Hmm?"

"What other stuff?"

Bev threw her mother a stern glare.

Mavis had had just enough wine to brush her off with a flip of her hand. "She has a right to know."

"Mom," Bev warned, reaching for Mavis's flapping hand.

Mavis evaded the grab. She focused a slightly bleary gaze on me, an earnest look in her eyes. "Most things we think are fairy tales exist, Aggy. Most of it is real."

I thought about that for a minute as a tense silence filled the room. I got the impression the two women were waiting for me to either run screaming from the room with my ears covered or tell them they were crazy. They'd have been shocked if I told them what was actually going on inside my head.

I took a deep breath and expelled it, something loosening inside my chest. "Have you ever heard of a Lares?"

Bev stiffened, her eyes sliding to her mother's, but Mavis said, "Thank the goddess. We were starting to think you'd never get there."

12

ALTHOUGH THE FATES WILL TAKE
THEIR TOLL...

"You knew all this time?" I shrieked. "Why didn't you tell me?"

"Your father..." Mavis began, then clamped her lips together.

"We were told you needed to come to the knowledge in your own way, in your own time," Bev told me. "When you bought this place, we really hoped that meant you'd accepted your legacy. But then you never said anything." She frowned. "We didn't know what to think."

I put my head in my hands and groaned. "You have no idea what's been going on."

A bell pealed through the building, and my head came up in surprise. *No! Not again!*

Monty ran barking toward the front door.

Bev winked at me. "Surprise!"

I blinked, confused. "Surprise?" Then I realized

the bell had sounded different. Close to the sound of the infernal bell in my belfry, but more like a... I felt a grin slide across my face. "A doorbell? When did you manage that?"

"I have my ways," she gave me a smug smile. "Do you like it?"

"It's perfect!" Lurching around the table, I gave her a hug. "Thank you so much."

"You're welcome. It was my pleasure."

"And she *does* mean it was her pleasure," Mavis said, waggling her brows. "She's dating the electrician who did it."

Bev's lips twitched.

I hurried down the hallway and opened the door a crack...just wide enough to allow Monty's head to stick through but nothing else. I was surprised to see a woman standing on my porch. She was dressed in a denim shirt over a crisp white tee-shirt and wore a tool belt over heavy work jeans. Scuffed boots completed the no-nonsense picture, but the wispy blonde hair and vibrant green eyes that crinkled in the corners when she smiled kept her from being defined by her clothes. "Hi," she said. "I'm Trish." She offered me a clean but calloused hand. "I'm the contractor."

The way she said that told me she'd had to explain to more than a few potential clients that she was indeed the contractor they'd been expecting. When I didn't open the door any wider, she added,

"We had a six o'clock appointment? I'm a little early. Sorry. I finished up at the last job quicker than I expected."

"Oh," I said. "Of course. I'm a bit muzzy right now." I started to open the door wider and then remembered why I hadn't. "Are you okay with dogs? If not, I'll lock him in my room."

Trish's grin widened. "Love them. I have five myself."

"Five?" I opened the door and Monty ran out to greet her, tail wagging as he sniffed around her boots. "You're my hero," I told her, laughing. "I have my hands full with just this guy."

Trish crouched down and ran a hand over Monty's sleek head. "He's a beauty. What's his name?"

"Monty," I said, grinning fondly down at my dog. What can I say? The quickest way to my heart was to love my dog. I was kind of simple that way.

"What a handsome boy you are, Monty."

He kissed her on the nose and returned to sniffing her boots.

"He smells my dogs," Trish explained. "I have two doxies myself." She cocked her head. "Is he a standard size?"

"He is."

Trish nodded. "You don't see too many of them anymore. Most people have tweenies."

Nodding, I said, "When I got him, the breeder

was almost apologetic about the fact that he'd be bigger. I like his size. He's big enough that I don't feel like I'm going to break him, and small enough I can still carry him around."

"Hey, girlfriend!" Bev said, wrapping Trish in a hug.

"Hi, Trish!" Mavis said.

"You all know each other?" I asked, surprised.

Trish nodded. "We're in the same coven."

I blinked. "Coven?"

Bev made a small sound, and Mavis wrapped an arm around me. "Remember what I told you, honey. It's all real."

"Oh, oh, did I spill something I shouldn't have?" Trish asked, looking worried.

"Not at all," Mavis assured her, linking her arm with the contractor's. "Let's get you a glass of wine, and we can get started."

Trish wielded the retractable tape measure like the pro she was. She nodded as the measure snapped back into place. "Two windows would give you the placement you want on this wall. And we'll set them about three feet off the ground, so you can run shelving underneath if you want."

I nodded. "That sounds perfect."

She glanced up at the ceiling. "I know someone who can copy the style of the lights and ceiling fans in the other room. I'll just get pictures of them before I go."

She turned to the back wall. "That wall isn't load-bearing, so it won't be a problem to move it. The only issue with putting a master bathroom there might be the plumbing. It's currently located adjacent to the kitchen, which isn't too surprising. I'll have to see if we can move it without too much trouble." She frowned. "I didn't check before coming in. This building's not on a slab, is it?"

"No. I have a basement," I barely kept from grimacing. The one time I'd been down there, the space had totally creeped me out. I had no plans to do anything with the area except avoid it.

"That's good. We should be able to run the plumbing wherever we want to then."

"So, no issues?" Bev asked hopefully.

"I don't see anything." She slid me a look. "Has anybody checked the roof?"

"I had the place inspected from top to bottom before I bought it," I told her. "He said it was getting a little long in the tooth, but I should be able to get another three to five years out of it."

"That's a bonus. It was too dark for me to see it when I came in, but I'm familiar with this church. As long as there haven't been any leaks?"

I shook my head.

"Good, then I concur with his assessment. Have you picked out an exterior door yet?"

"Not yet. I'll try to do that this week."

She nodded. "I know a concrete guy who can create a sidewalk to the shop door for you. Do you want to bring it directly from the parking lot or branch it off the sidewalk leading to your front door?"

I thought about it. "I know it would be cheaper to branch it off, but I think I'd rather give the shop a totally separate entrance. Maybe even plant some tall bushes to divide it from my front door." Since Bev had talked me into separating the store from my living space, I'd really embraced the idea.

"Sounds good," Trish agreed. "I know a landscaping gal when you're ready for those bushes."

We headed for the front door, Trish making notes in her book. She walked into the sanctuary and snapped several pictures of the fans and light fixtures.

"You said you were familiar with this church," I nudged the contractor when she came back. "Did you belong to it once?"

Trish glanced at Bev before answering. "No. We actually used to hold our coven meetings here."

I slid Bev and Mavis a look.

They flushed. "We couldn't tell you about the meetings without telling you about the coven thing," Mavis explained.

"Yes, you could have," I argued, my voice tight with irritation. "You could have just said you held meetings here."

"And you would have said, Oh? What kind of meetings? And then we would have had to lie to you. Just not mentioning it seemed like a better option," Bev argued.

Trish sighed. "I did it again, didn't I? I'm really sorry."

"Don't be sorry," I told her. "It's not your fault my family doesn't tell me anything."

Bev bit her bottom lip. Mavis turned red in the face.

"Well, I'll get going," Trish said. She threw an apologetic glance toward my rotten, lying family. "I'll get a quote to you within a couple of days. Is that okay?"

"It is. How long before you can start the work?" I asked.

"I didn't bring my project schedule, but..." She glanced at her phone, tapping an icon and perusing what I assumed was a calendar. "Week after next? By then, I should be done with the addition I'm currently working on."

I grinned. "That'll work."

"Good. I'll verify that date and include it on the quote when I send it." She took the hand I offered. "I look forward to working with you, Aggy."

"Me too," I told her. Excitement made my hand-shake a bit more exuberant than planned.

Trish just smiled, taking it in stride.

When the contractor was gone, I turned to the two subdued ladies standing behind me in the foyer.

Mavis opened her mouth and then closed it, giving me an apologetic look.

True to her nature, Bev dove right in. She'd never been one to walk away from an issue. "Your father asked us to let you come to things in your own time and your own way. We didn't like it, Aggy. We argued with him incessantly about it. But when he left..."

"Why did he leave if he knew this was hanging over my head?" A new feeling of betrayal swept over me. My father was either the magical parent, or he at least knew what I was. He'd left me with Mavis and hadn't even allowed her to tell me about my...what had Gren called it? My legacy?

"He had to go, honey," Mavis said in a soft, sad voice.

"What could possibly have been more important than his own daughter?" I asked. "And why didn't he take me with him? Here I am at forty-five, and I'm just finding out that the old stories he used to tell me were real."

I blinked. I hadn't given those stories a minute's thought until just then. It was as if they'd been brushed from my memories. "Why am I just remem-bering those old stories?" My voice was soft. I hadn't meant the question for them. But Mavis wrapped her arms around me.

"He told you all about your legacy, honey. But you resisted the truth. You kept insisting they were just stories. Ultimately, he realized he couldn't push you into accepting your legacy. He told us that when you were needed, you'd be called to your place."

I gently pushed her away as a memory resurfaced. "Did I research Lares when I was in High School?"

She grinned, nodding. "When you were fifteen. You got an A on that paper, and you deserved it. It was extremely detailed and well-written."

I sighed. My instincts had been right even if my conscious brain had fought it. "Wait?" I said. "Did you say dad told you I'd be called when it was time?"

Both women nodded. I sighed. "Did he say anything about the thirteen thing?"

They looked at each other again, and irritation flared. They'd never made me feel like an outsider before. But I got the impression the two of them were performing some kind of silent communication, leaving me out of the loop. "Tell me!" I demanded and then forced myself to calm, adding, "Please?"

Bev took a deep breath and launched into what sounded like something she'd read somewhere. "In the thirteenth month of the thirteenth year, beginning on the thirteenth day, the new Lares will be seated. And at her side will be a council drawn to her rule. On the thirteenth peal of the bell and for thirteen subsequent events, the beginning of the Lares' dominion will be challenged by a unique array of challenges. By the act of winning the trials affecting her domain, the newly seated Lares will install herself permanently as the guardian of her territory, and none shall unseat her except by foul and reproachable means."

I shook my head. "Thirteenth month? Were they using a different calendar when that was written?" I laughed at my little joke. The laughter died when I saw the expressions on their faces.

Mavis shrugged. "You've heard of a leap year?"

I frowned.

"Magic uses a mystical lunar year rather than a calendar year as humans do," Bev explained. "During certain years, instead of an extra day, the mystical lunar calendar adds an extra month."

"So, I'm guessing this is a lunar leap year?"

Bev and Mavis both nodded.

"And I'm in the process of being 'seated'?"

They nodded again, letting me work it out in my head.

"This is a mystical lunar leap year, which means there are thirteen months instead of twelve. I moved into the church on the thirteenth day of the month." I scanned a look at them. "Thirteenth year?"

"The last leap year was exactly thirteen years ago."

I frowned. "Okay, so..." I mumbled to myself, working through the equation. "Thirteenth year, thirteenth month, thirteenth day..." I looked skyward, in the direction of the belfry. "The thirteen peals of the bell started five nights ago." I grimaced. "I have eight more nights of these trials?" Rubbing a hand across my eyes, I groaned. "I'm not going to make it."

Bev shook her head. "Not necessarily. From what I've read, the bell serves both as a warning of danger to come and an announcement of a test you must pass. Some of your trials will likely happen by day. And I'm assuming some days may have more than one trial."

If she was trying to make me feel better, she wasn't succeeding. Still...I thought of the internal peals when the little girl had been in danger. The warning about Reverend Dodson's presence, and the single peal when Wanda showed up. Maybe I didn't have as many challenges left as I thought.

"Tell us what's been happening," Mavis said.

"That story," I told them, "will require more wine."

13

AN UNDERSTANDING FORGED
WITH LOVE…

B ev filled our glasses again and sat down. Across from me, Mavis' face was ashen, her eyes filled with worry. "This is horrible. I can't believe you have to go through thirteen nights of monsters and battles to the death to take your seat as Lares for Rome."

"That can't be right," Bev said, agreeing.

I shrugged. "I don't know anything about anything, so I can't tell you if things are going to get worse or better."

"What about this council?" Bev asked. "What have you pulled together so far?"

My lips twitched. "I have a naked gnome and a twenty-one-pound dachshund."

I'd meant it as a joke, but Mavis shook her head. "And two witches."

I looked back and forth between them. They

both nodded. "We're not leaving you to deal with this alone, honey," Mavis told me.

Tears burned my eyes. I clasped their hands and sniffled. "Thank you."

"Who else?" Bev asked, "You have to have more than that."

I thought about it for a minute and said, "Gren!"

"Who's that?" Bev asked.

I told them about my elusive sidekick.

"Oh, he sounds yummy," Mavis said, winking at me.

I choked on my wine. Coughing violently, I shook my head. When I tried to speak, my voice came out slightly strangled. "He's just a friend." I frowned. "I think."

"Who else?" Bev urged. She wasn't going to be distracted from her point no matter what.

I loved that about her.

I shrugged. "My bat in the belfry."

They stared at me for a beat and then barked out a laugh.

"You always were a little crazy," Bev admitted.

The front door slammed, and we all stilled.

Footsteps pounded down the hall, and Bev rose from her chair, light glowing at her fingertips.

My eyes went wide at the sight. I looked at Mavis and she made a "whatever" face. I stood up too, looking around for a weapon.

Monty jumped up from his spot under the table

and trotted jauntily down the hall, tail wagging. He didn't seem worried about whoever it was.

Wanda stopped in her tracks when she saw Bev's glowy hands, her eyes going wide. "What the actual fudge?"

"Wanda!" I eased around the table, not wanting to somehow accidentally set off Bev's own personal laser light weapons. "Ladies, this is Wanda."

Mavis stood up and headed for the young girl, beaming. "Hello, dear." Before Wanda knew the danger awaiting her, Mavis had enveloped her in a hug. "It's so nice to meet you."

Wanda looked past Mavis's shoulder at me, her eyes wide with panic. Her arms hung limply at her sides as if she'd never been hugged before and wasn't sure what to do.

"Okay, mom. Let's give her a little room to breathe," I said, laughing. I narrowed my gaze at Bev. "Wanda's a friend," I said with meaning.

The glow dissipated from Bev's hands.

Mavis finally released the girl, and Wanda glanced toward the hallway as if considering an escape.

"Are you hungry?" I asked the teen.

She shook her head, but I couldn't miss the way she glanced toward my refrigerator.

I gave Mavis a look and she nodded. "I brought lasagna. You're going to love it, dear."

Wanda sent me another panicked look. I

shrugged. "Mavis is an unstoppable force. You might as well sit and eat. I'll get you something to drink. What would you like?"

Wanda scanned a look at the last inch of wine in the bottle.

Bev grabbed it and poured it into her own glass. "Maybe a soda?"

"I can get it," Wanda said. She was frowning, but I saw the way she eyed the gooey hunk of lasagna Mavis dished up for her. "I'll just pop this into the microwave for a couple of minutes," Mavis said, smiling at the girl.

Watching her with Wanda brought back memories. She was treating the teen exactly the way she'd treated me at fifteen, when I'd lost my mom and rarely saw my dad. Like she was a skittish colt Mavis was trying to soothe. And feed. Lots of feeding. To Mavis, food was love.

It had worked for me, but, I suspected Wanda might give Mavis a run for her money.

Bev stepped close and spoke softly. "Who is this girl?"

I shook my head. "She just showed up here. Gren and I fed her PB&J sandwiches and tried to pump her for information. She wasn't very forthcoming, I'm afraid."

"A runaway?"

I shrugged. "That's what I think."

Bev's narrowed gaze stayed on Wanda, watching

her too carefully. I wanted to ask her why, but Wanda returned and sat down at the table with her can of soda.

"Here you are," Mavis said, putting a heaping portion of pasta in front of her. She placed a napkin on the table and put silverware on it. "Eat up. You're too skinny."

Wanda stiffened at the comment about her weight, but Mavis sat down next to her at the table and started making small talk. Wanda soon started eating. After a first, tentative bite, the lasagna disappeared very quickly.

Mavis took the empty plate. "Ice cream?"

"Mom!" Bev objected.

Mavis glared at her daughter. "I saw a gallon of swirl in there?"

"Yes, ma'am," Wanda said.

I blinked in surprise. The teen had called me Dude. She was calling Mavis ma'am?

Bev grabbed my arm and tugged me down the hallway. When we were out of earshot, she said, "Someone's spelled her, Aggy."

Horror spiked in my chest. "Spelled? What kind of spell?"

"I don't know. I can't get a read on it. It's something I haven't seen before."

"How do you know?" I asked out of curiosity.

"It's hard to describe," Bev screwed up her face as she tried to come up with an explanation I'd understand. "You know how they draw squiggly lines in the cartoons to show a stinky smell?"

My brows shot skyward. "She has squiggly smell lines?"

"No. Not really. But there are spell lines there."

"Girls! Come get your ice cream," Mavis called out. There was a distinctive tone in her voice. One I remembered all too well. Mavis thought we were being rude.

"...we used to hold our meetings here," Mavis was telling Wanda when we came into the room. "I've always loved this church."

Wanda looked up at us, her eyes turning wary when they caught on Bev. But she slid her gaze to me and smiled shyly. "I didn't know you were opening a shop."

I sat down and picked up my spoon. "I am. I make candles."

"Cool," said Wanda.

We ate in silence for a beat. Remembering how the girl had disappeared the night before, I said, "Did you see the bat when you went upstairs last night?"

Wanda's kohled eyes were dark pools of innocence when she looked over at me. "No. It wasn't there."

"Did Aggy tell you about the ghosts in the graveyard?" Mavis asked.

Wanda turned her way eagerly. "Dude!"

There it was. I smiled.

"Really!" Mavis looked at me. "How many would you say there were, honey?"

"Too many to count," I said, frowning. "They were coming from everywhere. Isn't that strange?" I asked Bev.

She swallowed a bite of ice cream. "It is, a little. I'd expect only the ghosts from your little graveyard to join in."

"That's what I thought too."

Mavis shook her head. "Aggy's dom...um..." She glanced at Wanda. "Her property covers much more than that. This is the seat of her...ah...influence. But not the entirety of it."

She was right. I'd been focusing only on my property. I needed to think bigger. Much bigger. "How big is Rome, exactly?"

"About ten miles in every direction from here. The church is dead center," Bev said.

Mavis nodded. "That makes sense."

"Why did the ghosts come?" Wanda asked.

"There were..." I wasn't sure how much to tell her. Just because she'd been spelled didn't necessarily mean she was magic. "It was just a little disagreement in the yard."

She stared at me for a long moment and then nodded. "It was the lost ones, wasn't it?"

I leaned across the table, surprised. "What do you know about them?"

She seemed to take my question as a request for information rather than an explanation of how she knew of their existence. I decided that would work too. Information was something I was woefully short on.

"I know they live in the woods behind the church."

I nodded, and she took it as encouragement.

"I heard they're looking for something and they're turning into giant douche nozzles 'cause they can't find it."

"You don't know what they're looking for?" Bev asked.

Wanda shook her head. She licked her spoon and placed it into the bowl. "No. But everybody seems pretty keyed up about it. I actually heard one guy say they were in trouble if the guardian didn't come soon."

Guilt sent a flush into my face. I stood quickly and grabbed the empty bowls.

"What guy?" Bev asked. "Where?"

I could picture Wanda punching her bony shoulders toward her ears in a shrug. "Just some guy on the street. I don't know. He said this area had always had special protection from up above. But they must have done something to annoy the Powers because it had been like the Wild, Wild West for years." She frowned. "I'm not sure what he meant by that."

"It was before your time," Bev said, taking a tiny

bite of ice cream. "A television show. I used to watch the re-runs after school."

Mavis nodded.

My stomach twisted. I suddenly wished I hadn't eaten so much food. Guilt was a physical presence in my body, tying my belly into knots from the inside.

Doubts tumbled one over the other through my mind.

I'd failed the people of Rome. I'd ignored my legacy for decades while they'd needed me. I'd wasted too much time worrying about moving into the church. I should have done more to stop the devils. What if I couldn't do what I needed to do? What if I just ended up failing them again after arriving much too late?

I suddenly couldn't breathe. I smacked my wet hands down on the edge of the sink and dragged air into lungs that felt like they'd locked up on me. Stars burst before my eyes. My vision grayed. I swayed on my feet.

I was aware of voices behind me...soft hands grasping my arms. I fell backward but didn't crash into the vinyl flooring. Then, I realized someone was still gripping my arms, lowering me down, so I didn't fall.

The last thing I saw before I passed out completely was Wanda's pale, drawn face leaning over me.

Her lips were moving, but I couldn't hear the

words. The overhead light burned my eyes, making them water and blurring my vision. My chest heaved as panic took me completely over. I thought I might die.

Then somebody said, "Sleep."

And I slept.

"What if she isn't okay?" a worried voice asked.

"She'll be fine," a deeper voice responded. "She has simply passed the first stage of her seating."

"I wasn't aware the seating was supposed to kill her," responded an angry voice.

Someone sighed. "Sorry, Dudes. I didn't mean to literally scare the life out of her."

"You didn't," said the deeper voice. "You just happened to ignite true understanding."

I twitched, fighting my way out of the fog my brain had succumbed to. Licking my lips, I said, "Water?"

A small, furry body launched itself at me. Monty kissed my arm with frantic enthusiasm. My dog was an emotional licker. When he was upset or stressed, he licked.

I managed to grab him before he started on my face. "Okay, buddy. I'm all right." He sank down next to me on the bed, his soft, warm body pressed along my leg.

Big, hands gently lifted me and shoved some pillows behind my back. "Drink," Gren commanded, and I felt the smooth lip of a glass against my lips. I grabbed the glass and drank deeply. "Thank you."

"Of course."

I forced my eyes open and jolted in surprise. I was on my bed, in my bedroom. And the room was crowded. I took in the faces around my bed. Mavis, Bev, Gren, Wanda, Niele, Reverend Dodson looking very corporeal for a ghost, the bat...hanging upside down from the top of the closet door.

I yelped, grabbing a pillow just in case. The creature was staring at me with those yellow eyes and it made me very uncomfortable.

Gren grabbed the pillow. "Nobody here wants to hurt you, Madam Lares."

I frowned at him. "I thought we agreed you'd call me Aggy."

He inclined his head. "We did. In private. This is a meeting of your council. Formality is required."

I grimaced, pushing myself upright against my headboard. "Why do I feel like I've been hit by a truck?" I asked nobody in particular.

"You've accepted the first part of your legacy," Niele said, beaming at me.

"What does that mean, exactly?" Wanda asked.

I skimmed a look her way, surprised to see her in the group.

Niele slid his smile to the girl. Thankfully, he had one of my towels draped around his nakedness. That had probably been Mavis' doing. Relief slid away and I had a serious "Ew!" moment. Those towels were new!

"There are four levels to pass in gaining a legacy," Gren explained. "Understanding, Acceptance, Outreach, and Response. Madam Lares gained Understanding of her role tonight. It is only a matter of time before she succumbs to the next."

I narrowed my gaze on him. "Are you telling me I won't be seated until I reach the fourth level? Because there aren't that many days left in the thirteen."

Gren shook his head. "It would be optimal if you reached the fourth by then, but most do not."

"So, what's the significance of reaching each level?" Mavis asked.

"An array of things," Gren answered cryptically. "For this first level, Madam Lares will gain a modicum of control over her magic. Part of that includes completing her council."

"What exactly does this council do?" I asked, feeling the tightness of panic swelling in my chest again.

Gren shrugged. "Basically, we support you in whatever you do."

"That seems pretty vague," Bev said.

"It is," Reverend Dodson said. "For now. That is of necessity. It remains to be seen what role each of us will play under her authority."

Wanda narrowed her kohled gaze on him. "I'm not sure why I'm being included in this. I don't have anything to offer her."

"Indeed you do," Niele said, still grinning. I suddenly wanted to know what was making him so blasted happy. "You have already performed a role. You created the catalyst to bring her to Understanding, level 1."

The girl shrugged, looking eminently unhappy. "That was a mistake. It doesn't mean anything."

"There are no mistakes in the Lares' dominion," Gren told her gently. "Madam Lares' dominion is preordained. As is that of her council. You were here because you were fated to be here. You are part of this."

The girl's frown deepened. She looked agitated, her skinny shoulders drooping. "I...I have to go," she suddenly announced, spinning on her heel. I watched her all but run out of the room.

Gren didn't seem concerned, so I let it go for the moment. Goddess knew I had other things to worry about. "I'm not sure I understand..."

Niele laughed enthusiastically.

I glared at him and decided to change the form of the question I was going to ask. "Does anybody have any foresight about these midnight kerfuffles? I don't feel adequate to the task of dealing with them. Is that normal?"

"You've succeeded so far," Gren told me.

"Only by sheer luck," I answered. "I have no idea what I'm doing."

"And yet, you called the lightning to you, vanquished a demonic fog, saved a child from devilish magic, and bested a lost one in the Mystical Wood," said a deep voice I didn't recognize.

All eyes turned to the man standing just inside the door to my bedroom. I jolted back, wishing I had something aside from a pillow to throw at him. "And you protected the spirits in your hallowed ground from evil," he added.

"I had a lot of help," I told him, my tone more defiant than I'd planned. I was getting really tired of people just showing up in my house without being invited.

The new guy smiled, showing large, white teeth. The canines were longer than normal, like a dog's. The man had long, wavy blond hair and was dressed in black, something that looked like a cape thrown over his broad shoulders. He looked like he'd stepped out of the pages of a historical romance novel. Our visitor took two steps into the room and stopped, giving me a low, elegant bow. "Madam Lares, I am Ferral. It will be my honor to serve at your side."

I frowned. "Ferral? What are you doing in my house? Where did you come from?"

Rather than answer my questions, he turned a dark silver gaze to Gren.

To my surprise, Gren sighed. "He is to be your advocate."

I looked from one man to the other, noting the tension in Gren's handsome face and the cool arrogance burning in the other man's eyes. "My advocate?" Glancing around, I saw the slack-jawed look Mavis was giving the newcomer and the naked interest in Bev's eyes. Niele had dropped into a low bow, and the reverend inclined his head, his eyes sparkling with intrigue.

Even Monty trotted down his doggy stairs and ran to Ferral, tail wagging.

Gren and I seemed to be the only ones not ecstatic to see the newcomer. I suddenly lost patience with the situation. "Okay, that's it!" I climbed out of bed as gracefully as I could, which, given the fact that my foot caught in the blankets and I nearly tumbled to my face on the ground, wasn't very graceful at all. "Everybody out of my bedroom. This is undignified." I made shooing motions. "Out, out. We'll reconvene in the living room." I glanced at Mavis. "Will you be in charge of drinks and snacks?"

Mavis patted my arm. "Of course, honey."

I watched them leave, grabbing Gren's arm to

stop him from following. When we were alone, I lowered my voice. "What's the deal with this Ferral guy?"

Gren pursed his sexy lips, his expression not matching his next statement. "It's a deep honor to have him on your council."

I narrowed my eyes on him. "That didn't answer my question."

"It sort of did."

I screwed my face into a glower.

Gren's gaze softened. "I am constrained in what I can tell you, Aggy. I promise I will watch him closely." He grabbed my hands and lifted them to his lips, anointing each one with a soft, lingering kiss before turning away and leaving.

Was that supposed to make me feel better? Why did the guy need close watching? What was going on?

I barely kept from stomping a foot in irritation. Every man I'd ever known had loved to gossip. Especially when it came to dissing a potential rival for a job or romantic interest. Why did I have to get the one man in existence who apparently had no interest in dishing on another man he clearly didn't like?

Stupid male.

The sound of flapping wings brought my gaze shooting up to the peak of the ceiling. My eyes widened. The bat hung upside down from its new spot on my light fixture. Its eyes glowed yellow in the soft light way up there. "Do you have an opinion?"

It extended its wings, waggled them a little, and then settled back to sleep with a squeak.

Well then. "You'd better not poop on my bed," I warned him. And then went to splash cold water on my face.

14

SHALL KNOW HER BOUNTY FROM
ABOVE...

F ive minutes later, facilities visited, face splashed, and hair returned to some semblance of control, I walked into the living room. My bare feet made no sound against the smooth coolness of the wood floor. Despite the silence of my approach, everyone in the room looked up when I entered, all eyes watching me as if I held the secret to world peace.

The sensation of being watched was definitely disconcerting. That was probably the leading factor in why I promptly stubbed my toe on the leg of the coffee table as I headed for the empty chair they'd left me.

I gritted my teeth against the sudden, bright pain and barely resisted hopping around, holding my foot like an idiot. Though, I did surreptitiously rub the damaged digit on my other foot as I glanced over the assembled group.

Mavis, Bev, and Niele sat on the couch. The Rev was looking over my bookshelves, examining the selection of hard and softcover books. My face heated as I thought of the sexy romance novels on the center shelf, hoping he wouldn't notice. No such luck. I watched him pluck one from the end...the really hot ones...and felt as if my face might catch on fire.

Gren and the newcomer stood behind the couch, arms crossed over their chests and identical glowers riding their handsome faces.

They looked like entry guards at the Queen of Hearts' palace.

Off with their important bits!

I fought a grin at the thought, clearing my throat.

Monty was over by the alcove, chasing a big moth that was fluttering against the glass. The bat wasn't there. It was apparently still in my room.

Unable to resist, I said, "You're probably all wondering why I called you here."

Bev snorted out a laugh.

Mavis grinned.

Gren's glower slipped a tiny bit.

Ferral's glare deepened.

No sense of humor. Got it. The guy was going to be a laugh a minute.

"We need to plan, Madam Lares," Mr. Unhappy growled. "It is nearly Midnight."

I nodded. As much as I hated being reminded of my "thirteens" problem, I knew he was right. And part of me was glad I wouldn't have to face the next nightmarish situation alone. "We need a plan, yes. But first, I need some information."

"What kind of information?" Mr. Unhappy asked. He narrowed his gaze on me as if he suspected my request was some kind of trick.

"These nightly crises...do we know ahead of time what they're going to be? Is there some way to plan for them?"

Ferral seemed confused by my question.

"I mean, is there some kind of pattern to them? Are they predictable?"

"That's an excellent question, Madam Lares," Niele gushed.

"No," Ferral said, ignoring the nearly naked gnome as he ruthlessly dashed my hopes. "Each seating is unique. In your case, you were brought to your legacy in response to events that were already set into motion. In most cases, a new Lares has time to acclimate and prepare for the thirteenth series. But, your reluctance to embrace your legacy has put everyone in a bind." He all but growled the last part.

In a jolt of unwelcome clarity, I realized he blamed me for the current situation. He thought I was... All the blood ran from my face. "You think I'm a coward."

The man didn't deny my accusation. His fine lips tightened, and his chin tilted slightly upward.

I fought the urge to slap his smug face. Rage flared through me and I surged to my feet, moving around the chair to pace the available space. I was vaguely aware of the wind picking up outside the building, its angry breath rattling the glass of the oversized windows and jostling the trees around the church. Branches scraped across the side of the building as they were bumped into motion by the rabid wind.

It wasn't until lightning flared across the distant sky that I realized trouble was possibly on its way.

Gren was suddenly standing in front of me. I jolted to a stop, my form tense and my fists clenched.

"Madam..." He pulled air into his lungs and lowered his voice, softening his tone. "Aggy. Your enemy is not in this room."

I blinked, casting an angry look toward the smug jerk across the room. "You could have fooled me."

"I am here to be your advocate," Ferral said in a cold voice. "Not your best friend."

Something crashed against the side of the house and the lights flickered. The wind growled and boiled against the structure, rattling the very bones of the old church.

Mavis and Bev stood, their expressions worried.

"Honey, you need to calm down."

I glanced at Mavis and my anger softened under a new emotion. Guilt. She looked scared. Of me.

Like turning a spigot of hot water to the off position, the realization cut through my rage, and I stilled. The tightness in my chest loosened.

The wind outside died.

A lightbulb went on in my head. Had I been the cause of what was happening outside?

"Honey?" Mavis said, her voice close. I looked up to find her staring at me with worried eyes. "Are you okay?"

"I..." I glanced past her to the ramrod-stiff man standing behind the couch. "I'm fine." Then I shook my head. "No. I'm not fine." I strode toward Ferral, only stopping when the couch kept me from going any closer. I stabbed a finger at him. "Look, you clearly don't think much of me. But I can live with that. In fact, I really don't care what you think."

His eyes widened slightly at that, but the cool arrogance never wavered.

"Aside from some random story my father told me when I was little, I knew nothing about any of this guardian stuff. Nobody told me I had a legacy waiting. No one bothered to inform me that I had magic. The one person in my life who should have prepared me for this role didn't do it. In fact, I barely know the man. He's been gallivanting around the world for most of my life. So, I'm really sorry that you're disappointed by my lack of action on this. But believe me, I'm fighting to catch up."

On some level, I realized I wasn't being entirely fair. I'd been the one to reject the information my father had tried to share. But I couldn't help feeling like he could have tried harder.

Ferral's expression softened slightly. But not much. His answering smile was little more than a sneer. "You should have known..." He stabbed a thumb into his chest where I assumed his heart would be. If he had one. "Your instincts should have guided you here much sooner. This..." He lifted his hands and looked around. "Has been here, waiting for you. For decades. Yet you immersed yourself in human nonsense. You chose not to embrace the warnings of your heart. For that, yes, I hold you in low regard."

Dual growls throbbed on the air. One of them came from the tiny, stalwart warrior at my feet. The other came from me.

The air around me heated suddenly and I thought I'd done something to the atmosphere again, but I glanced around and found Gren at my back, Mavis at my side, and Bev standing to face the man behind the couch.

Even Niele walked over in his towel to stand with me.

I pulled courage from their warm, supportive presence. Sucking in a careful breath, I pointed to the door. "Leave. If you don't support me, I don't want you in my house."

Ferral's glare softened a bit more. He inclined his head. "You did not let me finish. It is true that I do not like your reticence to accept your legacy. But..." he hastened to add when the entire room tensed against him. "I would be a fool not to recognize what you have accomplished in a very short time. You have already begun to perform your duties, even extending your protection into the town of Rome. That is commendable. I was given a choice to come to you or to take another commission. I chose to come to you." He bowed his head slightly. "I have made my choice, Madam Lares. I will not let you down."

Well then.

His declaration having taken all the wind from my sails, I sagged downward. "Fine."

Some of the tension leached out of the air. Mavis and Bev sat back down. To my horror, Niele did too, his towel shifting so that I was no longer sure how much real estate it was covering. I really needed to find a solution to his "boys" knocking around wild and free.

Something that didn't include thorny vines. Or my new towels.

I sat and Monty jumped up onto the chair next to me. Gren stood beside my chair, his hard gaze locked on Ferral.

Sides had been drawn. To my surprise and secret delight, Mr. Unhappy seemed to be standing alone. Though he was infuriating, I was glad he was sticking with me. Despite what I'd said to him, I needed someone who could provide advice on the magical world I found myself in. Notwithstanding his permanent scowl, Ferral would be a good source of much-needed information.

I drew in a long breath and slowly released it, feeling tension sliding away with the breath. "Okay, I think I have eight more events to survive to complete my seating."

"I've basically been winging it up to this point, but I'd love it if somebody had an idea for how we could take some of the sting out of the situation."

Mr. Unhappy shook his head, his jaw tight. "You must conquer each and every challenge during the thirteens. There are no shortcuts."

"She must conquer them, yes," said Gren. "But there is no rule that says she cannot use assistance."

"What kind of assistance are you speaking of?" Ferral asked, looking dubious.

"From her council, of course. We are her hand-selected aides and advisors. We are considered part of her team."

Mr. Unhappy thought about Gren's proposal and, predictably, shook his head. "It is unprecedented."

"Are you saying a Lares' council can't help her?" Bev asked.

"I'm not saying that..."

"What good is a council if we can't help?" Mavis asked, scowling at Ferral.

I was pretty sure, given the startled look on his face, that he was glad to have the couch in between him and the female members of my little group. "I didn't say..."

"Lungren is correct," Niele said, tugging unhappily on his towel.

I fought the urge to cover my eyes, just in case he accidentally tugged it off.

"It is acceptable for a Lares' council to aid in the thirteenth challenges. In fact, it's standard practice."

"I'm well aware..." Ferral began.

"In the event of a challenge of any kind," the Rev quoted in his dramatic, "preacher" voice. "The Laresic Council is called upon to take their place at the side of their Commander. Any who elect not to do so will be released from the Lares' service and stripped of their knowledge pertaining to the Lares and her dominion."

Mr. Unhappy exploded. "If you'd let me finish a single sentence!"

We stared at him, causing him to flush with embarrassment.

"As I was trying to say. No other Lares has been called to her seat in the midst of a full thirteen before, so we have no documented ruling on the amount of aid her council can provide."

I frowned. "So what does that mean? Are you arguing for or against my team helping?"

"I am saying that there is no rule supporting what you are proposing." He held up a hand to stop us as every single one of us opened our mouths to argue. "But, there is also no rule against it. Therefore..."

A bell pealed through the house.

We all looked at each other, eyes wide.

"It has begun," Ferral said, his tone onerous.

"Isn't that the doorbell?" Bev asked.

The bell pealed again.

We blinked at each other for a minute. The sound was similar, but the doorbell was slightly less robust. She was right.

I pointed my finger at her and winked. "I'll get it."

I opened the door to find contractor Trish standing on my doorstep, along with a dark-haired man who had intense golden-brown eyes and a sexy stubble over his lean cheeks. "Hi, Trish," I said, skimming a meaningful look toward the man. "Did I forget about a meeting?"

Trish shook her head. "No. I..."

A deep, robust *Gong* resonated through the church, the sound thrumming along my nerves and throbbing on the air like magic.

Trish nodded toward the belfry. "We're answering the call."

Her companion nodded. "Madam Lares. I am Luke. I wish to join your council. If you will have me."

Gong!

I felt the urgency in the bell's call flowing through my veins.

Glancing from one to the other of the newcomers, I felt something slide between us. Something that felt good and strong and warm. Like family.

I wrapped Trish in a quick hug and offered my hand to Luke. "Welcome. As you can hear, the party's about to start."

They offered me matching grins and then followed me inside the church...a cold, hungry fog nipping at their heels.

15

A DEVIL'S BARGAIN MET AND DASHED...

The fog was around our knees as we filed out of the house and stood on the patio, senses attuned to the magic on the air. Monty's frantic barking came from inside the house. I'd locked him in my bedroom to keep him safe.

He was really mad.

"Lost ones," Gren said in a soft rumble that would have sent heat roiling through me if not for the words he'd spoken.

Luke spoke up next. "I smell a human."

Smell? Curse Swear! I should have asked him what his particular skill was. My bad.

Mavis and Bev were silent, but when I glanced their way, I saw that their lips were moving. They slowly lifted their hands and energy swirled away from them, a sparkling wash that ate the icy, coiling mist around us as efficiently as I consumed choco-late mocha cheesecake.

I caught Luke's gaze, and his expression was dire. "There's blood."

Rage and fear clashed together in my chest, robbing me of the ability to draw a full breath. I glanced at Reverend Dodson and he nodded, disap-pearing into the night with a soft pop of displaced air.

A warm hand found my shoulder. I looked up at Gren. "Get as close as you can to them without being seen." I told him. "We need to figure out our options,"

He gave me a quick bow and stepped away. Within two strides, he'd disappeared into the dark-ness, the remaining mist swallowing him whole.

Trish stepped forward. "The gnome and I can set some traps for them."

I nodded and, without warning, Trish disap-peared in a wash of light. When I could see her again, she had wings and was about twelve inches tall. It wasn't only her size and form that had changed. In place of her jeans and tee-shirt, she was wearing a long gown that fluttered around her legs and a bright blue bustier with a belt of knives. She held a knobby walking stick that was as tall as she was, and there was an opaline orb at the top that flared with jagged bolts of silver lightning. A double strand of what looked like shimmering droplets of water encircled her blonde head. Her slender form sparkled bright green and blue for a beat and then went dark, disappearing completely. I only knew she'd flown away by the diminishing sound of her wings. I looked at Bev.

"AWF."

At my look of confusion, Bev clarified. "She's an Ancient Warrior Fairy of the Unseelie branch. Deadly little things. And they set the best traps."

"But I thought she was in your coven."

Mavis shrugged. "Technically, she's not. But she's an earth fairy and we're elemental witches, so she hangs out with us."

"Oh." I felt a smile spreading across my face. "We have a fairy?"

Bev laughed. "We do."

Something nudged my hip, and I looked down without thinking. I squealed in a decidedly unguardian-like way.

Bright yellow eyes in an enormous furry head looked up at me. With its wide muzzle filled with really sharp white teeth, the wolf looked like it was smiling.

At least, I hoped that was a smile.

"Luke?"

The big head lowered and lifted in a human-like nod.

My eyes went wide as I looked at Mavis and Bev.

They laughed. "Yes, we have a werewolf."

I fist-bumped them. "I'm in the cool club."

Their laughter cut off abruptly at the sound of a woman's scream. It curdled through the night, sharp and jagged with pain.

I forgot everything as I took off running.

Not on my watch. Not on my land.

I had cool *and* deadly friends. And I intended to use them

The fog had thinned to the point that we could finally see the graveyard. The hallowed area was surrounded by a white picket fence, the paint chipped and faded over time. The fence had a single gate, slightly crooked with hinges that had seen better days. Niele kept it secured with a big padlock to keep deer and other foraging animals out. If humans wanted inside, it wouldn't be hard for them to break in. But the big uglies, Niele had assured me, couldn't step onto the consecrated ground, so a bigger fence wasn't necessary for them.

The fiends from the woods formed a monster wall around the small graveyard, their eyes glowing with evil zeal through the darkness. I did a quick count and came up with a dozen of the ugly things. The biggest one...the one that had attacked Monty and me in the woods, stood in front of the gate. He was holding a large, flaming torch in one enormous hand.

Behind the lead fiend, her pale skin seeming to glow in the moonlight, lay a crumpled and bleeding woman. She was draped over a tombstone, her head hanging over the other side and dark hair obscuring her face. But I didn't need to see her face to know who it was.

I'd recognize the skinny black jeans and tunic anywhere.

"Wanda," I whispered, horror choking off my voice.

"Give us the key," the leader demanded. "Or the girl will die."

I started forward, rage making my heart pound and my vision sharpen. A hand landed on my arm to stop me, the grip of Ferral's long fingers like steel bands. "Hold, Madam Lares," he said in his deep, quiet voice.

I tried to tug free of Ferral's grip, but the effort wasn't nearly as forceful as I'd hoped. My rage faded slightly as something magical slipped through me, sliding warm fingers along my spine. Soothing, yet irritating.

"Giving them the key will endanger many. The girl is one life. You must be smart about your next play."

His words turned me stiff with rage. How dare he dismiss Wanda's life so callously? How dare he discount her worth like that?

But, despite my instinctual reaction to his words, the tone of his voice was like a balm. It soothed my anger enough that I was able to breathe. Clearly, there was magic in his tone. Or I'd have already sent a lightning bolt up his a...

"Are you really suggesting she should let them kill poor Wanda?" Mavis ground out.

I glanced at my surrogate mother, shocked at the sight of her shaking with rage. I'd only really seen Mavis angry twice since I'd known her. The first time was when a mean girl in high school had sprayed my new outfit with red spray paint in shop class because the boy she'd liked was paying more attention to me than her. I was currently witnessing the second time.

"Be still, witch. I am addressing the Lares."

Unfortunately for Ferral, he'd forgotten to put his magic into that command. I turned and smacked him in the center of the chest with the flat of my hand, infusing him with enough electricity to make him turn pale and stumble backward. "Don't ever speak to my mom like that again."

Coughing and doubled over, Ferral held up a hand. "My apologies, Madam..."

"Shut it!" I said as my magic grew beneath my skin, a living, breathing entity that was barely contained by the thin veneer of my flesh.

The trees high above our heads swayed in a violent rush of wind. In the distance, lightning speared the sky. Power spread through me in a wash, demanding and uncompromising. I needed to unleash it, or I was going to explode. I lifted my hands and fixed the head monster with a heated glare that I wouldn't be surprised to discover was glowing.

Ferral placed a hand on my arm. "No. Do not do it!"

I shook him off, his soothing tricks no longer working on me.

"Lares!" he yelled, giving me a shake. "See the magic threads between them!"

The energy flowing through my system like molten lava roared in my ears. Debris whipped past us as the wind scoured the area and my hair lashed painfully around my face.

I barely heard him speak to me. Barely noticed he was there at all. All I could think was that I needed to destroy the monster. I wanted to kill him! He'd hurt someone who was under my protection. He needed to die.

"Madam Lares!" Ferral yelled over the rushing of power that was making my skin bubble and sting. If I didn't unleash it soon, it would kill me.

"Look at the threads tethering them to her!"

Threads? I shoved the energy back, and the roaring softened. But needles stabbed my entire body from suppressing it.

I gasped, my knees weakening beneath me. Ferral caught me under my arms, holding me upright until my muscles found the strength to hold me up.

He bent close and spoke into my ear. "If you attack them, it will kill her."

His words slowly wound their way into my frantic thoughts and took root. "Threads?" My voice was raw, slightly breathless from the effort to withstand the pounding magic.

He nodded, pointing toward the scene in the graveyard. "Look."

My gaze followed his pointing finger to the leader of the lost ones and along an invisible path toward poor Wanda. Looking at her, I felt my muscles tighten again as a new wave of anger flared in my chest.

Ferral's hand tightened on my shoulder. "No. Look. See."

I looked. But I didn't see... "Ah!" I finally saw the micro-thin strands of magic trailing from the red-eyed demon to Wanda.

Ferral's pointing finger slid to the next lost one in the circle and the next. Each of them had a thread of magic connecting them to Wanda.

If you kill them, it will kill her.

He was right. They'd somehow magically tethered themselves to the young girl.

I gasped. "I almost killed her."

His hand slid off my shoulder. "Lesson one, Madam Lares. Assess before acting. Emotions can be useful, but without restraint, they are simply dangerous."

I closed my eyes and swallowed bile for what I'd almost done. I wanted to smack his smug face, but I knew he was right. Then my eyes flew open. "The others! We need to tell them."

He inclined his chin, infuriatingly calm. "They will not act without your order. We have a moment to consider our options."

Options. Right. Those things I didn't have.

"What options? If we do anything to them, we hurt Wanda."

To my shock, his dour expression slowly eased, and a smile spread on his face. It was a miraculous thing to see. When he smiled, he was actually very good-looking.

I shook off that thought, disgusted with myself. *Stay focused, Aggy! Stop acting like a hormone-crazed teenager. You're a middle-aged woman, for goddess sake.*

Suddenly, my mind cleared and I knew what we had to do. "I need to go to the belfry."

Ferral shook his head, and I fought the urge to throat punch him. "I'm getting really tired of this Dr. No thing you've got going on."

He laughed.

I felt my eyes go wide with shock. The man actually laughed.

When I yelled at him.

Okay. Well, if he liked that...

I bunched a fist.

"You needn't see your council to speak to them," he said softly. "You need only call for them."

"How do I do that?" Some of my rage eased under the magic of his voice. But I promised myself I'd call it back later and give him such a punch...

"With your magic."

I barely kept from mimicking his snotty tone, realizing it would reflect badly on my maturity. But curse! I wanted to in the worst way.

Instead, I closed my eyes and thought about the other times I'd managed to dredge up a little energy. I thought about what I wanted to do...felt the magic bloom in my core...and gave it a little tug.

It enveloped me in a warm wash of power, like heated water flowing over my chilled skin. I pictured the desired... Person? Creature? *Your presence is required*, I said in my mind. Nothing happened. I frowned. Your presence is required? Ugh! I mentally flagellated myself. Who talks like that? The thing probably wasn't coming because it was too busy LOLing.

The twelfth bell rang out through the night, its tones deep and vibrant. The fog that was beginning to grow again gave the sound an extra level of power, making it throb against my skin.

Filled with frustration, I tried again. *Hey, I need your help.*

Better? Or was it too bossy? *Please?*

There. That was better.

Nothing.

I could feel the seconds counting off before the thirteenth peal. We were almost out of time. And I was desperate to do something. I turned to Ferral and blinked, jumping backward on a yelp. "What in the goddess's...?"

Wings pulsated against the air, drawing my attention away from the vision of terror in front of me. The bat fluttered at eye height, its yellow gaze flaring brightly against the fog.

"I need you to save her," I told it, jerking my head toward Wanda.

The bat continued to stare at me for another beat of my heart and then popped away.

No, that wasn't quite right. It was still there, but it was the size of a large fly. A soft buzzing filled the silence, and the thing was suddenly gone.

I turned to Ferral, eying him carefully.

Bev and Mavis appeared on either side of me.

"Hmm," Mavis said.

"What the fudge?" Bev said.

I shrugged. "Suddenly, I'm glad he's on our side."

Focus, Madam Lares, Ferral said inside my head.

I blinked at the giant hound with glowing silver eyes. "Is that you talking in my head?"

Focus! He barked. No pun intended.

"Oh yeah, that's him," I said. Focus. Right. I turned to the graveyard as the last bell pealed. "Do your thing," I told the bat.

"You were warned," said the head monster. He lifted the torch, and the demons turned as one toward Wanda.

"Wait for it," I muttered, my chest tight. "Wait." My stomach twisted with fear. What if the bat hadn't gone to do what I wanted? What if it was just off eating random bugs and enjoying life? Oh, goddess. I fought the urge to chew on my nails. I totally sucked as a guardian.

The bat snapped into view behind the line of devils. It was...huge didn't seem to cover it. He was the size of one of those flying dinosaurs...what were they called? Anyway, he shot downward, grabbed Wanda in his...talons? Claws? I didn't know. I was getting a headache from all the thinking.

So. Much. Thinking.

Wanda lifted off the tombstone into the air, and I screamed, "Now!"

I started running, tugging energy into my hands as I ran.

Niele burst from the ground in a spray of dirt, his pale, muscular body naked except for a vest of flowers. Just my luck. He finally dons something resembling clothes, and it's over the wrong body part. Goddess, help me. But the gnome's delicate-looking vest must have been much stronger than it looked. The first devil he encountered lunged at him and raked two-inch-long claws over his flowery vest. The claws scraped harmlessly over the blossoms, and

Niele was on him, his own blade flashing in the night.

Ferral easily outpaced me, leaping onto the nearest monster and taking him to the ground. I left him to do his thing, not too worried about the outcome because I'd seen him fight that night in the woods. The enormous gray dog with the flashing silver eyes.

It would have been nice to know that was him. He and I were going to have a talk later. Right after I punched him.

A tree root as big around as my wrist snapped out of the earth and wrapped around the monster to the side of the leader, lifting him off his feet and slamming him into the ground head first. Lift, slam. Lift, slam. Repeat, repeat, repeat.

That guy was gonna have such a headache.

I glanced quickly at Mavis, who appeared to be on the other end of that magic root. I gave her a double thumbs-up. She had mad skills.

Another beast went down under the massive black wolf. The lost one's terrified screams were a welcome sound.

The next monster in line was enveloped in a shimmery net, which wrapped around him without any sound at all. The net was yanked by an invisible hand, and he was suddenly dangling from a high branch on the nearest tree. Behind me, Bev said, "That's what I'm talkin' about."

I laughed, feeling good as magic poured through me, filling me with energy, confidence, and an overwhelming need to kick some bad devil butt.

Gren? A moment later, he was walking out of the shadows, his expression grim. "There were more of them behind the graveyard," he announced. "At least a dozen. I took some of them out but the rest escaped back into the woods."

I wanted to groan out loud. How were we going to get rid of them all?

The massive torch-laden leader appeared in front of me as if he'd stepped from a wrinkle in space. I skidded to a halt, looking up, up, up into the fiery cesspools of his eyes. Drool dripped from his befanged mouth and hit the ground with a sizzling sound that did not bode well.

"We meet again, Madam Lares. It's a shame you will not survive our reunion."

Looking at the blood-covered claws wrapped around his big fire stick (Stop it. You have a dirty mind.) Some of my bravado fled me. I wasn't sure which would get me first. The teeth. The claws. Those deadly-looking horns. Or just the sheer musculature of the nearly eight-foot-tall monster.

I swallowed hard and gripped my magic with everything I had. The next few minutes were really gonna stink.

16

A TERRIBLE COST, A DANGER VAST...

I expected a full-frontal attack. The creature surprised me by lowering the torch and setting the grass on fire. It was no natural flame. The fire hit the grass and exploded outward as if the entire yard was doused in gasoline.

Watching the flames eat their way in my direction, I realized that I either needed to backtrack or find a way over them.

A quick glance at the sky told me I no longer had the option of using the pterodactyl bat for a ride. Jeezopete! There was never a dinosaur bat around when you needed one.

I was pulled from my thoughts by a searing heat nudging against my toes. Stumbling backward, I was surprised to realize the fire had already reached me. My gaze lifted to find the demon leader staring at me with his burning gaze.

"Give me the key and this will all end," he growled.

The wolf yelped, and I turned in time to see Luke go down. His yelp turned to agonized screams as fire ravaged his fallen form.

I didn't think. I acted on pure instinct. Flinging a hand toward Luke, I yelled, "Allay!"

The fire around Luke went out in a puff of charcoal smoke.

The wolf climbed to his feet and leaped onto the fiend nearest him, ripping the nasty thing's flesh with renewed vigor.

Movement caught my attention on the far side of the graveyard. Barely visible through the remaining mist, Gren leaped into the air and came down on top of something, a massive knife clutched in his hand. His gaze swung to mine and he smiled, the sight twisting heat through my belly.

The lead demon swung his torch to a spot behind me, and another scream rose over the cacophony of fighting. The high-pitched timbre sent chills along my spine. I swung around to find Mavis in the center of a column of flames. She was trying to make herself smaller, but the flames licked at her skin and hair as she tried to shrink away.

"No!" I started toward her, forgetting the monster behind me.

"Away!" I screamed, not even sure what I was trying to do. But the magic apparently didn't need specificity.

It was programmed to protect. My energy slammed into Mavis and coated her like a soothing balm, pulling the fire away from her skin and sending it into the air, where it dissipated with a sizzle and a soft gasp.

I grabbed Mavis's arms and looked her over with wild eyes, my heart pounding. She was fine. Mostly unhurt. Only a slight redness on her skin and a distinctly smoky scent remained. I pulled her into a hug. "I thought I'd lost you."

Bev slammed into us, wrapping us both in a hug. "Goddess! That was terrifying."

Mavis returned my hug for a beat and then pushed me away. "Go. You need to help them." She jerked her head toward Luke and Ferral, who were enclosed in a circle of fire, the flames reaching well over their heads.

I glanced at Bev. She was already weaving magic on the air. "We've got this, Aggy. Do what you need to do."

Nodding, I started running in the two shifters' direction, but before I could send my magic into the air, something hard and unrelenting dropped around me and snapped tight. Agony seared through me. My screams, husky with fear and pain, sheared the night. I tried to lift my arms but they were pinched firmly against my body. I struggled with everything I had, but the chains only constricted more when I fought to get free. Smoke and sparks rose off the metal where it touched my skin, and it felt as if I was being burned alive.

Smoke lay thick in the air. Fire raged around us. Enormous trees were on fire. Much of the grass was also in flames.

Behind me, matching screams told me Mavis and Bev were being attacked again.

I fought harder, my increasing struggles only wrenching the chains more securely around me. Agony pulled coherent thought from my mind and stripped me of sanity. I flung myself to the ground, trying to douse the sparks that were sizzling against my skin with soil. The scent of rich black earth filled my nostrils. Some of the pain did ease, the soil cooling against my flesh. The scent gave me a thought. "Niele!" I screamed, remembering how he'd burst from the earth earlier.

Nothing happened. I screamed his name in my mind and began to shove with my feet, scooting like an earthworm toward Bev and Mavis. Behind me, yelps and angry snarling reminded me I had four people to help. Not just the two in front of me whose struggles were ripping my heart in two.

Tears burned in my eyes. Tears of pain. Tears of fear. Tears of frustration. What kind of guardian was I if I couldn't help even one of my people?

The grass shivered in front of me, seeming to round and hump. I blinked, thinking I was seeing things. But no, it shivered again, leaving a mound of grass-covered earth in its path.

Like a giant mole track.

Niele?

I watched as the mound lengthened and grew, heading directly toward the horrifying creature standing in front of the gate. As my eyes met his, the demon opened his disgusting maw and smiled, exposing way too many teeth.

"The key, Lares! This can all end now. Just give me the key."

At that moment, I was glad I had no idea where or even *what* the key was. Faced with saving my mom and sister, I'd have probably given it to him. To my everlasting shame.

I shook my head, tears saturating the grass beneath my cheek. "Drop dead." The words emerged from my lips so softly, their passage through my raw throat having stripped them of power.

But he heard me.

His smile widened. The torch came up again, pointing directly at the house. "Say goodbye to the little warrior."

"No!" I screamed, arching off the grass.

The dirt in front of the demon exploded upward, and a naked man wearing a begonia blouse slammed into the leader, sending him stumbling backward to crash against the gate. Arms pinwheeling and eyes bugged wide, the fiend's big body fell into the graveyard and slammed to the ground.

He burst into black and red flames as soon as his flesh touched the hallowed ground.

A bright pink light flashed up around the fencing, and strings of power snapped out to wrap around the remaining devils, yanking them inward as it contracted. One after another, they all hit the sanctified soil and exploded into flame.

I sagged downward. Boneless with relief.

The chain around me loosened and fell away. The fiery prisons around my people died too. The trees and grass were extinguished with a soft whoosh, leaving behind only the choking wall of smoke

Then, slowly, even that began to retreat.

A pair of small, soft shoes appeared in front of me, and a slender hand lowered to help me stand. I let Trish pull me to my feet.

"Did you like my trap?"

I blinked. "That pink thing with the strings?"

She nodded, her grin blinding in the dark. "I think it was one of my best."

I couldn't disagree. "It was awesome."

She nodded. "It took a long time to create. I'm sorry I couldn't release it sooner."

I wrapped an arm around her shoulders. "No worries. It did the trick in the end."

We turned toward the house. I needed to let my poor dog out of the bedroom before he lost his cute little mind.

Bev and Mavis brushed ashes off their clothes and shook their heads at me. "We thought we were goners there for a minute," In direct opposition to her words, Mavis' eyes were sparkling.

"That was fun," Bev said.

I laughed at them. "I fully expect all of you to go running for the hills after tonight."

Trish tucked her arm through mine. "Not a chance. We haven't had this much fun since that troll broke into the coven meeting." She looked at Mavis and Bev. "Remember that, girls?"

Mavis snorted out a laugh. "How in the world could we forget?"

"He was a nasty little booger," Mavis agreed. "But he made a great bowling ball."

They all laughed, and I shook my head. "I don't even want to know."

Gren emerged once again from the shadows, his face and arms covered in dark blood. His stride was strong and sure, the deep lines around his mouth the only sign that he was tired.

I looked a question at him and he nodded, giving me a tired smile.

Luke and Ferral trotted into the trees. Maybe they needed to go shift somewhere and dress before joining us. Somehow I didn't see Ferral joining us butt-naked.

And speaking of naked...

We all turned and watched Niele stride across the yard.

Seeing us looking, he grinned widely and waved with *all* his parts. Disturbing.

Four sets of eyes narrowed. Four mouths turned grim.

"We have to do something about the gnome," I said.

The other three women nodded.

"Can't you get him to wear pants?" Trish asked.

"No," I admitted. "When I tried, he wove a diaper out of thorny vines. I think he did it just to mess with me."

Mavis winced. "Disturbing as that is, it's a dedication to making a point that I can respect."

Bev snapped her fingers. "I've got it. I know the solution." She turned on her heel and headed for the house.

Mavis took my other arm.

"What's she up to?" I asked.

"No idea," Mavis said. "But whatever it is, I'm sure it will get more creative with wine."

"Or maybe a beer?" Trish asked hopefully.

"Or maybe a beer," I agreed.

I nside the house, I released Monty, who shot out of my room and into the kitchen, where he forgot about being mad at me among a sea of legs that needed sniffing and fingers reaching to pet and scratch his cute furriness.

I left the others noisily gathering drinks and snacks and headed up to the belfry, hope flaring in my heart.

I hadn't forgotten Wanda. When I'd asked the bat to save her, I'd given it an image of the belfry, figuring she'd be safe from our unwelcome visitors up there since the church was built on hallowed ground.

I didn't draw a full breath until I saw her slender form draped across the floor beside the bell. With a sigh, I dropped to my knees next to her and checked for a pulse. Though she still slept, her narrow chest rose and fell in even breaths.

Thank the goddess.

I looked up and caught the yellow gaze of her savior. "Thank you. I owe you one."

The bat squeaked softly, its eyes seeming to flare with diaphanous light before shrinking back to normal size again.

"Who are you?" I asked. Clearly, the creature was much more than it seemed. But it just as clearly wasn't going to enlighten me.

"I'll figure it out," I told her...because something told me it was a she.

The bat just closed its eyes and went very still.

Wanda's form shimmered and turned translucent, like a ghostly spirit, before it disappeared altogether. I bit back panic, thinking of the times Wanda had come up to the belfry and then inexplicably disappeared. But she'd always shown up again.

"So, that just happened," I murmured.

At least, I knew she was okay. In the morning, I'd talk to Bev and Mavis about it. Between us, maybe we could figure out what was going on with the young girl.

I stood and, after a last look toward the flying rodent attached to the ceiling, I turned and started toward the stairs. "'Night Bat."

I didn't get a response. But then, I hadn't expected one.

The sound of laughter drifted up to me, easing the last of my fear and frustration from the night's events. I pulled air into my lungs and released it with a smile. We'd survived another night. Only a week of nights left before the thirteens ended and I was officially seated as Lares, guardian of Rome.

It was a thought that was both exciting and terrifying. But a challenge I was eager to accept.

Accept...

Gren's earlier words drifted through my mind:

"There are four levels to pass in gaining a legacy: Understanding, Acceptance, Outreach, and Response. Madam Lares gained Understanding of her role tonight.

It is only a matter of time before she succumbs to the next."

Acceptance.

A warm wind brushed over my skin, sparkling motes of magic saturating its gentle touch.

In time... a soft voice whispered on the wind. *All will be known.*

I jolted to a stop, my gaze sliding toward the bat again and narrowing with suspicion. "Was that you?"

The bat didn't so much as twitch at my question.

After another moment of watching, I shrugged and headed down the stairs. As soon as I opened the door at the bottom of the staircase, I wished I hadn't.

Ferral's fun-killing face stared at me from across the room, dour and judgmental. "Madam Lares, we need to talk."

Ugh!!

17

WHEN ALL SEEMS LOST AND DEATH IS NIGH…

"We won't survive another battle like tonight's."

I sipped some water and fought a yawn. The adrenaline had worn off, and it left me exhausted. "I know. That was bad."

Rather than appease Ferral, my words seemed to make him even madder. He slammed a fist down on the kitchen table, causing me to jump. I straightened in my chair, glaring at him. "What is your deal?"

"You are not taking this seriously! Do you understand how many levels of horrible tonight could have been?"

"Of course I understand. I just told you I did. What exactly do you want from me? Would you be happier if I collapsed on the floor, snotty and sobbing?"

He looked confused for a minute by my question.

Maybe the snotty and sobbing thing had overloaded his circuits. "I want you to..." He scrubbed a hand over his face and started to pace the kitchen. "You could have been killed."

"I am aware." I scowled in his direction. "Everyone could have been killed. But I did the best I could. I'm treading water as quickly as I can." To my abject horror, tears burned my eyes. The last thing I wanted to do was start crying, thereby proving to him I was a wimp.

I blinked rapidly, turning my head away from Ferral so he couldn't see my tear-filled eyes. "I'll accept any suggestions you have, Ferral. I want to survive the next several days. I want all of us to survive it. But this is all new to me."

Despite my best efforts, my voice broke on the words. I clenched my fists in my lap, silently deriding myself.

Ferral and I were saved from continuing our conversation by footsteps and laughter in the hallway.

Bev, Mavis, and Niele exploded into the kitchen, Niele pulling up the rear.

"Voila!" Bev said as she and Mavis spun apart. Niele stepped forward as they cocked their hips, presenting him with game show hands.

I eyed the gnome and felt my eyes go wide. "What in the world...?" Niele was wearing some kind of fuzzy green underpants.

"They made me drawers," Niele said with a grin. It sounded odd hearing him say the word "drawers." Mavis used the term, so I guessed he'd gotten it from her.

"They certainly did." My lips quirked up in the corners. "What are they made from?"

Mavis looked like she was going to explode. "Moss! My daughter is a genius."

Bev's grin widened and she mock-bowed. "Thank you, thank you."

Niele did a happy little dance. "They feel wonderful," he told me. "And they are of nature, which feeds my soul." He ran his fingers over the soft garment. "I shall wear them only on special occasions..."

"No!" We all chorused together.

Niele looked a little worried by the vehemence of our responses.

I tried a carefree smile. "Wear them whenever you're around the church," I said. "I'm sure Bev will make you more when you wear those out."

Bev nodded, giving him a wink.

I mouthed, "Thank you," to her as Niele hesitantly agreed.

"We must plan for tomorrow night." Ferral announced.

Gren eyed me. "Tomorrow will come soon enough, Advocate. The Lares is exhausted."

Mavis nodded. "We are too. Shall we meet back here early evening?"

I nodded. "Six o'clock? That will give us time to accomplish whatever is needed to buttress our position."

Ferral frowned but didn't argue.

Gren smiled. "Listen to you, talking all military-like."

"Listen to you talking like a normal human," Bev teased Gren.

Gren's chuckle made my insides go soft and squishy. "I guess my dad's love of all things military wore off on me." I blinked as a thought hit me. "Can you all let yourselves out? I need to make a phone call."

Bev's eyes went wide. "Now? It's three o'clock in the morning."

I gave her a grim smile. "I'm pretty sure this person will be awake."

***

"Hello?"

I nearly hung up the phone. It was too late/early, and I was too tired for the conversation I was about to have. But I knew I couldn't put it off any longer. "Hi, Dad."

"Agnes. How are you?"

I winced at the name. He was the only one who

ever called me that. I hated my full name, and my moms and Bev had been okay with calling me Aggy because it made me happy. My father insisted on using the full name. It had been his mother's name, so I was stuck with it. "I'm..." How was I? Tired. Sore. Overwhelmed. Strangely exhilarated about the changes in my life while still a little terrified. "I'm fine. How are you?"

"You know how it is, honey. What can I help you with?"

And there it was. The "I'm too busy to be bothered by the likes of you" voice. I bristled and nearly hung up the phone. It had been that way for as long as I could remember. Even at sixty-three years old, Andrew Lenore was too wrapped up in his own life and interests to include me.

I bit back an angry response, turning my anger back where it belonged. To me. I'd known I was too tired to have a conversation with my dad. I should have waited until I'd rested to call him.

"I'll make this brutally succinct so you can get back to your life, Dad," I told him, my voice tight. "I'm in the middle of my seating for Lares of Rome right now. It's not going well because I was unprepared. I was hoping you'd have some words of wisdom for me."

Silence met my stark statement. For a moment, I wondered if I'd made a mistake. Maybe he wasn't magical after all. But if not, surely he'd known about the legacy. He'd tried to tell me about it once. Hadn't he?

My father sighed, the sound long and drawn-out. "I thought you'd never get there. I must say, I wish it had been at a better time."

That did it. "Seriously? You're going to give me a hard time for not finding my way to something you should have told me about, oh...I don't know... decades ago?"

"Agnes..."

"I had no idea, Dad. I've been completely ignorant of everything. And now I'm in the middle of the thirteens, and I..."

"Wait!" he interrupted. "How long have you known about your seating?"

I managed to rein in my anger and bite out, "Ten days, I think." So much had happened to me since moving into the church. The days seemed to blur together.

He sighed again. "Goddess."

"Yeah. And we've got this woods full of lost ones who keep attacking us on the thirteenth peal of the bell every night, demanding some sort of key..."

"Wait!" he interrupted again. "The devils have invaded your dominion?"

"Yes. But I'm more interested in hearing about this key. I don't intend to give it to them, but it would be nice if I knew what it was."

"Have you even had time to find your council?" My father's voice sounded stressed.

"They mostly kind of found me."

"Mavis and Bev?"

I stilled. "You knew about them?"

"Of course, Agnes. If you hadn't been so resistant to your legacy, you'd have seen their magic too."

Torn between the fascinating revelation of being able to see magic and his unfair characterization of my motivation, I felt anger rising again. "How dare you!"

I could almost picture him shaking his head and flipping a hand dismissively in my direction. "There's no time to be indignant now," he said in his bossy "dad" voice. "The fact is that I tried to tell you about the family legacy. Many times. You didn't want to hear it. So I let fate decide when you'd come to it. Unfortunately for everyone, it seems the Powers didn't have your comfort and safety in mind when choosing the time of your seating."

My traitorous brain fed me the unwelcome thought that my unfortunate marriage and subsequent divorce had probably been part of why fate had overlooked me until it was almost too late. Naturally, I didn't share that revelation with the man on the other end of the line. I'm not a complete idiot. "Can we stick to the problem at hand, please?"

"Yes. We can. As for this key...it's not what you think it is."

"How do you know what I think it is?" I asked a little defensively.

"You were picturing a metal key. Probably one of those big, old-fashioned skeleton keys. Weren't you?"

I chewed my lip and didn't respond.

"Yeah. I thought so. No. This is nothing like that. It's actually a note."

Frowning, I said, "A note? You mean, like a letter?"

"No. A musical note."

"Okay, I didn't see that one coming."

He laughed, and the sound took me back to my childhood, to the days when he still did that kind of thing. Before my mom got cancer and he took to the road to pretend she wasn't sick. "It's actually a common mistake. The key the lost ones are searching for is a particular note from the celestial choir."

"There's really a celestial choir?" I smiled at the thought. That had to be something to see and hear.

"Yep. The term 'choir' is deceiving, of course."

"Of course," I said. Everything in my new world was deceiving.

"Their role is security for the Celestial plane and protection of mankind. Part of that security is keeping the key for the gates to the Elysian realm. Their music is much more than a celebration of divinity as human religions depict it. It can actually be a weapon and a tool to keep intruders out of the Elysian realm."

I leaned back against my pillows and dropped a hand onto Monty's soft back. The poor little guy had worn himself out stressing over being locked in my room earlier. He was snoring softly. "So how did this key get lost in the first place?"

"It's not lost, Agnes. It's a spare. Occasionally, one of the Lares or other guardian types in the earthly plane needs to get through the gates. The key is here for that purpose."

"Why wouldn't the choir just sing them in?"

He laughed again, but the sound was less amusement and more irritation. "You don't think they'd assemble the entire celestial choir for one of us peons, do you?"

Apparently not. "If what you say about the key is true..."

"It is."

I ignored his arrogant tone and went on. "Then why park it here? Rome is tiny. This is just a small country church that hasn't even been occupied for months. Why here and not some big church somewhere in a larger city?"

"Small and remote is much safer than large and busy," he said. "And Rome..." He sighed. "Rome was built in the epicenter of a magical vortex. Several lei lines flow into that area, converging very near your little church, I'm afraid." He hesitated, and I could almost feel his reluctance to continue through the phone line. I waited, knowing he'd get to it in his own time.

"Rome is a hotbed of mystical activity, Agnes. It's a very challenging spot to be a Lares. I have no idea what the Powers were thinking, placing you there."

I took umbrage at his inference that I was less than capable. Despite the fact that, currently, it was true. "They must have been thinking I could do the job."

His bark of laughter was edged in hostility, and I had to wonder why. "You haven't even been seated, and you've nearly lost your dominion," he said. "Probably more than once. Am I right?"

I frowned. "I haven't lost it yet."

"Agnes, two other Lares have tried to hold that dominion. Two better-trained guardians who'd spent their lives before being seated perfecting their magic. They were more knowledgeable, younger, and stronger than you are. How can you hope to succeed where they both failed?"

"Thanks for the vote of confidence," I snapped out.

He sighed. "Honey, I'm not trying to shatter your confidence. I'm just trying to keep you alive. Walk away from the seating. Let the Powers fill the seat with someone else. It's not the right battle for you right now."

The man had known me, sporadically, for forty-five years, and he still had no idea who I was. The best way to get me to do something was to tell me I couldn't do it. I simmered in silence for a beat, trying to figure out if I was capable of continuing the conversation.

I decided I'd had enough "advice" from the old man.

"Okay. Well, thanks for the information. I'll be seeing you." I hung up before he could respond and then turned my phone off when he called right back.

I snuggled up next to Monty, too angry to sleep, and thought about how I could protect a magical key to the Elysian realm, whose location I didn't know and identity I couldn't fathom.

18

AND IN THE END, A CHILD'S FAINT CRY...

An enormous gray dog trotted across the grass in my direction, its big paws sending glossy droplets of morning dew into the air as they landed.

Monty jumped up from his spot under the table and stood, wagging his shaggy tail at the beast.

To my vast surprise, Ferral lowered his head and touched Monty's nose with his own, sending the little dog into paroxysms of happiness. Ferral took a step back and light flashed, splashing heat over me, my breakfast of cold cereal and yogurt, and Monty. The little dog dove under the table as Ferral stepped out of the blinding light and lowered himself to a chair, tugging on the sleeves of an immaculate charcoal suit.

Well, that answered the naked-after-changing question.

He looked at me as the light faded behind him. I

arched a brow. He accepted my one arched brow and raised me with a second. "Is there a problem?" he asked, the picture of perplexed innocence.

I shook my head and scooped up another spoonful of cereal.

He eyed the mixture, grimacing. "What is that?"

I started to respond, but my mouth was full. Swallowing, I wiped my lips with a paper napkin and said, "Granola and sliced banana mixed with vanilla Greek yogurt. Would you like some?"

He grimaced again. "I thought this might be a good time to discuss our options moving forward."

Sighing in resignation, I stood and grabbed my mug. "I'll need more coffee for that discussion. Would you like some?"

"Coffee? Yes, please. It's a nasty habit I've picked up from interacting with humans."

I didn't bother to ask him how he'd like his coffee. I was pretty sure he'd be a black as tar kind of guy.

As I waited for the coffee pods to brew, I watched the shifter through the window over the sink. I was pretty sure he didn't know I was watching him because he looked around and then reached into my bowl, pulling out a chunk of banana with his fingers and dropping it into his mouth. I could tell he wanted to hate it, but after another furtive glance, he stole a second bite.

I quickly assembled another bowl and placed it

and the two coffees on a small wooden tray, carrying it out to the patio.

I shoved my breached bowl in his direction, handing him a clean spoon and his coffee. He flushed when he saw me settle my own fresh bowl onto the table. His gaze had a guilty look when it caught mine.

I scooped up a bite of sweet, crunchy goodness. "So, I'm assuming you have some thoughts?"

He spooned up a bite too, chewing thoughtfully. After swallowing, he said, "We cannot assume the lost ones are gone. Lungren informed me there were at least a dozen more of them we didn't capture or kill last night. He believes there are more than that."

My breakfast suddenly took on the weight of a rock in my stomach. I forced myself to keep eating. I'd need the calories for whatever lay ahead. "Okay, so they'll be back tonight."

He shrugged, pushing his empty bowl away and sitting back. He crossed his long legs at the knees and observed me, looking like something that just stepped out of a high-end men's fashion magazine. "They were badly damaged in our battle. Their numbers have been reduced to the point I think it's likely they'll lay low for a couple of nights at least."

My eyes widened with hope. "So maybe it will be a quiet night?"

He laughed. It wasn't a cheerful sound. "This close to the thirteenth night, you can rest assured there will be something bad waiting for us at the last peal of the bell."

"Wonderful," I muttered unhappily. I finally gave up on the cereal, pushing it away.

Ferral grabbed it and dug in.

I hid a smile behind my hand. It apparently wasn't only coffee that he let "humans" corrupt him over. I cleared my throat and muted the smile. "So, what do you think it will be? Trolls? A building-sized marshmallow man? A giant sea monster?"

When he gave me a disbelieving look, I pointed to a glossy puddle near the edge of the porch. "There's a puddle there. The way my luck has been going, the Loch Ness Monster probably lives in it." I'd meant the words as a joke, but they'd come out sounding bitter.

I actually wasn't feeling bitter. Much. I was just tired. And the conversation with my dad had left me feeling unsettled.

Ferral stared at me a long moment.

I fidgeted under his intense regard, finally looking him in the eye. "I suppose you're going to call me a coward and lecture me about my worthiness to be Lares?"

To my vast surprise, he shook his head. "Not at all. That decision has already been made. It's a wasted exercise to question it. It is now simply a case of moving through the last set of challenges with as much grace and dignity as possible."

Thinking over the events of the night before, I snorted out a laugh. There hadn't been much grace or dignity in any of what we'd done. But we'd survived another night. And the key...wherever it was...was still safe.

"Tell me about this key," I said.

I'd braced for his refusal. After all, he'd seemed reluctant to tell me anything on the subject up to that point. To my surprise, he nodded. "The Powers hid the key in this area two hundred years ago. Its location has been a secret since that time. But, somehow, the lost ones recently discovered the secret. Which is why you were called to service at this late stage."

"What exactly does that mean? Called to service? I certainly didn't get a message from the Celestial main office that I needed to get off my wider-than-I'd-like-it-to-be middle-aged butt and buy a church."

He tilted his head like the canine he sometimes shifted into. "Did you not?"

"I didn't. If Troy hadn't walked away from our marriage..."

"Troy is your husband?"

I shook my head. "Ex-husband now. Anyway, if I hadn't been left on my own at age forty-five, I might never have bought this church. I wouldn't have considered starting my own business. I would have never..."

"Pursued your dreams?" Ferral asked, his voice unexpectedly kind.

"Pursued my dreams," I agreed. I thought about the sequence of events, and shock robbed me of breath. Reaching across the table, I grabbed his hand. "They didn't do something to Troy, did they?" I had zero regrets that I was on my own, forging my own way. I was happy to be single again. But that didn't mean I wanted Troy to have been turned into a vegetable or worse by some all-powerful body because he'd had the misfortune to have been inadvertently keeping me from claiming my legacy.

Aside from my deep regret if that happened, Mavis and Bev would be devastated by his loss.

Ferral's gaze never wavered from mine. I thought I could read the answer in those silver eyes. And I didn't like what I was reading. But he finally shook his head. "He was simply encouraged to do what he'd been wanting to do for a long time. He is well."

Relief made my muscles soften. I sagged back in my chair. "Okay. That's good."

"So, Madam Lares. About tonight..."

I nodded. "Tonight. What are you thinking?"

Despite a full evening of planning, I was a jittery mess when I heard the front door slam and heavy footsteps coming up the hallway. Smiling, I recognized the ungraceful, almost angry footfalls. I looked up from the diagram I was perusing as she came into the kitchen. "I'm glad to see you're okay."

Wanda shrugged. "It takes a lot to dent me."

"I'm glad. Are you here because you want to help tonight?"

She frowned. "Tonight? I...um..."

My eyebrows lifted. "Or are you just here because you have to be?" I watched her carefully. Since first setting eyes on the teen, I'd felt like something was slightly off about her. Then Bev had told me she was under the influence of a spell, and I'd taken a closer look. I'd realized sometime the day before that I was seeing a hazy aura around the people I interacted with. And each aura was different. Different colors, distinctive edges, unique vigor. Some throbbed, some wavered, and others almost danced.

Wanda's aura was washed out, a dull kind of gray-blue, and it sat perfectly still around her.

"You've been spelled to come here every day, haven't you?" I asked quietly. I'd given it a lot of thought since my realization that she wasn't functioning under her own steam. She always arrived at the same time of day. She stayed about the same length of time. And she didn't leave so much as disappear. Added to some of the things the teen had said, there could only be one explanation.

Wanda's expression was shocked. She fixed me with wide eyes and shuffled nervously in place. "Why do you say that?"

I gave her a look.

She fidgeted some more and then sighed. Heading to the refrigerator, she tugged it open and pulled out a soda. Popping the top, she turned back to me and leaned against the counter. "It's a Groundhog Day curse. I'm locked into visiting every day at the same time, and the spell usually pulls me out around the same time every night."

"Usually?"

"Yeah. Once in a while I get stuck here overnight." She shrugged. "I think the spell has a random glitch in it."

Odd. My mind filled with questions. The first one was the most immediate. "But last night...?"

"I don't know what happened last night. I popped out as usual, but something dragged me back. I remember having a nightmare about some really ugly dudes." She grimaced. "And this horrible bird thing. It was massive." I winced when she shuddered, guilt forcing my gaze down to my hands. "Then I woke up this morning with no idea what happened after the nightmare." She shrugged.

Thank the goddess for small favors, I thought. "Okay, let's leave that for the minute. Tell me about this spell."

"Curse," she corrected me. "It's a curse."

I nodded. "Curse. Got it."

She was quiet for a long moment, staring at the cold can of pop in her hand. And then said. "My mom isn't quite human."

My brows lifted at the odd beginning to her story, but I stayed silent.

"My dad didn't stick around long after he realized what she was." A wave of pain ran through her expression and disappeared. It seemed to be an old wound, healed over but still tender. "He stayed in touch with me for a while. Until..."

I felt my chest tighten, knowing where she was going with her story. I fought the urge to ask her to stop. But I knew she wouldn't fully heal until she'd shared her story with someone else. Then, I'd do whatever I could to end the curse.

She shook her head. "When he found out I was like her, he called me a freak and even implied I wasn't his kid."

A single tear mapped a silvery trail down her pale cheek. "I was okay with that. At that point, I was pretty sure I didn't want to be his kid anyway."

I couldn't really blame her. "He didn't deserve you," I said, fighting tears myself.

She shrugged, her narrow shoulders rounding. She seemed to want to fold up into a microscopic spec and disappear. "When he left, my mom did some things she shouldn't have. She ticked off the wrong people. And it came back to bite her."

"What happened to her?" I asked.

"I'm not sure exactly. Two...people, I guess... came in the middle of the night and took her. The only thing I remember is somebody standing over me when I was in my bed. I couldn't really see who it was, but I remember the voice. It was terrible, like something straight out of Hell, and the person wore some kind of long dress and a cape. Like a fairy-tale witch. The witch put a hand with long curved nails over my face and said, 'You will suffer the sins of your mother, who never moved beyond the largest mistake of her life. Therefore, your sentence will be to keep living a single event from your memories. You will live that event until your physical form gives out. Or until you find the secret of the curse and break it.'"

"Then a cold, nasty finger touched my forehead, and there was a bright light that blinded me for a long time. When I woke up, my mom was gone. I cried all day." She shook her head. "I should have done something, but..." She angrily shoved tears off her face. "I'm useless. Even the thing I relive over and over again is stupid."

"What is it?" I asked. "What are you reliving?"

She gave me a self-deprecating laugh. "I used to help this pastor once in a while." She swung a hand around as if to indicate the church. "He used to preach here a few years ago. I must have been thinking about him when that thing cursed me. So I relive coming to the church to help with whatever Pastor Joel asked me to do." She looked at me, apparently misreading my sorrow for pity. "I told you it was lame."

"You haven't heard from your mom in how long?"

"Three years." She looked around the kitchen. "I've been coming here for three years. It was pretty boring until you moved in." She gave a watery laugh. "That bat has been my best friend, so that should tell you how pathetic I am."

I blinked desperately to dispel the tears I didn't want her to see. "You're not pathetic. Even cursed, you're still trying to help people. I'd call that pretty awesome."

She looked away to hide the pleasure my words gave her.

"So," I said, trying to lighten the mood. "You and the bat, huh?"

She laughed again. "Sometimes the bat's not there, but usually some kind of flying thing is up there. Once, it was a raven. He was pretty cool. There was also an owl. He was really pretty. I found a bunch of pigeons once. Have you ever noticed how stupid pigeons look? They have tiny round eyes, and there's just this whole blank thing going on."

I chuckled and we fell quiet, lost in our thoughts.

Silence spread out between us. Wanda didn't seem willing to break it. I batted around several ways to give her encouragement. Her situation was heart-breaking, and I wanted so badly to make it better. But, everything I came up with sounded like false comfort. Finally, I just stood up and pulled her into a hug. She was stiff against my embrace for a few beats, then she slowly softened, her bony arms wrapping around me hard enough to make my bones creak.

We stayed that way until the front door slammed shut and Bev called out. Wanda stepped quickly away, running the back of her hand over her face to scrape away the tears. I squeezed her shoulder, marveling at the almost emaciated quality of her frame. Mavis was right. We needed to fatten her up. "We'll fix this," I told her. "You have my word."

She lifted a world-weary gaze to mine, her eyes filled with doubt as she shrugged again.

"Hey!" Bev said, breezing into the kitchen and scanning a look over Wanda and then me. "What's up?"

"Wanda and I were just dishing some gossip. Too bad you missed it."

Bev frowned. "Was it good? Come on, ladies, share."

I winked at Wanda. She rolled her eyes. But not before I saw the twinkle of pleasure there.

"All right, be that way," Bev said in mock affront. She held up a couple of greasy bags. "I guess I'll eat all these donuts myself."

Wanda moved faster than any human should be able to move and snatched the bags.

"Hey!" Bev said, laughing. "Save one for me."

Wanda stuck a donut into her mouth and moaned in pleasure. "I'mf bweally bglad byou moofed in," she told me, spitting donut crumbs.

"Well, that's something else we agree on," I said, snatching a bag out of her hand.

19

A FAITHFUL GUARDIAN'S TOUCH
WILL QUIET...

"Mom's going to be a little late," Bev told me as she made us both a cup of coffee to go with our donuts. "I don't know what she's doing, but she's definitely up to something."

I felt a smile cross my face. Mavis on a mission was a wondrous thing. I'd expected her to be afraid or leery after the previous night's events. But when they'd left me the night before, the older woman had a sparkle in her eyes that I hadn't seen for a long time. "Whatever it is, I'm sure it's epic."

Nodding, Bev dunked her glazed donut into her coffee. "What's the plan for tonight?"

"Without knowing what we're going to be facing, it's kind of hard to plan. Ferral wants to put a giant containment spell on the whole woods."

"That's a great idea," Bev said. "Between Trish,

me, and mom we could get it done in three or four hours."

I glanced at the clock. It was after six PM. That would be cutting it a little close. I nodded. "We'll have to make that decision soon."

The front door slammed, and Trish's voice called out. "Helloooo?"

"In the kitchen," Bev hollered before I could respond. I had a mouth full of donut and was happy to let her be my greeter.

Trish and Luke came into the kitchen, looking refreshed and ready to go. I really wished I felt the same way. A dogged sense of unease had painfully tightened my neck and shoulder muscles since I'd woken up, and it wasn't easing, despite a long bout of yoga and copious amounts of pain killers.

"Oooh!" Luke said, "Donuts." He grabbed two powdered sugar pastries and shoved one into his mouth.

"Coffee stuff is over there," I told them, pointing toward the panting coffee maker at the end of the counter. Bev had helpfully set out sugar and cream, along with an assortment of pods and mugs.

Trish headed for the coffee. "Do we have a plan for tonight?"

The back door opened and Niele came inside, his cheeks moist and covered in soil. The moss of his new "pants" looked like it had returned to its natural state. The smell of fresh earth wafted through the room as he approached. "Welcome, all!" He gave us a smile and a wave.

"Hey," I said to the gnome. "Help yourself to a donut."

Grabbing a cherry danish, Niele nodded to Trish when she handed him a mug and flushed red beneath his earthen makeup.

"We're just waiting for Gren and Ferral," I told everybody. "Then we'll go over the plan."

"And mom," Bev reminded me.

I nodded. "Unfortunately, we might have to start without her. We only have a few hours to get prepped for tonight." I frowned. "It would be really helpful if we knew what was coming."

The door opened again, and Gren and Ferral strode through.

Gren's dark eyes found mine and settled, heat flaring in their depths.

I shuffled uncomfortably in my seat. It had been a while since a man looked at me like that, and I didn't trust it.

He was probably just showing me respect for my position.

There was no way a man as sexy as Gren would look twice at a slightly fluffy forty-five-year-old woman who was in way over her head and flailing.

I really needed to lay off the romance novels. I was starting to imagine things.

"Good morning, everyone," Gren said with a brief flick of his dark brown gaze around the room.

The group responded with a chorus of murmured greetings.

Wanda took herself to a corner and stood staring at everyone with wary eyes, nibbling her third donut.

What I wouldn't give to have a teenage metabolism again.

Ferral eschewed both coffee and donuts and leaned against the farmhouse sink, crossing his muscular arms over his chest and looking at me.

That was my cue. "Okay, now that everybody's here, we need to discuss our plan for tonight."

"Do we have one?" Bev asked, grinning.

"We do. Sort of. As I said before, without knowing what we're going to be up against, it's hard to plan. But..." I glanced at my adviser. "Ferral had an idea how to minimize the possibility that we'll undergo another attack like last night's."

Taking my cue, he nodded. "I propose we set a containment spell around the wood. Just until the thirteens are over."

Stunned silence met his proposal, which surprised me a little. Then everyone seemed to explode at once.

"You can't," Niele screamed.

"That's a terrible idea!" Luke growled.

"It's sacrilege," Trish yelled.

"No," Gren said very quietly. "It's out of the question."

I looked at Bev, raising my brows.

She shrugged. "It would make things much easier."

"Easier!" Niele ground out. "Do you know what that would do to the thousands of woodland creatures in the Mystical Wood? The sprites, the fairies, the gnomes?" He advanced on Ferral with his fists bunched. "You will not close them in with the lost ones. They'd never survive."

Bev held up a hand, "Don't get your moss in a twist, gnome. There has to be a way to protect them..."

"No! It's out of the question," Niele barked back. "I'll fight you to my death over this."

I grimaced. It was out of character for the gnome to react so violently. He must really believe it would be bad.

I looked at Trish. "He's right," she said in response to my unasked question. "It would be a bloodbath. And if by some miracle, the devils didn't kill them outright, the magic the lost ones used to try to escape would destroy the wood, killing every living thing in there."

"I have people living there too," Luke said, his voice still growly with anger. "It's one of the reasons I'm fighting this battle. Someone needs to expel those monsters. But killing all the innocents in the wood isn't the way to do it."

"We can protect..." Ferral began.

Gren's hand was wrapped around the Advocate's throat before he could finish the sentence. "No." The overhead lights flickered and the soft sound of fluttering wings filled the room.

I looked around for the bat but didn't see it. A faint shadow in the shape of enormous wings rose above and behind Gren, pulsing around him.

I blinked in surprise. What *was* he?

The two men squared off, their faces like granite. Where Ferral had the advantage on Lungren in weight and bulk, Gren was taller by a few inches and seemed the stronger of the two. At some point during the silent battle of wills, Gren suddenly seemed larger than Ferral, though I couldn't pinpoint the moment it had happened.

"Is that even allowed?" a small voice asked. "I thought the Lares had to vanquish her enemies alone during the thirteens."

Wanda's question sucked the tension from the air like a magical vacuum cleaner. The lights stopped flickering, and Gren and Ferral turned to the teen still standing in the corner. When she saw us all looking at her, she shrugged in her self-deprecating way. "Before we kill each other trying to come up with a plan to help, maybe we need to consider whether it will even be allowed."

"The girl has a point," Bev muttered.

The front door slammed, and footsteps hurried down the hall. "Hello? I'm not too late, am I?" Mavis entered the room, a wide smile on her face and a crystal ball clutched in her hands. She let out a relieved breath, her pretty round face slightly flushed. "It took some doing, but I've got what we need to even the score a bit."

She set the ball down in the center of the table and stood back, beaming at me.

I lifted my brows in silent question.

Mavis blinked. "Oh. Sorry. I forgot you aren't inside my head. Heh." She pointed at the ball, which swirled with liquid silver against a deep, unrelenting blackness. The ball was about eight inches in diameter and vibrated softly against the wooden tabletop.

"I have a friend who's an oracle..."

"An oracle?" I shook my head. "Why am I not surprised?"

"I don't know," Mavis responded, grinning. "Anyway, she agreed to read the next few days for me and..."

"Wait!" Gren held up a hand that, I was happy to see, was no longer attached to Ferral's throat. "You convinced an oracle to read the future for you?"

"I did. As I said, she's a friend..."

"Oracles don't have friends," Ferral growled out.

That was enough to finally wipe the smile from

Mavis's face. "Oh, I get it. You're an oracle bigot as well as an all-around grump?"

I was pretty sure she expected the advocate to deny the charge. He simply shrugged.

Jerk.

"Mom, you have to admit there are good reasons not to like oracles," Bev said.

I didn't know anything about oracles, but I could see why people wouldn't want to hang with somebody who could tell them when and how they were going to die. But that was a discussion for another day. "What did the oracle tell you?"

After a final glare toward Ferral, Mavis allowed her happy expression to return. "She foresaw the challenges we'd face for the rest of the thirteens." She frowned. "Well, all but the last one. For some reason, she couldn't see that one."

Hope flared in my chest. "If we know what we're up against..."

"We'll know how to fight it," Trish said, nodding.

Even Ferral appeared pleased by that news. But he hid it well. "Young Wanda had a point," he groused. We must verify that use of an oracle doesn't go against the rules of the seating."

Mavis flapped a dismissive hand. "Verify away, grump. The oracle read *my* future, not Aggy's. Since I'm a member of the Lares Council, I'm allowed to help her. And, technically..."

"It doesn't fall under the parameters of outside aid," Gren finished, nodding. "It just might work."

"I still believe we should make sure," Ferral insisted.

I nodded. "I agree. Can you take that on, please? The rest of us will figure out how to tackle whatever is going to happen tonight."

He gave me a shallow bow and strode from the room. I didn't know where he was going or what he was going to do. But I smiled at the sigh of relief that ran through the room when he left.

"Okay," I said. "Let's get started." I locked at Mavis. "Mom, how do you fire this thing up?"

20

A TERRIBLE FOE, EMOTIONS RIOT...

Of all the things. Ugh!!! I stared out over the sea of writhing, black and yellow and green, spotted, striped, and painted reptiles covering the church grounds. Their muscular bodies writhed and boiled over the grass like the foul contents of a witch's cauldron.

"I hate snakes," Trish mumbled unhappily.

"I'm pretty sure none of us love them," Bev agreed.

"I don't mind regular snakes," Wanda said, her bored expression not even wrinkled from what she was seeing. "But I prefer it if there aren't thousands of them."

"Amen and amen," Mavis said.

"Keep in mind, those aren't regular snakes," Gren said. He jerked his chin toward the graveyard.

"Notice there isn't a single one on consecrated ground."

I lifted my brows. "Then why couldn't we just hide inside the church until dawn? Why do we even need to vanquish the things?"

"If you do not, they'll still be there in the morning," said a grumpy voice from behind us.

I turned to find Ferral striding into the kitchen. "What did you find out?"

He sighed. "The news is not good, I'm afraid." He looked around the room, his expression filled with regret. "We cannot use the information from the oracle…"

Everyone exploded into conversation at once.

I held up a hand to stop them. "Let him finish," I told my team.

Ferral inclined his head in thanks. "We cannot use it directly to defeat the Lares' foes. What we can do is use it to form a plan for protecting her as *she* conquers them."

"Well, isn't that just a skunk's behind?" Niele mumbled.

I sighed.

"Yeah," Bev agreed, rubbing my back as my pulse shot into the stratosphere.

"I was afraid of that," Luke said. He stared at the ground.

Wanda raised her hand, and everybody looked

her way. "I think I might have a way that we can help Aggy *and* keep her safe."

When nobody rebuffed her, Wanda pulled something out from behind her back.

I frowned at the curved piece of dented and pocked metal. "Is that the centerpiece from the outside table?" I'd found the thing in one of the kitchen cabinets when I was moving in and had almost thrown it out. But it had a certain kitschy kind of charm, and I finally decided to use it as decoration.

Wanda chuckled. "It's not meant to be a centerpiece, Aggy."

"Then what is it?"

"A rhyton," Mavis breathed. "Of course."

Wanda nodded. "These things were mostly used as drinking horns. But ancient Lares sometimes transformed them into musical horns. The rhyton's melody controlled the enemies of their dominion."

"Like a Pied Piper?" Niele asked, looking skeptical.

Wanda nodded. "It doesn't work on higher-level monsters, but the snake has a much simpler genetic makeup." She jerked her head toward the mass of thrashing creatures in the yard. "Those guys probably came from the Garden of Eden line of snakes. Hell's version. They're not the same type of snake every Lares throughout time has depended on as a symbol of fertility and prosperity for their domains.

But, I think if you used the horn on those guys out there..."

"You could change their inclinations from evil to good," Ferral finished for her, nodding.

Bev's gaze was narrowed on the teen, her expression speculative. "You sure do know a lot about this," she said to Wanda.

The teen's gaze slid away and she shrugged. "I read stuff."

"But what do we do with that many snakes?" I asked. I wasn't sure I was convinced by the whole drinking horn thing. It sounded like an impossible task. "There must be thirty thousand of them out there."

"You lead them away," Wanda said, shrugging.

"To where?" Bev asked.

"To Rome," Gren said. His expression turned from dire to hopeful. "That just might work."

I shook my head. "There's no way I'm going to infest Rome with thousands of snakes."

"Well, you could take them further into the country, but then your people won't benefit from the prosperity they spread," Wanda said.

We hashed it out until the snakes started flinging themselves against the side of the building. But it wasn't until a particularly meaty one smashed through the window and landed in a writhing, hissing coil in my kitchen sink that we decided we'd run out of time.

"Okay, it's the best plan we've got," I said. "Let's do it." I tore my gaze from the snake that was slowly slithering out of my sink to look at the others. "How do I do this?"

Wanda handed me the horn. "Think Pied Piper."

Narrowing my eyes at her, I said, "Seriously?"

She peaked a dark brow.

Sighing, I murmured, "I'm way too old for this."

A familiar warmth enveloped me, and I looked up to find Gren mere inches away, his expression soft. "Madam Lares, you are exactly old enough and not a minute older."

Despite the ugliness ahead, I couldn't help smiling. "Thanks, Gren."

He gave me a shallow bow. "Now, before you go to battle, you'll want to gird your loins."

My eyes went wide, and I barely kept from looking southward to said loins. "Um."

He flushed as he seemed to realize I'd taken him literally. Pointing to my legs, he said. "You'll have a few dangerous moments before the beasties are enthralled..."

I thought he was being optimistic. I was pretty sure I'd have more than a few minutes. I'd probably be buried under a mountain of the nasty things, trying to blow on my horn with snakes hissing in my ear long before I got them enthralled.

I saw a flash of movement out of the corner of my eye and whipped around to find Ferral, in his enormous gray dog form, with a massive snake drooping from between his jaws.

Ugh!!

I handed Gren the horn and spun on my heel. "I'm going to gird. If you all get bored, feel free to kill a snake or a thousand."

Bev and Mavis hurried after me. I wasn't sure if they were trying to get away from the snakes trying to breach the broken window or because of a sense of sisterhood.

The three of us rushed into my bedroom, and I flung open the doors of the too-small closet. We stared in forlorn silence at the mess in there.

Bev whistled. "Girl..."

"I know. But there's no coat closet, so I had to put everything in this one measly space."

Mavis suddenly dove toward the floor and came up with the knee-high leather boots I'd bought for a rare night out with Troy. I grimaced at the memory. I'd had too much to drink and barfed on my pretty new boots. I hadn't worn them since. "These will do the trick," Mavis told me, her eyes gleaming. Then she wrinkled her nose. "What's that smell?"

I snatched them away from her. "Never mind. I cleaned them like ten times."

Bev laughed. "Are those the boots you horked on? Troy was hysterical over that, you know."

"Jerk," I mumbled under my breath. He'd teased me incessantly about that unfortunate night for weeks afterward. "I've seen him pretty drunk about a hundred times, you know. I never teased him about it."

Mavis patted my shoulder. "It doesn't matter. Maybe some of the snakes will pass out from the stench and run away."

Bev snorted.

I glared. "I'll need something from the knees up. Some of those suckers out there are ginormous."

We eyed my closet for another minute and then started grabbing stuff and flinging it toward the bed.

We left my room a disaster area and returned to the kitchen about ten minutes later. I pulled up the rear because...well...honestly, I was walking like C3PO from Star Wars, and it took me longer to navigate the hallway. I was the sta-puft marshmallow woman from the knees up, and Captain Jack Sparrow from the knees down. There are very few times in middle age when having slender calves becomes a negative.

I was living through one of those times. The contrast between my upper and lower sections was stark...bordering on comical.

The room at large was speechless when they looked at me. They'd probably never seen a mature woman (or any woman, let's be honest) dressed in a puffy snowsuit and "kiss me sailor" leather boots with three-inch heels. I was worried about those heels. The last thing I needed was for one of them to sink into the ground and fling me beneath the writhing mass. But I didn't have it in me to break the sexy heels off. Despite the stench and the potential for horrible death, I loved those boots. They looked really kick-butt with my above-the-knee leather skirt.

"Goddess on a gourd," Wanda said. "You look like something that's been spliced together from several bad adventure films."

"Hey!" Bev objected. "Those movies are classics."

The teen rolled her eyes. "If by classic, you mean ancient."

"I resemble that statement," I told her. "I grew up on those movies."

Wanda snorted.

"Excuse me, Madam Lares," Niele said. He pointed to my boots. "May I?"

I opened my mouth to ask him what he meant, but he didn't wait for my response. Reaching down, he wrenched one foot off the ground and I nearly toppled over. Luke grabbed my arm to keep me upright as I felt a quick wrench on my boot.

"What?" I looked at the heel in the gnome's hand, my eyes wild. "What have you done?"

"Survival over beauty, Madam," he told me.

Then, quick as a wink, he went around behind me and wrenched the other heel off.

I nearly cried.

Wanda shoved the horn into my hands and headed for the door to the belfry. "Good luck. I'll be on lookout upstairs."

My council surrounded me, forming a perfect circle. Fortunately, Ferral spit the dead snake out before joining us. Unfortunately, he left it bleeding on my floor. Though the sink was currently roiling with the things, spitting mad and trying desperately to escape, so I figured the dead one was the least of my worries.

"Use your instincts," Mavis told me, giving my arm a squeeze. "You've always had great instincts."

I sighed and nodded. Closing my eyes, I said a silent prayer that my instincts lived up to Mavis' good opinion of them. I let my thoughts drift, trying not to think about the disgusting reptiles slamming against my house and the circle of people waiting for me to do something. It wasn't easy. In fact, I was starting to be afraid I wasn't going to be able to pull it off when Gren's voice drifted to me through the silence. It was deep and smooth and filled with encouragement. The pleasing timbre worked its way beneath my skin and sparked the magic I'd had trouble finding by myself. "Feel the energy, Aggy. Bid it to rise and meet the moment."

Power rose in soft spirals toward my hands. I

watched it rise with my inner vision, inserting my will into the gentle coils of energy to give them vitality. A moment later, the skin of my hands heated, prickling with the infusion of unaccustomed power.

The metal horn began to soften beneath my touch, and I envisioned a musical instrument I'd never seen before. The form of it had to have come from some unknown well of information tied to the past. The far distant past. When the horn stopped changing, it began to cool. I opened my eyes to see something I wouldn't have been able to describe but somehow recognized.

The musical instrument was much bigger than I'd expected, very thin and curved into a letter "G" with what looked like carved bone bisecting its form and a wide flat lip around the larger opening at the top. I didn't need to ask Gren or Ferral what to do with the horn. I somehow already knew.

Slipping it over one shoulder, I gripped the bone piece with one hand and placed my lips around the mouthpiece. I blew softly into the horn, and a gentle melody of high-pitched notes emerged from the bell near my head.

There was movement in the sink, and several long bodies rose straight into the air, swaying gently to the music I was creating. Their snakey jaws were open wide, fangs glistening, and tongues sliding out to taste the music on the air.

I moved toward the front of the church, my team

following. When I reached the front door, Niele pulled it open. He bowed low, murmuring, "May the goddess smooth your way, Madam Lares."

I pulled the horn from my lips and looked out over the ground I needed to cover. Snakes. As far as the eye could see. Thousands and thousands of them.

They surrounded the building.

My heart was beating so fast, I thought I might pass out.

A warm hand found my shoulder. Another touched my arm. Then another, and another. An enormous wolf pressed against one thigh. A huge silver dog leaned against the other. Monty whined pitifully from behind the closed bedroom door. Poor baby, he only wanted to join the fun.

Trish buzzed overhead in her warrior fairy form. Gren gave me a brisk nod.

Taking a deep breath, I put the horn to my lips again and stepped outside.

21

EXTEND HER HAND TO SEVER VICE...

Running out the door behind me, Niele leaped into the air and dove, his body piercing the earth as if it were butter. The ground ahead of me suddenly bowed upward in a wide path of raised dirt and grass. Snakes flew into the air wherever Niele went, some falling below the earth and disappearing from sight.

On either side of me, Ferral and Luke ripped writhing bodies away from my legs, flinging them into the distance.

Trish sent sparkling jets of her energy toward the ground, the pulsing energy beating against my skin and repelling the attacking snakes.

I knew that Bev and Mavis worked their magic at the back of the procession, flinging retaining webs over as many snakes as they could to delay them until I could find the right music to control their activity.

Even with all of their help, dozens of writhing, muscular bodies slammed against my legs and body, the sound of ripping fabric rising above the melody of my horn.

I blew harder, building the power of the music until I couldn't hear anything beneath it. The night was dark, with a heavy bank of clouds covering the moon's silvery glow. For once, the ever-present fog didn't rise.

The sky shifted above my head, a cool evening breeze bringing with it the distinctive scent of flying rodent. The bat had joined the battle.

The size of a very large Raven, the bat swooped and struck at snakes rising up around me, giving them a different target for their animus as I struggled to find the right notes in my mystical tune.

Slowly, in fits and starts, the music began to take hold of the mass of snakes. The attacks against me abated. As I stepped down onto the road leading into town, the snakes formed two wide queues behind me and my people fell to the sides, watching for any disruptions they might need to squash.

But there was no further trouble.

As we passed the first, tumbledown farm house, dozens of snakes turned off and slithered toward the house, giving me a moment's pause. The music stuttered as I worried over the snake's intentions.

The mass pressed closer, some hissing aggressively before I started to play again.

My council moved toward the house, only the bat and Trish hovering nearby in case I needed their help.

We needn't have worried. The grass beneath the diverging snakes turned a deep, lush green. Trees sprouted flowers and grew several feet as a handful of large snakes slithered into their branches. The crumbled sidewalk repaired itself beneath three bright yellow snakes. The paint on the house brightened. A crumbling chimney was rebuilt. The frame straightened and stood tall again under the slithering attentions of dozens more reptiles.

As the fortunes of the old white house improved, the reptiles that had offered the new prosperity turned to dust and blew away on the air.

The next home gained fresh concrete in the drive and a new garage door to replace the one that was broken and sagging.

We hit the edge of town and I watched in awe as what had once been a popular ice cream shop regained walls and a roof, had its chimney rebuilt, and its lawn and parking lot repaired from the devastating fire that had robbed its owners of a livelihood.

I moved on, the music becoming the air I breathed. All around me, Rome straightened its time-worn shoulders and lifted its sagging chin.

Brick shone brighter beneath the street lights. Potholes disappeared. Paint brightened. Window glass rebuilt, dying trees revived.

With every repair, snakes dissolved in the wind. Finally, a mile outside of Rome, on the other end of the small town, I saw the last of the creatures dust the air.

I was so exhausted by then that I didn't have the strength to stand. I fell to my knees on the freshly repaired road, my brain almost too fractured from weariness to notice the pain shooting through my knees.

I was dimly aware of someone taking the horn from me.

I heard concerned voices and felt the warmth of several bodies surrounding me. But I couldn't keep my eyes open, and my muscles were liquid beneath me.

I didn't even manage surprise when a heated pair of arms pulled me gently off the ground, and with a powerful jolt, carried me into the sky.

I let myself give in to exhaustion at that point, trusting that whatever was happening to me would be all right.

It wasn't as if I had the strength to stop it anyway.

A particularly persistent bird trilled happily beyond my open window. The creature sang gaily into the brightness of a painfully sunny day, clearly happy to be alive.

Covering my face with a pillow, I embraced pleasant thoughts of throttling the stupid creature.

Monty nudged my arm with a cold, wet nose.

I ignored him and the idiot bird and rolled over.

Monty nudged me again, clawing at my thigh.

"Ouch!" I told him, shoving him gently away.

He bounced enthusiastically, filled with canine glee that I was awake.

If he started trilling like the bird, I was going to suffocate myself with the pillow.

Five minutes of determined trilling and nudging later, I gave up and threw the pillow aside. "Alright, alright, you little tyrant. I'm getting up."

My dog whipped around and flew down his doggy steps, bouncing around my legs as I shoved myself, groaning, into an upright position.

My whole body hurt. Being a middle-aged super-hero sucked rotten lemons.

I hobbled down the endless hallway to the kitchen, where I let Monty out to do his business and slapped blindly at the coffee maker until it was spewing delicious midnight brew into my favorite mug.

Something flapped against the window, and I jolted into full consciousness. The glass was whole again. Had I dreamed the whole thing from the night before?

I quickly realized I hadn't when I opened the cabinet to drop the spent coffee pod into the trash and saw a pile of broken glass on top.

Okay. I wasn't losing my mind. Not yet anyway. I'd get there soon enough.

I took my coffee outside and lowered my achy body into a chair at the round iron table.

The sound of wings flapping had me looking up as an enormous black bird landed on the table.

"Ah!" I said, my muscles contracting to flee. But the pain that immediately burned through me from the action kept me rooted. It would hurt too much to flee. I'd just throw hot coffee at it if it attacked.

No. Bad idea. I needed every drop of that liquid healthcare. I'd gulp the coffee and throw the mug at it, I decided. I had other mugs.

Decision made, I took a big drink that scalded my innards all the way down to my stomach.

"Jeezopete!"

The bird lifted its wings and danced sideways, shiny black eyes riveted on me.

"You'd better not poop on my table," I told it.

The raven cocked its sleek black head and ruffled its feathers. We had a staring contest for a minute. I gave in first. "What's the deal?" I finally asked.

The bird fluttered its wings, lifting off the table a few inches as Monty ran up to the table, barking excitedly. The little dog lifted to his hind legs and bounced, trying to see the bird better.

Aside from being startled by Monty's arrival, the raven didn't seem concerned by his presence.

I finished my coffee and realized I had a new problem. Trying to ignore my full bladder, I squirmed in my chair. For some reason, I was reluctant to scare the raven off. I couldn't shake the feeling that it was trying to tell me something.

"Okay, bird," I said. "I really need to pee, so if you have something you want to say, say it fast."

The raven opened its beak wide, and a melodic trilling sound emerged.

I blinked. "That was you outside my window this morning?" I laughed. I'd known ravens were extremely intelligent, but I hadn't realized they could sing. "Can you talk?" I asked the bird.

It lifted one foot and spread its beak wide, trilling into the morning like a songbird.

Shaking my head, I grabbed my mug and headed inside. "Have a great day," I told the bird, feeling silly for talking to it.

"Great," said a deep voice. The single word sounded for all the world like sarcasm.

I whipped around, and the raven stared at me with its black eyes. "Was that you?"

Silence.

I danced from foot to foot. "Sorry, I really need to pee," I told him as I opened the door and all but ran inside. As I passed the open window over the sink, I heard the deep voice speak again, saying the word "pee" as clear as day.

Jeezopete.

An hour later, after a long, hot shower and some toast, I headed into town to hit the grocery. Having so many people in my house every day was draining my food resources. The significance of what we'd done the night before hit me as I drove past the farmhouses around me and then the homes and businesses on Rome's main street. Everything looked shiny and new.

People walked along the sidewalks, engaged in lively conversation or briskly walking pets, and everyone looked happy. I doubted they'd noticed the changes directly, since that would go against every-thing I understood about magic. But, on some level they'd assimilated the positive energy, and it had made their day better.

I smiled. Suddenly everything we'd gone through the night before seemed worth it. I only hoped the coming night's challenges would be worth it too. That thought made my breakfast toast sit heavy in my stomach. But I shoved the unease away and parked in the freshly paved grocery store parking lot.

I was halfway to the door when the raven dropped from the sky and perched on my shoulder.

"Ah!" I twitched violently, causing the big bird to

drift upward in alarm and then settle back down again. I lifted my arm. "Shoo!" I said softly, trying not to draw the notice of others. The last thing I needed was to become the town's designated crazy raven lady.

"Morning, Aggy!" someone called.

Face flushed with humiliation, I looked up and smiled weakly at a woman putting groceries into her car. I recognized her as someone I'd gone to high school with. She waved and smiled, very friendly.

I waved back, my face beet red. "Hey. How's it going?"

"Pee!" quoth the raven.

I dropped my face in my hand, "Sweet goddess take me now."

The woman only laughed, giving me another wave.

I stood there in shock, watching her drive out of the lot.

"Hey, honey," Mavis's cheerful voice said. I whipped around, my passenger giving a surprised little "caw."

Mavis eyed the bird. "Honey, why do you have a raven on your shoulder?"

I threw up my hands. "I have no idea. The thing showed up this morning, and now it wants to go everywhere with me."

"Pee!" quoth the raven.

Mavis barked out a laugh. "Why is it shouting pee?"

"Ugh!!"

She looped her arm through mine. "Never mind. There must be a reason. Just go with it."

"But I have to do my grocery shopping. I can't just go in there with a raven on my shoulder."

"Why not?" She swung an arm around the parking lot. "Nobody seems to care."

I sighed. "I guess we can give it a try."

Sure enough, though several people waved and greeted us, not a single person seemed to notice the giant black bird on my shoulder. Which was a very good thing because the stupid bird had started mimicking my pee dance before he shouted out the word to the entire universe.

Mavis was laughing so hard she was crying.

"I'm glad my humiliation is entertaining to you," I groused.

That only sent her into new spasms of helpless laughter. "You should take this show on the road, honey," she said, patting my arm.

I shook my head. "Har."

Mavis helped me load my groceries into the car and then followed me home to help me unload them. Thankfully, the bird flew off when I climbed into my car. He reappeared at home, but only to land on the patio table and make a lot of noise.

"He seems to have adopted you," Bev said when

she arrived a couple of hours later. "Did you feed him?"

"No!" I said too emphatically. "I'm not that stupid."

She only shrugged, then winked at her mother.

Mavis giggled. She slid a pan of biscuits into the oven and lifted the lid on the bubbling deliciousness on top of the stove. "Dinner will be ready as soon as those biscuits are done. Do you want to check the crystal ball now? Then we can start putting together a plan of attack."

I nodded in agreement. "Let's do it."

22

AND EASE A SOUL NOT ONCE BUT TWICE...

"It's blank," I said, frowning. "What does that mean?"

Mavis chewed a fingernail, looking worried.

Staring into the murky blackness of the divining ball, Bev wore an unreadable expression. The two women were giving me polar opposite reactions. And I didn't know how to deal with it.

"Maybe it means nothing's going to happen," Mavis said in a hopeful tone.

Bev continued to stare mutely at the ball.

I wrapped an arm around Mavis's shoulders and kept my gaze locked on Bev. "Tell me," I urged her, my stomach twisting. "I need to know."

She flipped me a glance, her expression dire. Still, it took her another minute to speak. Sighing, she sat back in her chair. "I think the Powers have spoken, and they want you to complete the rest of your challenges alone."

The knot in my belly twisted tighter. That was what I'd thought too, though I hadn't wanted to put it into words. I inclined my head. "Okay." I cleared my throat and crossed my arms over my chest, feeling my heart try to beat its way out of my chest. "All right then." I gave them a forced smile. "If that's the way it has to be..." My throat clenched, and I couldn't finish my brave declaration.

Tears burned Mavis's eyes. "I'm so sorry, honey."

I nodded, swallowing with difficulty. "I think this calls for a cup of coffee."

Bev's eyes went wide. "No wine?"

I gave my head a single shake. "Not tonight. I need my wits about me."

The two women nodded. Though I insisted they should have their accustomed wine, they supported me and drank coffee too.

The front door opened and closed and footsteps came down the hall. Trish's and Luke's expressions were grim.

Niele, Gren, and Ferral looked equally morose.

Wanda arrived as usual at dinnertime but begged off eating and went straight up to the belfry.

Mavis placed the food on the table and instructed everyone to fix their own bowls. We ate. We chatted quietly. We even tried to laugh a few times. But a pall had fallen over the group, and it fed poisonous doubt into my soul.

Even Monty was subdued. He only half-heartedly begged for handouts and then fell asleep beneath the table before all the food was gone.

For a dachshund, that was the equivalent of being on his death bed.

None of them seemed to believe I could fend off a challenge on my own.

And I was starting to think they were right.

The bell sent its first warning into the night at exactly Midnight. We stood in the front foyer of the church, a collection of people with unhappy expressions. As I drew myself up and took a deep breath, all my friends...my council... moved close, giving me silent support.

"Keep the goddess close," Gren said as I reached for the door.

I nodded, took another deep breath, and stepped outside.

The night was quiet except for the familiar song of the crickets. A soft breeze slipped over my fear-heated skin as I walked across the yard, soothing some of my nerves. I had no idea why I was moving toward the gravel roads that crossed in front of the pretty white church. It seemed I was being led by some instinct that was older than I was, forged in the pages of history and the passage of time.

A fluttering of wings told me the raven had arrived. I flinched only a little when the creature landed on my shoulder and gave me a deep-throated caw. Glancing sideways at the bird, I said, "You know you're not supposed to be here, right?" I asked softly. Still, I was glad for his fearless presence.

He cawed again, lifting his shiny black wings. The tips of his feathers caressed the side of my face, and I couldn't help feeling as if he'd meant for them to.

In the distance, behind the dull, melodic clang of the bell in the tower, loud music and shouting filled the night. I frowned in that direction. What in the world?

My foot stepped down onto the pure, white gravel, which didn't seem to get dirty no matter how many vehicles rolled over its surface. I stopped at the edge of the road, despite an insistent need to keep walking. The music and voices told me a car was coming. If I stood in the center of the road, one of two things would likely happen.

The car would strike me.

Or they'd crash trying to avoid me.

Neither outcome seemed preferred.

The raven on my shoulder rose into the air on a strident caw, whipping my face with his wings.

I sighed, knowing I had to trust my instincts,

even if I thought they had to be wrong. I moved into the road, feeling the stones warming encouragingly beneath my sneakers. Dead center of where the two roads crossed, I stopped and closed my eyes.

The eleventh peal sounded.

A deep rumbling and the sound of massive tires on gravel approached from my right.

Laughter and too-loud music approached from my left.

My eyes flew open as I realized what was about to happen. The raven flew away, landing in a tree whose branches overarched the crossing.

My pulse pounded. Head whipping around, I watched the enormous yellow vehicle barreling toward me from the South. A joyful shout sliced through the air from the North, and my gaze shot that way. An SUV that seemed filled to bursting with drunk teens threw up rock dust and snaked from side to side as the inebriated driver tried to sing, drive, and wave his beer bottle out the open window at the same time.

The big yellow bus was full too, a cacophony of animated voices rising above the roar of the engine and the crunch of oversized tires on gravel. The voices sounded young. School-aged kids, no doubt returning from some kind of athletic event or outing.

Kids.

Lots of kids.

And, if I didn't do something, they were all going

to die.

How could they not see each other?

As often happens on narrow country roads, both vehicles claimed the very center of the road. Expecting little traffic in the quiet countryside at that time of night, neither one seemed inclined to moderate their speed.

I looked back and forth between them as peal number twelve struck, its power reverberating along the invisible lines of power that led from the belfry directly to me.

It thrummed in my chest, overriding my terror of failing and forcing me to react.

I lifted my hands, said a quiet prayer to the forces behind our fate, and pushed air from my lungs. Energy bubbled inside me, unfocused and brimming with unmet purpose. I tugged on it as the thirteenth peal throbbed through the night.

Kids talked and laughed with excitement.

Music danced toward me on the night air, the bass notes mapped to the beating of my frantic heart. Tires crunched over the snow-white stone, drunken laughter rippled on the tension-filled air.

Panic flared over me, and the seconds ticked away.

At the last possible moment...as the bus driver finally noticed the oncoming SUV, a horn blared into the night, slicing off the happy shouts from the car.

Mere seconds from impact, the thirteenth peal cut through the cacophony on the ground, and the bus's huge front end was suddenly in front of me.

As if in slow motion, the bus moved on past, a frozen portrait of horrified faces framed behind the row of open windows. Wide eyes and rounded mouths bore testament to their impending deaths.

My hands moved. Reasoning cut off as flying rocks sliced against my skin and dust choked and blinded me. The SUV began to skid, its back end sliding sideways on the unstable gravel surface.

I saw it all happen.

The massive impact.

The horrible crunching sound.

The inhuman squeal of ripping metal and the shrieks of pure, unadulterated terror and horrific pain.

I had less than a second to change that future for us all.

I stood there, arms up as the two vehicles met in the center of that road, and only the flick of a wrist and a single muttered word turned the horror back on its heels and changed imminent death to vibrant life.

My lips formed a word, *Skew*! And my arms swung toward the road, a single heartbeat before metal hit metal, and the lives of far too many young people were sliced away by hideous destiny.

When I blinked again, the SUV was barreling

down the crossroad, perpendicular to their previous route. Unscathed. The shouts were raucous and happy, and the music faded as the distance grew between them and me.

The bus had slowed some as if an unseen force of common sense had made the driver realize he was being careless with his precious cargo. But it moved on, heading into Rome at a more sedate speed.

I collapsed to the ground, boneless with residual terror and weak from the enormous expulsion of power.

I'd done it! They were all safe.

For a long moment, the only sound was my ragged breathing and the natural melody of crickets returning to their song.

Then I heard the soft thump of wings on the air. The raven settled down onto the gravel in front of me, wings flapping and clawed feet moving awkwardly across the rough surface in a familiar dance. "Pee!" he cried in his deep voice, dark eyes sparking with golden light.

"Goddess!" I breathed on a bark of laughter. "You too? I'm pretty sure I need to change my clothes." I fell backward onto the road, laughing so hard I barely even noticed the pristine rocks digging into my flesh.

It was over. We'd all survived.

Only a few more challenges ahead.

ONE BY ONE AND TWO BY TWO...

My eyes popped open way too early the next morning, and I sat bolt upright in my bed with the residue of a bell toll still sifting through my consciousness. I held my breath and waited for another peal, but none followed.

Maybe I'd dreamed it. Goddess knew I probably had PTSD from the whole near-miss event out on the crossroads the night before.

I took mental and physical inventory. Aside from a few cuts on my legs and arms from flying gravel, I was physically fine.

Emotionally...? Yeah, I was okay. No lingering stress. In fact, I felt really good.

Energy poured through my cells, and I suddenly found it hard to stay still. I shoved back the covers and swung my legs over the side, earning a confused glare from Monty. I patted his soft behind. "Come on, sleepyhead. We've got work to do."

I had no idea what work, of course, but every cell in my body was keyed to movement and action, and I was helpless against the call.

I knew as soon as I stepped into the kitchen that something was wrong. The house was unnaturally dark, even for five o'clock in the morning. The window over the sink usually framed the moon, its silvery glow burnishing everything in the room with gentle illumination. But the window was dark. Deep, unrelenting dark. I reached up and flipped the switch just inside the kitchen door and then screamed.

It took my shocked brain a beat to figure out what I was seeing. When it finally clicked, I knew I was looking at my next challenge.

Locusts.

I turned on my heel and headed for the front door. Opening it just wide enough for Monty and me to fit through, I stepped out into a post-apocalyptic landscape of endless flying bugs and ravaged plant life.

The grass was all but gone, the succulent green stalks eaten down to the dirt. The leaves in the once-lush trees were gnawed and scourged. I lifted my gaze to the fields across the road and saw nothing but a sea of rabid insects, manic with their need to pillage anything green and edible.

My heart sank as I watched the once lush fields, one filled with vibrantly healthy corn stalks and the other a dense carpet of soybeans.

The plants were almost completely gone.

"No," I breathed, my chest tight. Why hadn't the warning come sooner? How was I going to fix the damage that had already been done?

The nasty grasshoppers clogging the air around me separated in a panicked wash of air as the raven dropped from the sky and landed on my shoulder. I turned my head just in time to see him open his beak and swallow a wriggling locust down his gullet.

"Ew!" I complained, flapping a hand at him. "Go do your eating somewhere..." My words were sliced off by the arrival of an idea.

The raven pecked the air and snatched another bug, swallowing it whole.

"No," I murmured thoughtfully. "What I need is more of you. Lots more."

I eyed the distribution of bugs, and my nascent idea matured. I looked at the raven. "I need your help. I hope you don't mind when I do this..." Letting my Lares energy expand to fill me, I lifted a hand and cupped the air in front of him. "More," I told him. And then pictured what I wanted.

At first, I thought I'd failed. But a moment later, the locusts rose into the air in a cacophony of clattering wings and then scattered as what looked like a hundred ravens descended from the sky, hungry and relentless.

It was good. But it wasn't enough. "More," I said again. And a minute later, "More."

I pictured ducks in my mind, having remembered a documentary I'd once seen where a foreign nation had brought in masses of ducks to get a plague of locusts under control. I pictured the picturesque little town of Rome and sent the ducks there.

I pictured chickens and sent thousands of them into the countryside.

By the time it was done, I was tired, but not as tired as I'd been after previous challenges. Maybe I was growing into my magic. Dropping to the concrete steps at the front of my little church, I watched the birds do their work. I'd lost *my* raven with the first order for more birds. He'd dived into the roiling mass of bugs and disappeared.

I really wished he'd stayed with me. I needed someone to scout the countryside from above to tell me how far the plague had spread.

As if my thoughts had called him, the raven returned, landing heavily on my shoulder.

"Ugh!" I told him. "You feel like you've put on the scourge seven."

He focused beady gold eyes on me, and I blinked. When had that happened? "You know, like the freshman fifteen?" He continued to stare at me. "Nothing?"

I shook my head. "No jokes for the bird. Got it. Humor is wasted on you." I swung my arm across the visible landscape. "Can you do a flyover and see if I need more help? I don't know how far this infestation reaches."

With a powerful sweep of his wings, the big bird left my shoulder and shot skyward. I didn't have any idea if he'd gotten my message. Maybe I was just fooling myself. But he didn't seem to be snatching bugs from the air along the way, so there was that.

I watched him go for a moment and then twitched in surprise when my vision went black. I jerked to my feet in shock and fear, nearly falling off the step in the process.

Color swam back into my world in a series of dizzying flashes before stabilizing into a pretty pastoral scene that passed by beneath me at a disorienting speed. It took me a moment to realize that I was seeing the countryside around me, with a bird's eye view.

As the raven circled the town of Rome and what was probably a couple of miles in every direction, it quickly became obvious that I had the infestation contained.

The picture show blinked off without warning, and I fell back onto the step again, nearly crashing backward with the impetus of my fall. Disoriented and dizzy, I kept my eyes closed for a few beats. When I opened my eyes again, the birds and bugs were all gone.

Unfortunately, so was just about every bit of vegetation, as far as my eyes could see.

"We need an influx of fairies," Trish said.

I looked up from the pad where I'd been noodling ideas for how to repair the destruction the locusts had left behind. I'd been hoping for a magical fix, one that would repair the damage before the farmers and townspeople woke to discover the devastation.

"Fairies?" I asked.

She nodded, grabbing a rewarmed, leftover biscuit from the night before. "Earth fairies have an affinity with all growing things. They can put it to rights within a few days."

I frowned. "I was hoping we could come up with something a little faster. I'm worried about what the farmers will do when they see the fields. They're going to be devastated."

She nodded. "We can put a glamour on the damage until the fairies get it fixed."

I liked the sound of that. "Can you take care of it?"

She nodded and grabbed another biscuit, wrapping them in a paper napkin. "I'll go do that now."

"Thanks, Trish." I gave her my first genuine smile since seeing how much damage the stupid bugs had done.

"No problem."

I watched her leave, my shoulders drooping with weariness. I needed more coffee. Heading for the coffee maker, I glanced at Bev. She was standing in front of the sink, staring out at the grass-free dirt and naked bushes and trees. "Has Niele seen his flowers yet?"

I followed her line of sight to the pitiful remains of the greenskeeper's flower beds. "I don't think so. He's going to blast right out of his moss diaper when he sees them."

She nodded in silent agreement.

Whoomp! There she is... my phone exploded into the silence.

I eyed Bev and she barked out a laugh, raising her hands in surrender. "Don't look at me. I don't know where she gets the ringtones either. I'm just glad she only tortures you with them."

Whoomp! There she is... Answer the phone.

"The woman is well beyond the age of being technically savvy. Somebody's got to be teaching her these things," I accused, narrowing my gaze on Bev.

She shook her head and laughed.

Whoomp! There she is... Answer the phone. You're being rude!

I hit the Answer button. "Har!"

I was greeted by Mavis's infectious laughter. "That one's a personal favorite."

"I'm going to find out where you're getting these ringtones, and I'm going to start laying them on you."

"There, you see? I knew you loved them."

Shaking my head, I didn't bother fighting a smile since she couldn't see it anyway. "What's up?"

"I just wanted to let you know that the town's all in an uproar about the locusts."

I sighed. "I was hoping we could put a pretty gloss over the mess before they saw."

"Too late. But Bev and I can do a wide-reaching 'clueless' spell. I'm assuming Trish will call the fairies?"

"She's in charge of that, yes. What's a clueless spell?"

"We plant a suggestion that there's no issue with certain things. In this case, anything green or growing outside. Their brains just stop noticing those things until we remove the spell. Anybody who's already noticed will forget."

I chewed my lip, hating to play with people's minds like that. "It won't do any long-term damage?"

"None at all. It's a very gentle spell. To be honest, honey, you'd be doing some of them a big favor. The annual Best Rome Rose contest starts next month. Several of the townspeople are avid gardeners. They'll be suicidal when they see their flower beds."

"Okay, do it then. Thanks, mom."

"My pleasure. Send my daughter home, will you? We'll get that spell baked up and sent out by late morning."

I hung up and relayed Mavis's request to Bev.

My sister-friend looked me in the eye. "Are you sure you'll be all right alone today?"

"I'm not alone. I have Monty."

She eyed me carefully for a moment, then pulled me into a hug. "Call if you need anything."

I nodded. "I promise."

After Bev left, I decided I'd spend some time soaking in the clawfoot tub and then do some of the small things around the house I hadn't had time to do with everything going on.

I was pretty sure I wouldn't be given any more challenges for the day.

The thought cheered me considerably.

Which was why, when the bell started pealing a few minutes later, the summons hit me really hard.

24

THE LARES' RESOLVE WILL SEE IT THROUGH...

I found myself standing in front of a door leading to the dungeon of the old building. My entire body felt encased in ice. Dark, dank spaces terrified me. When I'd moved into the church, I'd resolved never to go down into that horrible moldy-smelling place.

Never.

But the peal of the bells was calling me to that place. Like a hypnotic force, the call was making it almost impossible for me to resist. Before I realized I'd moved, my hand was clasping the ancient brass handle of the door and pulling it open.

A horrible stench rose up out of the basement... a wave of putrid air straight from the grave.

Ice slid along my nerve endings, robbing me of breath.

Without a single thought of moving, I was

halfway down the stairs. My hand was wrapped around the cool roughness of an age-pocked wood railing. My bare feet were leaving bloody smears on the grayed wood of the steps.

I hadn't even felt the moment when a thick sliver of the aged wood sliced through the heel of my right foot.

Behind me, still at the top of the stairs, Monty whined.

Even my stalwart companion, my furry hero, resisted coming down those stairs.

I stepped down into loose earth, the feel of it like cool silk against my skin. The smell of the grave was stronger down there, and the lack of real light was disconcerting.

Wrapping my arms around myself, I looked around, rubbing vigorously at gooseflesh brought on by the cold and my bone-deep terror of the situation I'd been sucked into.

"It's a test," I reminded myself in a strangled voice. "This is just a test to make sure I have the stuff to be a Lares. I'll be all right. Everything will be fine." Unfortunately, my breathy, cracking voice wasn't very convincing.

Part of me wanted to throw up my hands and surrender. That same part wanted to yell at the Powers guiding my seating that they had the wrong girl. I wasn't woman enough to deal with whatever they were about to throw at me.

The atmosphere seemed to bubble with menace. The air was like the foul breath of the worst kind of poltergeist—the exhalation of a deadly spectral menace.

A shadow shifted behind me. A long, low moan wound past, the sound equal parts terror and pain. I jerked around to face it, and twisted my ankle in the soft soil.

"Ouch!" I tried to lift my leg to rub the injured joint but nearly fell over in the process. "Cuss!" I complained softly.

One of the truly unfortunate things about reaching middle age was the loss of balance that came with it. I had no idea why I could barely stand on one foot anymore, but I was pretty sure it was something the Devil instigated, along with wrinkles and saggy boobs, to mess with our psyches as we aged.

A burst of icy air ripped the mundane concern out of my mind. It swept the hair off my face and sent the wormy scent more deeply into my nostrils. When I lifted my head again, I gave a shriek and tried to backtrack. My ankle gave out and I landed on my butt in the dirt.

I crab-scrambled backward as the horrible specter hovering above me moved closer. He was stooped, with claw-like fingers and hate-filled eyes. His face seemed set in a permanent sneer, and he advanced on me as if he wanted to inhale my last breath.

I kept scrambling until my back hit the edge of the bottom stair. I didn't dare risk a glance backward as Monty exploded into shrill barking, clearly alarmed.

The specter opened its mouth and a horrible garble of watery speech spewed forth. I couldn't understand a word of it, but the way he reached those claw-like hands in my direction sent me into a panic. I tried to stand, but my ankle wouldn't hold. With sheer determination, I managed to grab the railing before I fell again.

Behind the man, the air thickened and formed into a second ghost. The nearly translucent woman had dainty features that were covered in what looked like blood, but it was black. Her chest was deeply sliced, a hunk of some kind of thick glass sticking out of the wound.

She had kind eyes, and she seemed to be trying to say something to me. Her lips were moving, but only wormy air came out.

When she saw the man she cringed away, her hands coming up as if for protection.

As he turned to her, I felt the need to protect the woman.

But something felt wrong.

Choose, a disembodied voice said on the wind.

"What?" I looked around. "Who is that?"

Choose, the voice said again.

"Choose?" I wracked my brain, remembering that I was being tested. All of my challenges to that point had been external. I'd needed to protect or save someone. Which made sense if I was a guardian deity. But who was I supposed to protect in the current situation? Me? The hostile ghost did seem to want to hurt me.

But could he? Really? I straightened a bit at that thought. If I was a Lares, could they do anything that would harm me?

I didn't think so. And, if that was true, then I was there to protect one of them.

Choose.

Not protect. Choose. I looked around. "But what does that mean?"

Taut, uncomfortable silence met my question.

I really needed a better explanation for what I was supposed to do, but it didn't seem like I was going to get it.

Great.

The two specters turned as one and started forward. They were coming for me. Both of them. My newfound backbone softened into jelly again, and I tried to climb the steps. I managed one step before my ankle tried to buckle out from under me again.

Choose.

Irritation had me biting my tongue against an

angry retort. It was a test. I needed to figure out what I was supposed to do. Choose. Choose what? Or who?

A sudden memory flashed through my mind. Prescient words that had seemed to mean nothing at the time.

Human beings are fallible, Aggy. We're flawed. But our true spirits are hidden throughout our lives. Our physical presence serves as a mask rather than a window into our souls. Do you understand?

Reverend Dodson had been telling me about two of his parishioners. What were their names...?

Mary! That was the woman. And the other one was...Dix!

I looked at the two specters, realizing with a start that they'd come within two feet of me. I could see the spectral pores on their gray skin, smell the grave on their forms. The icy breeze they seemed to create wound around me with deadly efficiency, chilling me to my bones.

"Mary and Dix," I said aloud.

The woman smiled, her eyes sparkling.

The man's snarl deepened.

Their proximity locked my muscles into place. I couldn't move. Couldn't stop them as they floated closer, hands outstretched and mouths opening in dual screams that made me want to run shrieking from that horrible place.

Choose! The disembodied voice said again, the tenor of the command growing more insistent.

I looked from the woman to the man as their terrifying forms wrapped around me, encasing me in ice. My heart stuttered in my chest, slowing and beating more erratically by the second.

Choose!

I looked into the enraged face of Dix Walters. Then I rolled my eyes to see the soft smile on Mary Martin's bloody face. But something ugly sliced through one of their gazes. Something that dredged another memory out of the terrified muddle that was my thoughts.

She loved her husband, cherished her children, and was active in Rome charity circles...

But Mary Martin had killed her whole family, I remembered. She hadn't been at all what she'd seemed.

Masks...

Yes. Masks, I remembered. And I chose.

Throwing out a hand, I sent a wave of energy into Mary Martin's deceptively docile form, sending her flying away from me on an enraged howl. At the last moment, just before she slammed into the slimy concrete wall and dissolved into mist, her gentle, attractive face contorted into the face of a monster. Showing her true character beneath the mask.

My horrified gaze slid to Dix Walters and saw the

relief there. He gave me a slow nod, turned away, and his spectral form disappeared.

You chose wisely, my dear.

I was so exhausted that night, I barely roused myself from sleep at the sound of the first gong. I wanted to cry. "No," I murmured sleepily. "Not again."

But there was no second gong. Nor a third, nor a thirteenth.

Only one.

And then the whispered words inside my head, which brought me out of sleep more thoroughly than a bucket of ice water.

Um, Mrs. Lares, gardan of our town, we need you. Please, gardan Lares, save Daddy, Mommy, Davie, and me from the bad man.

The words shot through me like liquid energy and I sat bolt upright, Lungren's name on my lips. "Gren! Now!"

I shoved back the covers and yanked on slippers, then grabbed my keys and ran toward the driveway. I was only faintly surprised by the sound of wings on the air, though it did occur to me that they were much larger wings than I was used to hearing. The moon disappeared behind a large shape soaring high above me as I unlocked the car and started to climb inside.

"Aggy? What is it?" Gren asked, his sexy voice filled with concern.

I turned to him. "I know I'm supposed to do it alone, but I won't be in time if you don't help, and I can't let them die. Please help me..." The words ran together. I discovered that I was short of breath when I was done with my plea. "Please," I all but gasped out.

He wrapped his warm hands around my arms, forcing me to look at him. "Be calm. It will be all right."

I frantically shook my head, my body rigid with fear. "I'm going to be too late..."

His gaze found mine and locked on until I was staring into twin pools of golden-brown light. "Do you trust me, Agnes, Madam Lares?"

I didn't hesitate. "Yes."

He nodded, reaching for me and wrapping an arm around my waist. "Close your eyes," he said in a deep, sexy voice.

"Gren, this isn't the time..."

"Trust me," he said. "Close your eyes."

With a sigh, I did as he asked.

The world shifted around me as we jolted upward. Sensation narrowed down to the comforting and familiar smell of Gren's skin, the sound of massive wings throbbing on the air, and the feel of the wind bathing my skin. I clutched his shirt as the axis of my world shifted, throwing me off balance. If Gren hadn't told me to close my eyes, vertigo would have taken me over. But he wrapped himself tightly around me and whispered words of comfort in my ear. His heart beat strong and slow against my cheek and, despite holding onto me, his body felt relaxed.

"What are you?" I asked, my voice lost in the wind.

His body shifted against me as he lowered his head, his breath sliding soft and warm across my cheek. "That, my beautiful Aggy, is a story for another time."

I would have argued, but suddenly it was over. Gren set me down onto concrete that felt rough against my slippers. The sudden loss of the wind left me feeling slightly dazed, my ears ringing.

My eyes flew open. I glanced quickly around. I was standing in front of a medium-sized cedar home with flower boxes on the windows that contained only empty stalks from the locust infestation.

The front door of the home was ajar and hung at an odd angle.

One window was broken, and a small table lay in pieces in the barren front yard.

Without a thought for my purpose, other than to help the child who'd summoned me, I turned and ran up the steps to the small porch, pushing my way into the house.

I stood in the tiny entrance area and listened to the stark silence. A beat later, I heard the soft scuff of a shoe against tile. My gaze turned toward the sound. I moved, my steps quick and my breathing slow and quiet. A soft rumble had me jerking to a stop. It had been like a growl but human rather than animal. Then a voice, broken and dripping with hate.

"You thought I wouldn't come back, dear brother? You thought I wouldn't take from you what you took from me?" There was the sound of something hitting flesh and a pain-filled grunt. "Where are they? You might as well tell me where, Jackson. If I have to search, it won't go well for them."

There was a panting sound and the swish of fabric across something hard. Probably the floor. "James, I told you, it wasn't my fault they died. I'm hurting just as much as you are. I loved them too."

I eased closer, my senses filling the space between the two men in the other room and me. The energy I threw out picked up stark fear. I suspected it was the fear of a husband and father who wanted to protect his family.

I also picked up hate, irrational rage that blotted out any love the second man had ever known for the brother he was clearly attacking.

And, amazingly, I picked up love from the man

on the floor. He still loved his brother and didn't want to hurt him.

I took a deep breath. *Gren?*

I'll get them, Aggy.

He would protect the children and the wife. I could put them out of my mind.

I took a deep breath. And stepped into the room.

One of the men, dirty blonde hair in disarray and pale eyes wild with emotion, held a baseball bat in two hands as if he were stepping up to the plate. His stance was rigid...aggressive. The second man was leaning against a wall, curled in on himself as if in great pain.

Both men looked up at me, identical expressions of surprise on their faces.

I gave them a smile. "Hi."

Their eyes narrowed. The one with the bat said, "Who are you? Why are you in this house?"

I pointed to the guy on the floor. "I'm his fairy godmother."

The two men shared a perplexed glance. In their shared concern about my sanity, they found common ground they'd been unable to find before.

"Um," said the man on the floor.

The brother stepped closer, brandishing the bat. "You think you're a fairy godmother?"

My lips twisted as I considered how best to respond. "No. Not really. But I am here to help this man and his family."

He sneered at me. "Lady, you're loopy. Do you always go around protecting people in your fuzzy slippers and puppy pajamas?"

My ears tuned for the soft sound of small feet in the next room, I looked down at my fuzzy fuchsia-colored slippers and dachshund-covered PJs, grimacing. "Yeah, the slippers are a bit much, aren't they?"

He snorted.

I sent my will across the room, urging the man on the floor to move slowly and quietly toward the door.

I shrugged. "I would have gotten dressed, but someone beseeched me to come, and I didn't have time." Holding my hands out, I smiled again. "So, I guess this is what you get."

Smacking the bat against his hand, he barked out a laugh. "So, now you think you're some kind of deity?"

I sighed. "Yeah. I do. I know, crazy huh?"

Strong hands whipped around the doorframe and yanked the injured man into the next room.

Unfortunately, James noticed Gren pulling his brother to safety and howled his rage. He dove toward the door. But I was ready for him.

I threw up my hands and yelled, "Suspend!"

The man jerked to a stop, not a single part of his rigid body moving.

In the distance, sirens heralded the imminent arrival of Rome's finest.

I stepped closer, looking directly into the man's unfocused gaze. "Whatever you believe your brother did to your family, it's not your place to distribute justice. If he deserves to be punished for his actions, he will be, and you're better served staying out of it. More importantly, those children and their mother aren't responsible in any way. You'll pay for the damage you've done here. But that payment would have been much worse if you'd been able to exact your revenge on your brother. Because it would have been weighted under the additional baggage of your unrelenting remorse. Take your punishment, and then attempt to rebuild the relationship between you and this family. Believe it or not, your brother still loves you. It's your job to make sure you deserve that love."

I stared at him a moment longer, and then hurried outside to find Gren crouched down in front of a small girl with glossy blonde curls that danced around her plump, rosy cheeks when she talked. He held her tiny dimpled hands in his as her parents and older brother looked on.

"I asked her to come juss like Mrs. Plinkton in sunnay school said. She said we have a gardan and her name is Lares. That's a pretty name. I asked her to come and save Daddy and Mommy and Davie and me, and she did." The little face turned up to me, and she giggled. "You have funny jammies."

I grinned back at her. "I like them though. Do you?"

She nodded enthusiastically, her blue eyes sparkling. "Thank you for coming to save us."

Tears burned my eyes, and I shook my head. "I didn't save you, honey. Your daddy did. I just helped a little."

Lights and sirens speared toward us through the night. I shook the father's hand and hugged the tearful woman who was clutching her small son close. "Thank you," the woman breathed, tears clogging her voice.

"Take care of yourselves," I said. And then I looked at Gren.

He nodded. We hurried down the sidewalk, veering into the shadows as a sweet, clear voice called out. "Bless you, Mrs. Lares."

Gren grinned at me. "Mrs. Lares, huh?"

I shrugged. "I kind of like it." The sirens slashed into silence, and I jerked to a stop. "Curse!"

Gren frowned. "What?"

"I forgot to release the guy."

We watched the police enter the home and I counted to ten, then snapped my fingers, feeling the man with the bat blast out of the hold I'd put him in and then be immediately grabbed by the police. I turned to Gren. "Let's go. I'm beat."

He held his arms out and grinned. "Do you wish to fly Air Gren again?"

I laughed. "I don't suppose you're serving snacks?"

"No," he said, looking sad.

"Drinks?"

He shook his head.

"An in-flight movie?"

His frown deepened. "Sorry. But I know a place where we can get coffee and donuts."

"At this hour?"

He nodded. "I have an in with the owner."

"That's good enough for me. I hope they don't mind fuzzy slippers and PJs."

He winked saucily. "Since she's currently wearing both, I doubt she'll mind."

25

AND WHEN AT LAST DEATH'S COURSES RUN...

It was after dark when I woke up. I looked around, feeling groggy and disoriented. Monty wasn't in bed with me, and I could hear voices in the kitchen, though I could tell my friends were trying to stay quiet.

I shoved the covers back and headed into the bathroom, feeling guilty about sleeping so late.

Twenty minutes later, I emerged from my room. Freshly showered and dressed in jeans and a light sweater, I padded down the hall in bare feet.

My entire council was there. Every face turned my way when I entered the kitchen. Monty trotted over and licked my foot in greeting, his tail happily painting the air. I reached down and picked him up, burying my face in his sweet-smelling fur. I just needed one more moment of normalcy before I dove into things.

I could tell by the looks on their faces that something bad was coming. And I suddenly wasn't in a hurry to know what it was.

A long moment later, someone cleared his throat. With a sigh, I settled my dog to the floor. When I straightened back up, Bev handed me a cup of coffee. "Thanks." I forced my gaze to slide around the room. "Okay, give it to me quick and straight. What fresh Hell is waiting for me tonight?"

They silently stepped aside, showing me the crystal ball in the center of the table. It was no longer empty of prophecy.

But I immediately wished it was.

The swirling picture within the crystal was filled with familiar faces. Jade from the nail salon, Brett from the car parts store, Pete and Alice from the local grocery store, Michael from the bakery, my stylist Esme, sweet Margaret at Notions and Seams, our talented local seamstress. And behind them were at least a hundred other people. People I'd grown up with. People I'd known all my life. A few I hadn't.

I shook my head at the rage on their faces, feeling confusion as they lunged toward some unseen force beyond the crystal. They were armed with garden implements, knives, and a few guns. Front and center in the crowd, one really beefy guy who worked at the butcher shop held something that looked like an old-fashioned torch. They were literally brandishing pitchforks and torches.

"What is this?" I asked my team, dread coiling in my gut. "Are they under attack?"

My friends shared a look filled with sadness. None of them would meet my gaze.

"What?" I asked.

Finally, Mavis waved a hand over the crystal ball, and the picture inside the swirling mist changed perspective, sliding around until we saw the vision from the crowd's point of view.

My breathing hitched. My stomach wrenched painfully as shock and fear stabbed through me.

There was my pretty new home, its steeple piercing a charcoal sky with a fat silvery moon behind it. There was my team, arrayed at my back with grim looks on their faces.

And there was me, tears streaming down my paler-than-pale cheeks, standing alone in front of the enraged crowd.

They were definitely on the warpath, I realized. But, shockingly, the person they were threatening was...me.

I can't imagine what my eyes looked like when I lifted my gaze to look at my silent council. "It's not possible."

Gren placed a reassuring hand on my shoulder. "Aggy..."

I shook my head. I didn't want his reassurances

because they'd ring false. The ball hadn't steered us wrong yet. Even when it had gone black to tell me I had to work alone.

"Honey, maybe it's not what it looks like," Mavis said.

My right hand hurt, and I looked down to find that I was clutching the back of a chair so tightly my fingers were white. I forced the muscles to relax.

"We have enough power to stop them," Luke started to say.

Ferral and I both spoke at once. "No!" I went on, "We can't hurt them."

The advocate glanced at me, and something that looked like respect passed through his gaze. He inclined his head in a slight bow.

"But," Bev said, frowning.

I shook my head again. "Whatever this is, I have to handle it myself. I'm trying to prove I can protect them. I can't hurt them to protect myself. That would go against everything I'm supposed to stand for."

"But they have blood in their eyes," Trish said. "And a raging mob mentality. They'll kill you."

Her words smacked me between the eyes, hard. I flinched beneath them. "I can't," I said again, the words a strangled whisper.

Niele stood across from me. When I caught his gaze, he gave me a sad smile. Reverend Dodson hovered behind him. The specter nodded, looking resolved. As if it was a foregone conclusion I'd be in his realm soon. Ice slipped along my spine.

I turned to Gren. The pain in his eyes was nearly my undoing. "You are a tribute to your Lares legacy, Agnes Madam Lares."

My chest painfully tight, I straightened my shoulders. "Okay then. Is there any way to find out what they're going to be so mad about? Maybe I can prepare for it somehow..."

The front door slammed open. Fast, heavy footsteps came toward us. Just before Wanda stepped into the kitchen, her face grim, the bell gave off its first, fateful peal.

Gong!

We all stilled. The sound reverberated through the building, sounding much louder than it should have. I shuddered and looked at Wanda. "Are they here?"

She nodded. "Aggy, you can't go out there."

It was the first time she'd used my name. Along with her obvious concern, it touched me.

Gong!

I took a deep breath.

Gren's warm hand slid down my arm, and he clutched my fingers. "Goddess be with you, lovely Aggy."

Gong!

Tears slid down my cheeks. I scanned my friends

one last time and gave them a watery smile. "I guess it's showtime."

Mavis pulled me into an impulsive hug. Bev joined us.

Something thudded against the house, and a roar went up outside.

I pulled free and took a deep breath. I forced myself to start moving, knowing that if I lingered I'd lose my courage to meet the final seating challenge.

Gong!

The roar of rage when I opened the front door was like a slap to the face. My face heated as if it had been physically assaulted.

The crowd filled the entire front yard and the small gravel parking lot off to the side, bulging toward the road. The faces in front of me were contorted with rage, out of control, and mindless.

Gong!

I felt Gren come up beside me. "This isn't natural, Aggy," he said in a quiet voice. "These people have been spelled somehow."

I nodded my head toward the icy mist swirling around their feet and legs. "Look familiar?"

He expelled air. "The lost ones."

Gong!

Something flew from the crowd and hit me on the chest, splatting wetly. I looked down to see an egg spreading over my shirt and glopping to the sidewalk. The attack set off a barrage of additional attacks, ratcheting quickly from food to rocks and more dangerous projectiles. When a small, sharp knife flew unerringly toward my throat, Gren lifted his hands, and the blade stopped in mid-air. "Aggy," he pleaded in a strangled voice.

Silent tears slid down my face. "I can't attack them, Gren."

He shook his head, slashing his hands down to drive the blade into the concrete like it was butter. "There has to be something."

Gong!

I lifted my hands, using a gentle nudge with my energy to get them to quiet. It took them a few beats, but they finally quieted enough so that I could be heard. "Please tell me why you're here." My tone was as gentle as I could make it while trying to be heard across the entire yard. Not a single expression softened in the face of my question.

"You're a witch!" yelled someone from the crowd.

"Evil!" yelled someone else.

"You tried to kill Macklin Dart last night!" yelled another.

"And ran off before the police could arrest you," yelled the beefy butcher guy. His contorted face turned toward Gren. "With that demon."

Gong!

Voices rose into the night, enraged and hard to understand as they tangled together, slashing toward me.

"You tried to kill those children in the road!"

"You set fire to a child."

"...burned out our fields!"

"Satan worshiper!"

Then fragments of incoherent diatribes...

"Leave this town..."

"Wicked..."

"Banished."

"Rot in Hell!"

Gong!

The soft ripple of wings on the air brought my gaze up, and I watched the raven descend, his wings flaring out to the side as he did the pee dance on my shoulder. He turned a golden gaze to me and said, "Pee."

"You got that right," I agreed. I lifted my hands again, and silence slowly fell. "Please, you've got it all wrong..."

They bellowed their rage and surged forward, brandishing their weapons. Trish buzzed up beside me in her warrior fairy form. Mavis and Bev took up positions on either side of me, their hands knitting a spell together on the air.

I felt sudden alarm at their open use of magic. With the crowd accusing me of being a witch, the display seemed destined to make things worse. Trish recognized the censure on my face and shook her head. "We can't attack them, but we can protect you.

Besides, look at them. They're not even aware of what they're doing."

"Very astute of you, little fairy," said a gravelly voice from somewhere in the crowd.

Gong!

The fog quickly rose, covering the crowd in some kind of silencing spell. Their mouths continued to form angry words we couldn't hear.

The creature who moved toward us towered above the angry mob, looking to be nine or ten feet tall. A bony crown rose up behind his head, and his protruding cheekbones were sharp on his long, triangular face. The creature's red eyes glowed through the night. He had gray, leathery skin and goat's hooves for feet, his legs bent and malformed like the back end of a farm animal. When he spoke, he showed unnaturally sharp teeth with elongated canines. Black horns stuck straight out from the sides of his leathery forehead. He stopped at the front of the crowd, dragging a pretty young woman out with him.

I started forward when I saw her, recognizing the mother of the little girl from the night before.

Gren grabbed my arm, holding me in place. "Let's see what he wants, Aggy."

I knew he was right, but my instincts screamed for me to grab the dazed-looking young mother away from him. "Leave her alone," I said, rage making my voice tremble.

His grin was horrible. "Ah, such a soft heart, Madam Lares. That's very good for my purposes." He half-turned and indicated the crowd with a sweep of a muscular arm. "Such horrible beasts they are, aren't they, lovely Lares? A simple suggestion in the mist, and they turn on the one person who is meant to protect them above all things." He glanced my way again, cocking his head. "They'll kill you in a heartbeat, you know. They care nothing for you. Would you die to save them?"

I pressed my lips together, my heart banging against my ribs. Gren's grip on my arm turned nearly painful. I reached over and pried his fingers away from my flesh. "What do you want?" I asked, my throat constricting around the words.

His fiery eyes widened. "Want? Haven't we made that clear?"

"I don't know about any key. I haven't even been seated as Lares yet. You're asking the wrong person." I caught movement in my peripheral vision and spotted Reverend Dodson floating through the crowd. His lips moved as he passed through, and he had a large, silver cross clutched in one hand. The sight made it hard to breathe. He was giving the people last rites. I wanted to scream and claw at the monster in front of me. But I couldn't do anything. Not until I figured out what my next move should be.

The creature's laughter slid like rancid oil over

my skin, causing me to shudder with revulsion. "Please do not insult my intelligence," he growled out, the smile dying on his thick gray lips. Another sweep of his arm revealed several more lost ones in the crowd. Each one held an enormous, curved blade at the throat of one of the townspeople.

The crowd had gone docile and quiet, their eyes blank and their lips slack. They were totally under the power of that vile mist.

"What can we do about the fog?" I asked quietly.

"Working on it," Bev responded.

"The devils?"

"We have a plan for that too," Ferral said from behind me.

The tightness in my throat eased somewhat.

"Attend me!" the monster screamed. He lifted the woman he held off the ground with one hand and shook her like a ragdoll. I watched in horror as her head snapped back and forth. He was going to break her neck.

I started forward. "Leave her be!" He stopped shaking his victim but still held her several feet off the ground. She hung limp and lifeless in his claws. "The key, Lares."

I stopped far enough away from him that he couldn't grab me. "Let's go into my home and discuss it. You don't need all these people here."

His laughter slimed over me again. "You take me for a fool!" his enraged bellow was accompanied by a gust of wind that blew me off my feet. I left the ground and flew backward, slamming into Gren as he moved to cushion my landing.

"The key, Lares!" The monster bellowed again.

Someone screamed in pain and I looked up in horror to see a man crumple to the ground, his throat covered in blood. "No!"

I shoved to my feet and dove into the crowd, lunging toward the monster who'd cut the man's throat. Energy flared around me, and I watched with some satisfaction as his gleeful expression turned to surprise and then concern.

The mist rose again, and the crowd suddenly came alive. As if answering a silent call, every last one of them turned in my direction, their rage focused like a laser on me.

The man in front of me swung a huge fist toward my face. Pain exploded, and my head snapped back on the punch. Blood ran down my face, but I barely noticed. All I wanted was to get to the fallen man and the monster that had hurt him. Someone kicked my knee, and I felt it crack as pain detonated through my leg and into my hip. I hit the ground and rolled into a ball as the crowd surrounded me, kicking, spitting, and punching.

Aggy? Gren called in my mind, his voice filled with horror.

No! I responded. *You can't hurt them.*

Oh goddess, Aggy, he nearly moaned. *I can't let them do this...*

"Stay back," I said through bloodied lips. "Stay away."

A woman who'd been trying to tear my hair out screamed and suddenly lurched back as a small, black creature dove at her hair and clasped it with its claws.

More screams followed, and people scampered away from the bat, hands beating the air where it had been. But the bat was much too fast for them. And, though it did nothing but touch their hair and clothing, they retreated, arms flailing the air above their heads.

Gren appeared and helped me to my feet.

He pushed a strand of hair away from my face and grimaced. "Aggy..." His tone was so tender. I just wanted to sink against his chest and feel safe for a minute.

But we didn't have a minute.

More screams surrounded us. Screams filled with agony. They were hurting more people. "Gren! We need to do whatever we were going to do to get rid of these monsters."

He nodded. Lifting a hand into the air, he gave a shrill whistle.

Nothing happened.

I looked at him. He held up a finger.

Nothing.

And then the first devil screamed and erupted into flames. People ran shrieking away from the column of fire he created. Then another went up in flames. And another.

I smiled, realizing Reverend Dodson hadn't been doing last rites. He'd been consecrating the ground the demons stood on.

Finally, every lost one except the enormous leader was gone.

I looked at him, and my hopes fell as he rose above the ground, a wide grin on his evil face. "The key, Madam Lares."

His demand made rage flare to life in my chest. "You want the key? I'll give you the key!" I threw up my hands and energy burst from them like fire from a flame thrower. The wave of energy crashed into him, slinging him backward, and setting the air around him on fire.

Beside me, Gren said, "Leave him to me." I watched in awe as enormous black wings sprang from Gren's back and tested the air with two powerful beats before he shot skyward and exploded toward the hovering monster. The two slammed into each other with such power a concussive wave rippled away from them as they connected, rattling the glass in the windows behind me.

At that moment, a flash of golden light detonated, and the mist disappeared from the ground. Dual shrieks of happiness cut through the stunned silence that followed as the crowd tried to reorient to reality. I turned to Mavis and Bev. They gave me thumbs up, grinning. Bev blew on her upthrust thumb.

I laughed.

"Help him, please!" A woman cried out. My gaze jerked toward the sound. Several people crouched on the ground over the man whose throat had been cut. I ran toward them, panic making it hard to breathe. My mind replayed the man crumpling, the curtain of red washing down his throat from a lethal slice. A woman with a tear-stained face looked up at me, her hand hovering near a deep cut on the side of the man's throat. Blood coated her fingers and painted the ground beneath him.

I closed my eyes as panic rolled over me. What could I do for the man? I wasn't special. I was just a middle-aged woman who'd somehow fallen into a role I wasn't prepared for. I hadn't even believed in magic until recently. I still wasn't sure I believed everything I'd seen. There were times I felt like I'd been sleep-walking through the recent chaos, dreaming my involvement in everything.

The people in front of me were real. They weren't magical. But they somehow recognized me as someone who could help.

The crowd stirred and a little girl moved forward out of it, her clear blue gaze locked on mine. "Help him, Mrs. Lares. Help him like you helped my daddy."

My first instinct was to pull the little girl away from the scene on the ground. Sweet young children had no business seeing things like that. But there was something in the child's face. Something in the way she looked at me that convinced me she belonged there.

The soft sound of fluttering wings had me looking up as the raven landed lightly on my shoulder.

"Please, Ms. Lares," the woman on the ground pleaded. "People say you can help. I'm begging you to help my husband."

I forced my feet to move forward. The other people around the bleeding man stepped back. I felt the energy of my team moving up at my back, the realization that they didn't trust the crowd making my unease grow.

Laying one hand on the dying man, I tried to push my doubts aside. His life force rose up to meet my touch. Without having anything to compare it to, I thought it felt weak. It fluttered against my palm like the wings of the beautiful butterfly I'd touched in the wood. Even as I made the comparison, I felt his life slow and weaken beneath my hand.

He had only seconds of life left in him.

I tried pulling my energy forward to heal the wound. But it was impossible. I didn't know much about what I could do, but I knew with a stark certainty that I wasn't a healer.

I reached to cover the woman's hand. "I'm so sorry." The words came out strangled and too soft. But she turned her hand and clasped mine, giving it a squeeze.

"Aggy?" Gren's deep, husky voice made fresh pain twist in my chest.

His warm hand touched my shoulder as tears slid from my eyes.

A sob escaped me, and I shook my head. "I'm supposed to protect them, but I can't save this one man."

He squeezed my shoulder. "Maybe he wasn't meant to be saved."

I shook my head again, tears sliding in silent tracks down my cheeks.

The raven danced on my shoulder, his wings lifting as he moved.

Beneath my hand, the man's life eased quietly away.

The woman next to him gave a sob and threw herself over his body.

I was afraid to look into the little girl's eyes. I knew I'd see my failure there.

After a moment of respectful silence, people started to move away and walk back toward town. Someone picked up the body, and others supported the woman toward the road where a car waited.

After only a few minutes, I was alone with my team.

"Hello, young man," a familiar voice said. "They'll be here for you shortly."

My head snapped up at Reverend Dodson's words. I saw him standing with the man who'd died, his expression kind. The two of them were less than fully corporeal. The reverend had a hand on the other man's shoulder. His touch seemed to pull some of the confusion from the man's eyes.

I looked at Gren, and he gave me a smile. "You are tasked with guarding them, Aggy. But you are not tasked with changing their fates. If one of your people is supposed to die, they will. Then, you are tasked with guarding their souls until the Elysian realm comes for them."

I frowned. "The Elysian realm?"

A beautiful melody filled the air, the sound pure and sweet as a newborn babe. It engendered a feeling of life and love and promise. With shock, I realized it was coming from the raven, whose beak was open, his throat working gently under the notes.

Sudden clarity rolled through me. The raven held the key.

Light suddenly pierced the darkness, a golden light that spread across the sky and sent healing warmth down on our little party.

From within the light, a creature bathed in blinding light descended, golden robes gently drifting around bare feet and the vague impression of wings shifting the air in pale shadow behind it.

The celestial being drifted to the ground in front of the newly dead man and smiled, its perfect face gentle with love. "Welcome, Jacob Richards. You are anticipated and will be cherished."

A large, golden dog suddenly danced around the man, its form like a spirit but its enthusiasm as solid as the lump in my throat. An older woman stood beside the celestial being, her pale cheeks wet with silvery tears. "I've missed you so much, son," she told him.

Jacob Richards embraced his mom, hugged his dog, and then touched the fingers of the divine creature to rise into the light high above. He was going home.

Mavis sighed. Bev cursed softly. I gave her a look, and she flushed. "Sorry. That just slipped out."

I swiped at my wet cheeks, feeling better knowing that the man I'd failed was in good hands.

But I *had* failed him. And, for that, I wasn't sure I could forgive myself.

26

THE LARES' TEARS WILL SEE
IT DONE

I locked all the doors and didn't answer my phone for four days. I'd texted Bev and Mavis to tell them I was fine but needed some time to myself. So far, they'd honored that request, but it was only a matter of time before they bullied their way back into my life.

I was determined not to speak to anyone until I'd made a decision about moving forward. I had no idea if I'd passed my seating since I'd failed so horribly to guard at least one of my people. The radio silence from the Powers, whoever they might be, told me I'd probably failed.

I wasn't sure how I felt about that.

Every time I thought about it, a knot the size of a fist lodged in the center of my chest. At some point during the stressful and terrifying thirteens, my inclinations had drifted toward wanting to be what everybody kept telling me I'd been chosen to be.

The deep well of self-doubt hadn't run dry. In fact, it was pretty much overflowing all over the place. I didn't think I deserved to be Lares. I didn't believe I'd earned it. But if I was being honest with myself, I realized I *wanted* to be deserving of the title and the job.

With every fiber in my being.

Gong!

The sound of the bell jumpstarted my heart, and instinctive panic set in. But Monty ran barking toward the front door, and I realized it had been the doorbell. Not the Hell bell...as I'd taken to thinking of it.

That bell hadn't rung for four days and nights. In fact, nothing had happened at all for the last four days. It had been deeply and eerily quiet. I'd like to report that I'd used the time to get stuff done. Goddess knew I had lots of stuff to get done.

But I hadn't. I'd pretty much been a physical and emotional vegetable since locking myself in the pretty little church on the last night of the thirteens.

I ran my fingers self-consciously through my hair and tugged my tee-shirt down to smooth the wrinkles. I grimaced at the coffee stain on the pocket of the shirt. Unfortunately, there was nothing I could do about that.

Still, I dawdled. Hoping that, whoever it was, they'd just go away and leave me alone.

Monty ran back and forth between me and the door enough times that I decided opening it would be a kindness to the excited little dog.

But I wasn't in any way prepared for who I found on the other side once I had. I stilled in surprise, blinked, and lifted my eyebrows. Tall and slender, with midnight black hair that was threaded with silver at the temples, the man standing on my porch had a broad chin, liberally speckled with gray stubble, and bushy brows that peaked when he saw me. The eyes were as familiar as my own, and the quirk of well-crafted lips in a crooked smile was a blast from my past.

"Dad. Why are you...?"

"Agnes. How are you?" A quick flick of his gaze over my disheveled form told me he hadn't missed a single one of my flaws, but he gave me a gentle smile and leaned through the door to kiss me on the cheek. "Can I come in?"

"Oh. Sorry. Of course." I stepped back, giving him room to enter before closing and locking it behind him.

He looked around my home, eyes alight. "It's everything I imagined it would be."

I couldn't stop my grin. "Yeah?"

"Yeah." He pointed to the sanctuary turned living room. "May I?"

I nodded. "I'll take you on a tour."

The tour was quick, but he had lots of questions about how I was going to use the space and seemed excited about my shop.

"Handmade candles are a wonderful idea," he told me. "I still have the candle you made me in sixth grade."

I laughed. "The one that looks like a pile of dog poop?"

His eyes lit up. "That's the one. I cherish every slimy-looking inch of it."

He seemed to delight in my laughter. "Can I get you something to drink?"

He nodded. "Wine?"

I jerked my head toward the kitchen. Monty was already in there, sitting dutifully by the back door. I let him out, instructing him to stay close. He promptly ignored me, running toward the graveyard, where I'd noted the black cat was draped over a tombstone again. So far, the two of them had settled into a careful truce. But I had no illusions about who would come out on top if that changed. Monty had already come home with a tiny scratch on his nose after one encounter.

I handed dad a glass of wine and grabbed my own. "Would you like to sit outside? It's a beautiful night."

He agreed, and I led him to my little iron table on the porch. The metal horn was once again a faux cornucopia, filled with oranges and apples that Niele replenished from an unknown source every day.

The grass was lush again, and there was a new crop of vibrant flowers. The hedge sculpture Niele had done of me was also back. It appeared the fairies had performed their magic and repaired the damage the locusts had done.

We sipped in companionable silence for a few minutes. I watched Monty dance around the tombstone where the big black cat lounged, his posture eager and excited to make friends.

The cat's long tail snapped lazily against the monument in a silent warning for my dog to keep his distance. I smiled, knowing the friendly little guy would eventually win the cranky feline over. He was just that irresistible.

"So, it sounds like you had quite a seating."

I grimaced. "Did you talk to Mavis?"

He sipped his wine, staring toward the wood in the distance. "I saw her before I came here. She wanted me to tell you she was bringing lunch tomorrow."

I sighed. "I knew I couldn't keep her away for long."

"Why would you want to?" He frowned as if my words bothered him. I didn't know why. He'd been out of my life more than in it for years.

"I don't. Not really. I was just snagging some Me time."

He nodded. "Understandable. What you just went through dragged you through a wide range of really powerful emotions. Not everyone would have survived it as well as you did."

I shook my head. I might have survived, but I certainly hadn't succeeded. The bitter thought turned the wine on my tongue to vinegar. I didn't tell him, though. I didn't want to see his face when he found out I'd failed.

Instead, I eyed him. "You sound like you know something about the process? Is there a handy dandy instruction manual somewhere I could have used?"

He stared at me a long time before responding. When he finally spoke, his words stunned me to silence. "No. I wish there were. I could have used it during my seating."

I blinked. "Your..." Blinked again.

"Yes, Agnes, I'm a Lares too."

"But, why? How?"

He shrugged. "I was called just as you were."

"When?"

His expression folded into unhappiness. "Right after your mother died. I'm sorry, Agnes. I should have told you. But I didn't think you'd accept the idea of magic and our legacy. I was afraid you'd think I'd lost my mind."

"So you just deserted me?"

My tone was shrill. I clamped my lips together

on the sound, not liking it one bit. I was an adult woman. I had no business still harboring a grudge against my father for neglecting me.

"Mavis told me she'd keep you safe. You were always happy with her and Bev. I thought it would be a kindness to let you have a normal life until you were called to your seating."

"The seating that took my knees out from under me because I knew nothing about my *legacy* as you call it?"

He nodded. "Yes. I tried to tell you many times, Agnes. I know you don't believe that. But it's true. Your mind found ways to ignore the idea of magic each time. The Powers waited as long as they could to bring you in. And when you bought this place, at this location, they knew you were ready."

I laughed bitterly. "I wish I *had been* ready. But I'm not. I don't think I'll ever be." I turned to him. "I failed my seating, dad. I let someone die under my watch. I couldn't save him."

My dad stared at me, his hazel eyes, so like mine, filled with sorrow.

I shook my head. "I'm sorry I couldn't make you proud." It was true. Despite being well into adulthood, I really did care what he thought of me. I knew I should be embarrassed by that. But I wasn't.

He leaned closer, clasping my hand and giving it a squeeze. "You were always too hard on yourself," he said softly. Then he lifted my hand and gave the back of it a kiss. "You have never disappointed me, sweet Agnes. You are everything you are meant to be. Do you think it is a small thing to jump into the middle of a thirteens without any knowledge of your role and responsibilities? Do you believe anyone else could have done what you did?"

I frowned but didn't meet his gaze. I knew he was just trying to make me feel better.

"You have made me very proud," he went on. "So proud. And you are not responsible for deciding when someone should live or die. That isn't your job, my girl."

I took a deep breath and sighed. "It makes me physically sick that I failed him."

"You haven't failed anyone yet."

That brought my gaze up. "Yet?"

He nodded. "If the Powers came to you tonight and told you that you had passed, would you accept the commission? Would you become the guardian for Rome?"

I chewed the inside of my lip, digging for an honest response to his question. I hadn't thought I would. I'd told myself a dozen times since the final challenge that I couldn't be in the position to risk another soul with my inadequacies. I'd believed I was being honest with myself. But... "Yes," I said, surprised by my own words. "I'd take it in a heartbeat."

His smile was stunning. Though my father was a

handsome man...far too young-looking for a man in his sixties...the smile somehow made him look even younger. "That's very good, sweet Agnes."

I shook my head, wanting to cry. Didn't he realize he'd just stuck a knife into my gut and twisted it? "But they aren't going to tell me that, Dad. So it doesn't matter what I want."

He placed a hand, palm up, in front of my face. "Agnes Bethany Lenore..." he intoned in a voice that seemed to boom through the night, causing me to jerk in surprise. A soft glow surrounded his outstretched palm and a long wooden stick with a twisted metal grip at its center appeared in a flash of light.

I stared at the staff, my eyes narrowing. "What...?"

He held the staff toward me and said, "Do you accept the dominion of Rome, Indiana? Do you accept the role of guardianship of the people and places within your protectorate? And do you accept the council that was called to support and advise you in your role as Madam Lares?"

I stared at him, seeing the pride in his features and the telltale sparkle in his dark eyes.

"I..." I swallowed a lump as big as my thumb, staring at the beautiful staff. "I..."

He lifted his brows, his lips twitching with mirth.

"I didn't know I got a big, pretty stick," I finally said.

He gave in to the laughter. "You have to answer my question to accept the seating, my girl."

"Oh. Yes. I do!" I laughed. "I definitely do!"

And I did. Doubts, terror, chaos, pretty stick and all.

The End

DON'T MISS OUT

Stay up on all Sam's news by joining her newsletter, and get a copy of a fun mystery just for signing up!

SIGN UP FOR SAM'S NEWSLETTER!
https://samcheever.com/newsletter/

READ MORE MATURE MAGIC

If you enjoyed **What Devilry is This?** you might want to check out the next book in the series: https://samcheever.com/books/#maturemagic

Enjoy this taste of Book 2: What Voodoo Do You Do?:

I'm discovering that glossing over that whole "epicenter of a magical vortex" thing when I took this Lares job was a mistake. Looking back, that now seems like important information.

Whoever said midlife was a time for reflection and relaxation clearly wasn't an ancient guardian deity. I'd just started to think I was getting a handle on this whole Lares thing, and then the earth decided to open up into a giant, fiery hole of evil nastiness.

Talk about your hot flashes!

Add in a deadly new ally, a magical weapon I'm pretty sure I'll never get the hang of, and being forced to play "Where's the Voodoo Queen" while trying to deal with everything else...well...let's just say that crepey skin is probably the least of my worries.

WHAT VOODOO DO YOU DO?

Gong!

I jerked awake, the darkly melodic tones of the bell still reverberating through my mind. The sound was more than a warning. It was more than an invitation.

It was a summons.

On the heels of that realization, my cell phone rang. I shoved the covers off and swung my legs over the side of the bed, grabbing my phone. "Hello?"

Monty trotted past me and hit his doggy stairs, descending at a run and disappearing down the hall in the direction of the kitchen.

"Is this Aggy?" the voice on the phone asked.

"Yes. Who is this?" I didn't recognize the voice, but something about it rang a familiar note.

"Oh, thank heavens!" the woman said. Her voice was rusty as if she'd been pulled from sleep as she'd done to me. She coughed wetly as the force of her exclamation tore at her throat. When she spoke again, her voice broke beneath her words. "You need to save us. This is cataclysmic."

I stood and headed for the sweatshirt I'd thrown over a nearby chair. "I'm sorry. Who is this?"

"It's Molly. Molly Stanton. From Golden Years senior home. We need your help, Madam Lares. We're about to be overrun."

I hesitated, remembering Molly from my days of working at the senior facility. As I recalled, the eighty-something-year-old woman had been strange. Beyond strange. I suspected she had a touch of dementia. I glanced at the clock and grimaced. Three AM. "I can come in a couple of hours," I told the octogenarian. "Would that be okay?"

The tension in my shoulders relaxed as I realized the crisis I'd been expecting was probably just the creative imaginings of a woman with compromised faculties. I grabbed a hair clip off my bedside table and smoothed my straight black hair back, twisting it into a quick bun and clipping it to get it off my face.

Monty's claws tap, tap, tapped up the hall. The sound of something dragging along the floor as he ran sent a chill through my system.

"No! You have to come *now*. Please, Madam Lares."

I frowned at the title. Non-magical humans

didn't call me that. They didn't know about my newly-minted guardianship. When I'd worked at Golden Years, I hadn't had any magic. At least none that I'd known about. And Molly had seemed just as human as I was. Which, looking back, just might have proved the point I was missing. If I could become an ancient Roman deity in the space of weeks, there was no reason to assume Molly couldn't become something...more...too.

Monty trotted into the room with his leash clutched in his mouth, bounced up to me, and dropped the leash on my feet. He barked emphatically, his fringe of a tail whipping enthusiastically behind him.

The leash thing was new but not surprising, given that everyone and everything in my life seemed to be embracing a magical core. The bat in my belfry (not a metaphor, I actually had a bat in my belfry) was magical. My adopted mom and sister were magical. I had a magical raven that sometimes showed up out of nowhere. My gardener was a gnome. The sexy man candy in my life had wings. The contractor working on my renovations was a warrior fairy. And the ancient brass bell in my belfry (again, not a metaphor.) was enchanted.

I fully expected my single-serving coffee maker to someday sprout hands and make the coffee for me.

If only I could get my oven to make pumpkin muffins...

A sharp, terrified scream came through the phone line, followed by a roaring sound that rolled over the screaming and swallowed it whole.

"Molly?" I yelled into the resulting silence. "Molly? Are you still there?"

Down by my feet, Monty whined. He shoved the leash with his long, black and tan nose. "Woof!"

I paced my room, my nerves atwitch with the feeling that something cataclysmic had just happened. Without warning, the foundation of my pretty little church slash home slash business shuddered beneath a concussion so powerful it nearly threw me to the ground.

Monty lunged in my direction, dancing on his back legs in a terrified plea to be held. I scooped him up and ran toward the front door. Flinging it open, I ran out onto the small front porch and searched the darkness for anything that would explain the explosion.

In the distance, beyond the picturesque town of Rome, Indiana, the sky was lit with a pale red glow. Beneath the glow, the horizon burned gold and orange and smoke lifted to the slate-gray sky.

Fire! I grabbed my cell again and dialed 9-1-1. The phone rang and rang, but nobody responded.

Something was wrong. Very wrong.

Shoving the phone into my pocket, I said, "Come

on, little man. We need to go find out what's happening."

Golden Years Senior Home was an old facility. It had been in its current location since I was old enough to ride my bike into the country with my friends and head to the reservoir only a couple of miles away. Despite their age, the buildings had been well-maintained. The facility had gone through several owners over the decades of its existence, and each one had put his or her own personal brand on it.

A hodge-podge of styles and a mix of tastes, Golden Years was an ugly sucker, rising from the corn and soybean fields on either side of it like a boil on the verdant earth.

I climbed out of my car and eyed the building, not seeing any damage that would explain the explosions I'd heard. And felt.

The parking lot held only one car at that time of night...day...and the windows were mostly black. The door in the glass-fronted entranceway was locked, as expected, and a soft light inside showed no activity in the lobby.

Goochy Goochy Goo, Your Mom Needs you. Goochy Goochy Go, She Won't Take No!

Goochy Goochy Gum, You Know You Can't Run. Goochy Goochy Glee, You Know You Can't Flee.

"Curse, curse, swear!" Why did I leave her alone with my phone? I hit the button to answer the call from Mavis. "Mom. You know it's the middle of the night, right?"

Mavis and her daughter Bev had been my family in every way that counted since I'd lost my birth mom to cancer when I was fifteen. My ex-husband was Mavis's son. Their family had lived next door to mine back then. Mavis had opened her heart and home to me from the day my mother died, treating me like a daughter, even as Bev treated me like a sister and best friend all wrapped up in one. Neither of them had ever wavered in their support or love.

But Mavis had recently formed an annoying habit of changing my ring tone to weird, mother-themed songs when I wasn't looking.

"Actually, *Aggy*, it's early morning." Mavis didn't sound like her usual, sunny self, but I wasn't surprised, given that it was three-thirty in the curse, curse, swear morning! "What's going on? I felt something," she demanded.

"You felt that explosion?"

"Something exploded?"

"You didn't feel it?"

"No. What exploded?"

"If you didn't feel it, why are you calling me?"

"Because I felt...something."

I clamped my lips together, scrubbing a hand over my face. Monty dragged his leash past me and trotted over to a nearby bush to pee. "I'm standing outside the Golden Years Senior Home right now," I told her. "Molly Stanton called and begged me to come out here because there was some kind of danger. Then I heard an explosion."

Mavis's voice shook slightly, and I heard the sound of keys jangling. "Don't move from that spot. I'll be there in five minutes."

I opened my mouth to tell her everything looked fine, but was confronted by dead air. She was gone. Sighing, I walked over to the keypad on the wall and punched in the code to unlock it. Luckily, I'd recently resumed my regular visits to the home, bringing the ever-bubbly Monty along to enthrall and delight the residents. They'd given me the code so I could come and go as I pleased.

I stepped into the darkened building, listening to the soft whir of air moving through the ducts. As it had appeared from outside, the lobby was empty. That didn't surprise me since the night nurse stayed pretty close to the resident rooms in case there was an emergency. The place was only dimly lit via security lights over both exterior doors and a small lamp on the table next to the couch. I started toward the door into the resident wing. "Come on, little man," I told my dog. "Let's go find Molly."

Light flickered past the windows overlooking the courtyard, jolting me to a stop. Monty took off toward the light, barking a warning I couldn't ignore.

Flames suddenly bathed the air beyond the doors. I turned and started running, hitting the bar on the glass door with momentum and diving out into the fiery night.

I expected to see burning buildings. Or, at the very least, a large fire in the enclosed courtyard. But what I saw was much stranger than that.

And infinitely more terrifying.

Grab your copy of What Voodoo Do You Do?
https://samcheever.com/books/#maturemagic

ALSO BY SAM CHEEVER

If you enjoyed **What Devilry is This?**, you might also enjoy these other fun mystery series by Sam. To find out more, visit the **BOOKS** page at www.samcheever.com:

Mature Magic Paranormal Women's Fiction
(for more fun adventures with Aggy and Monty!)
Enchanting Inquiries Paranormal Cozy Mysteries
Yesterday's Paranormal Mysteries
Reluctant Familiar Paranormal Mysteries
Country Cousin Mysteries
Silver Hills Cozy Mysteries
Gainfully Employed Mysteries
Honeybun Heat Series

ABOUT THE AUTHOR

USA Today and Wall Street Journal Bestselling Author Sam Cheever writes mystery and suspense, creating stories that draw you in and keep you eagerly turning pages. Known for writing great characters, snappy dialogue, and unique and exhilarating stories, Sam is the award-winning author of 100+ books.

To learn more about Sam and her work, visit her at one of her online hotspots:
www.samcheever.com
samcheever@samcheever.com

www.ingramcontent.com/pod-product-compliance
Lightning Source LLC
Chambersburg PA
CBHW070537260626
47161CB00002B/418